DARKEST FIRE

Also by Tawny Taylor

Decadent Master

Wicked Beast

Dark Master

Real Vamps Don't Drink O-Neg

Sex and the Single Ghost

DARKEST FIRE

TAWNY TAYLOR

APHRODISIA

KENSINGTON PUBLISHING CORP.
www.kensingtonbooks.com

APHRODISIA BOOKS are published by

Kensington Publishing Corp.
119 West 40th Street
New York, NY 10018

All Kensington titles, imprints, and distributed lines are available at special quantity discounts for bulk purchases for sales promotion, premiums, fund-raising, and educational, or institutional use.

Special book excerpts or customized printings can also be created to fit specific needs. For details, write or phone the office of the Kensington Special Sales Manager: Kensington Publishing Corp., 119 West 40th Street, New York, NY 10018. Attn. Special Sales Department. Phone: 1-800-221-2647.

ISBN-13: 978-0-7582-4696-7
ISBN-10: 0-7582-4696-X

First Kensington Trade Paperback Printing: April 2011

10 9 8 7 6 5 4 3 2 1

Printed in the United States of America

DARKEST FIRE

1

Sin in stilettos hunted him.

In Drako Alexandre's lifetime, lust had worn many masks—fair and sweet, dark and exotic, male and female—but whatever form it took, it always, without fail, seized its prey. There was no escape. Yet, like the quail in Drako's favorite sutta, "The Hawk," Drako knew he would eventually break free from the predator's grip . . . and shatter its heart.

Tonight, the hunting ground was one of Drako's favorite haunts and lust was a redhead in an itty-bitty fuck-me dress, her mile-long legs bared to *there,* her full tits a sigh away from tumbling out of her dress, and a dozen erotic promises glittering in her eyes. She didn't know it yet, but the hunter would soon be the hunted.

Drako acknowledged her with a hard, piercing stare. In response, lush lips pursed in a seductive pout.

Yes, he'd have this one. But on his terms.

Let the games begin.

Eyes on the prize, expression guarded to keep her guessing, Drako tipped his beer back, pulling a mouthful of bitter ale from the bottle. As he swallowed, the heavy bass of the music thrummed through his body, pounding along nerves pulled tight with erotic need. Red and blue lights blinked on and off, casting everybody in the nightclub, male and female, in an alternating crimson and deep indigo glow.

Her gaze shifted.

His body tightened.

Oh, yeah. He liked this place. A lot. He slowly swept the crowded room again with his eyes. Writhing, sweaty bodies, mostly female, packed the small dance floor. Groups of people crowded around tables, the flickering red tips of their burning cigarettes dancing in the shadows.

"I've got the redhead," he announced.

"That's just as well." His brother, Talen, set his empty glass on the bar's polished top and shoved his fingers through his spiked platinum hair. "I'm not in the mood for this tonight."

"Not in the mood? Are you kidding me? Look around, baby brother." Sitting on the other side of Drako, Malek shot Talen a bewildered glance. About a dozen women gaped as his shaggy blond surfer-punk waves danced on a breeze.

Drako slid his quarry a heated glance, then twisted to flag down the bartender. "Yeah, well, if you spent half as much time working as you do playing, Malek, we'd—"

"Yeah, yeah, I've heard it before, big brother." Malek ordered another beer for Drako, then clapped him on the shoulder. "But like I say, life is short. You gotta live while you can." He slipped from the stool, peeled off a twenty, and handed it to the bartender. "Do either of you have a bad feeling about tomorrow's meeting with the old man . . . ?" Malek stood a little taller, tipped up his chin. "Ohhhh, yes. Talk to you later." Not waiting for them to answer his question, he headed toward the nearest flock of admirers.

"I think I'm calling it a night." Talen said, watching Malek gather a small herd of women around him.

"Okay, bro. See you at home." Drako checked his redhead again. She was still sitting at the table with her friend, but she was looking a little less certain of herself now. One hand was wrapped around a wineglass, the other nervously tugged at a lock of hair.

That was better. An aggressive woman did nothing for him.

Letting the corners of his mouth curl slightly, he lifted his fresh beer to his mouth and waited for their gazes to meet again.

Uh-huh. Much, much better.

He held her gaze, and everyone and everything else in the crowded bar seemed to slowly drift away, until nobody but his redhead existed to him. Electricity sizzled between their bodies, like heat lightning arcing between storm clouds.

Her tongue darted out, swept across her plump lip, then slipped back inside. She set her glass down and, breaking eye contact, leaned over to her friend sitting next to her. They both glanced his way. The friend smiled and nodded, and then the pair of them stood.

Their arms linked at the elbow, their gazes flitting back and forth between him and the back of the bar, they hurried in the opposite direction, toward the bathroom.

That was an interesting reaction. Nothing like what he'd expected. Was she playing him? Were they both?

Mmmm. Both. Maybe he'd have two women tonight. Two was always better than one.

He dropped a fifty on the bar. And with his beer clutched in one fist, he walked around the far side of the room, taking the scenic route to the dark corridor at the rear. He'd catch them out there, where it was quieter, more intimate.

His timing was perfect. Just as he rounded the corner, they clacked out of the bathroom on a breeze of sweetly perfumed air. They halted instantly, eyes widening, one pair a soft gray-blue, the other a deep brown.

Up close, the redhead lost a little of her charm. It was her friend who demanded his attention now. Her features were different—her almond-shaped eyes tipped up at the outer corners, the uncreased eyelids hinting at her Asian ancestry. Her full lips were plump and freshly coated in shimmering gloss. Her carefully applied makeup emphasized a set of picture-perfect cheekbones, and her slightly mussed hairstyle lengthened a slender neck, a tumble of silky blue-black waves cascading over her shoulders.

He'd seen her before. Where?

"Hi," the redhead said, her voice a deep and sultry siren's call.

He turned toward her again, catching once more the sensual promise glimmering in her cool blue gaze. Despite the invitation he read on her face—or maybe because of it—he found himself tiring of her already. His attention snapped back to the quiet woman next to him. An old David Bowie song echoed in his head, "China Girl." "I know this is the world's worst line, but don't I know you from somewhere?"

"I'm not sure." His China Girl stared at the tattoo on his neck, following the curved line up to his jaw. "I think I recognize the tattoo."

"My brothers and I have the identical design, a griffin. It's kind of a family thing. Our mother did the work."

"Your mother? How interesting." The redhead inched closer to get a better look, or so he assumed. "It's very sexy. I'm not crazy about tattoos, at least not most of the ones I've seen. This one's very different. All black, and gray and sorta... what's the word I'm looking for?"

"Celtic?" The brunette offered.

That brunette was spot on. Their mother had been 100 percent Irish. There could never be any doubt, with her mane of copper-colored hair and freckles. And the design she'd created for her three sons was as Irish as her maiden name, O'Sullivan.

The redhead scowled. "No, that's not it. I mean, yeah, it is Celtic, but that's not what I'm trying to say. Men with tattoos are a little... dangerous."

"Wicked." Something darkened the brunette's expression.

"Yes, wicked." The redhead's white teeth sank into her lower lip. "That's a good word."

Yeah, that was a good word.

He was feeling a little wicked something going on. And he could tell at least one woman was feeling it too. "Can I buy you ladies a drink?"

"Actually"—the brunette shot the redhead a nervous glance—"we were getting ready to leave—"

"But one more drink wouldn't hurt," the redhead finished, slanting a smile his way. "Thank you. By the way, my name's Andi and this is Rin."

"Good to meet you, Andi and Rin. I'm Drako. Let's find a table." He motioned for them to precede him out of the dark corridor. He followed them back into the crowded heat of the bar. As they shuffled and wound their way through the throng, his gaze meandered down the back of Rin's body, from the bouncing curls that tumbled down her back to a nicely rounded ass hugged in a snug black skirt. When she stopped to let a couple pass by, he leaned over her shoulder and whispered, "Maybe we can figure out where we've seen each other before."

A delicate fragrance drifted to his nose. Jasmine. It was refreshing, compared to the cloying blend of cigarette smoke and cheap cologne hanging heavy in the air and making his nose burn.

"Sure. Maybe." She hurried around a couple clawing at each other like bears in heat.

He smiled at her expression as she shuffled past them, her lips parting, cheeks flushing a pretty pink.

Damn, this was a hot place, in more ways than one. It sure put him in the mood to fuck, with all the gyrating bodies and hard, thumping music. A song he recognized started playing, a slow, sexy number, and taking advantage of the moment, he caught Rin's slender wrist.

She glanced over her shoulder.

"Dance with me." He didn't wait for her to respond, just tugged her gently until her body was flush with his. He looped one arm around her back, splaying his fingers over the base of her spine. He felt her stiffen against him, then relax.

She was petite, the top of her head hitting his chest at about nipple level. He liked how small and fragile she felt in his arms, how her little body fit against his.

And how she worked those hips of hers. Damn.

Sparks of erotic hunger zapped and sizzled through his body with every sway. He tucked his leg between hers and rocked his hips from side to side, melting at the feeling of her hips working perfectly with his. Her feminine curves conformed to his hard angles as she pressed tighter against him. He cupped her chin and lifted, coaxing her to look at him, to let him see that beautiful face, to maybe taste her lush mouth.

A second female body crowded against him from behind. A woman's hands glided down his tight thighs. Breasts flattened against his back. Within a second, his prick was hard enough to bust through brick, his balls tight, his blood burning like acid.

Rin's eyes lifted to his, and her lips parted in a natural pout, so different from the practiced expression her friend had donned for him.

That was it; he had to kiss her.

He tipped his head, his entire body tight and hard and ready. But just before his mouth claimed hers, she lurched away. He opened his eyes to catch the redhead slipping into her place as the music changed.

He twisted to find his delicate Rin, but she'd disappeared into the crowd.

"She's my friend," Andi shouted over the music as she undulated against him. "I won't say anything bad about her. But she's just not into this. She's so shy. Sorry." She smoothed her hands up his torso.

He was sorry too.

There was something about her. A quiet sensuality that didn't need to be forced. He hadn't been that intrigued by a woman in a long time. "No need to apologize for her."

"I'm guessing you like your women a little less aggressive?"

"Yeah."

"Got it." Her expression softened. "If you want to be the predator, I can be the prey. Let's play." Giggling, Andi slipped out of his arms and dashed into the crowd.

Now this was getting interesting.

Rin all but forgotten, he set out to hunt down his redheaded quarry in the black fuck-me dress.

Hunter. Prey. It looked like both of them would get what they were after tonight.

The next morning, Drako headed down to the library with a satisfied smile on his face and memories of one lush redhead strapped spread-eagle on his Saint Andrew's Cross.

Damn, that had been one of the best nights he'd had in a long time. Andi wasn't just a slut; she was a pain slut. The more he gave her, the more she begged. And that insatiability had applied to *everything*.

By the time they were through, both his single-tail whip and his cock had gotten a thorough workout.

He'd sent her home less than an hour ago, had taken a shower to wash away the lingering scents of sex from his skin, and was ready to face whatever news their father was about to deliver.

Whatever it was, Drako knew it would be major. The old man had said his good-byes ten years ago, after his brothers and his wife had been buried. He hadn't called, written, or even e-mailed his three sons since. Not that any of them could blame him. He'd paid his dues; he'd earned his freedom. Someday, they'd earn theirs too.

Until then, duty was duty. It wasn't like they had it bad.

When he entered the room, he found the old man sitting behind the desk—the one Drako considered his—hands clasped, waiting, silent, gaze sharp. It was damn good to see that face.

Malek was slumped in a chair next to the fireplace, looking like he'd had a long night—which he probably had. Talen was looking bright-eyed and alert, no doubt because he'd turned in early, like usual.

Drako knew he looked like Talen, but inside he felt like Malek. Dead dog tired.

The old man lifted his cool gray eyes to Drako and cleared his throat. "We can begin."

"Sorry I'm late." Drako snagged the closest seat and braced himself for what was coming.

Their father stood, hands on the desktop. "All three of you men know how vital your duty is. You've served well, protecting The Secret faithfully since my brothers and I stepped down over ten years ago. For that, you have earned my respect." He straightened up, crossing his arms over his chest. "But now it's time to prepare for the future." His assessing gaze turned to Drako. "Son, you're my oldest. The leader of your generation of Black Gryffons. You've proven to be an excellent leader—fearless, loyal, responsible and yet sensitive. I admire the man you've become."

Drako didn't know how to respond to his father's words. It had been a decade since the old man had paid him any compliment, let alone one so great. "As I admire you, father. You set a fine example, as the firstborn of your generation."

The old man smiled. After a beat, he said, "You've just celebrated your thirty-first birthday. In order to assure your retirement by your fiftieth, all three of you must father sons within the next twelve months. Which means you must take wives. Immediately."

Wives. Children.

Drako had understood this day would come, since shortly after taking his father's place as the leader of the Black Gryffons. Thus, he'd accepted it long ago. It was their fate, their duty, their honor.

But, gauging from Malek's barely stifled groan, at least one of his younger siblings hadn't been mentally prepared for the responsibility of wife and child yet.

"*Must* we all take a bride?" Malek asked. "If Drako conceives three sons, there would be no need for the rest of us to father children."

"Of course," their father said. "There's no guarantee he'll produce one, let alone three."

Malek's shoulders sank a tiny bit. "Okay, but today, marriage and children don't always have to come hand-in-hand—"

"No bastard child will ever be a Black Gryffon." Their father shook his head. "That's the law."

"I think the law's antiquated," Malek grumbled.

"Doesn't matter what we think." Drako stood, giving his scowling younger sibling a clap on the shoulder. "So what? You have to take a wife. It's not the end of the world."

"Depends on your perspective."

"Hey." Drako glanced at his father. "There's no law that says we have to be monogamous, right? I mean, if our wives know beforehand that we have no intention of limiting ourselves to having sex with just them, then we're good, right?"

Their father shrugged, eyes glimmering with an unexpectedly playful sparkle. "If you can find yourselves wives who are willing to live with that kind of arrangement, then more power to you. Your mother wouldn't. It was hell, giving up certain things, but I could never deny that woman anything." He sighed. "There are some sacrifices that are worth it."

"I hear you," Drako said, knowing fully well what kind of agony it had to have been. "Discomfort" was an understatement, but he respected the old man more than he could ever say for his commitment to their mother. Since at least the early eighteenth century every Black Gryffon had practiced some form of D/s, and many of them had taken multiple lovers. His father had done neither.

In the silent moment that followed, Drako studied the man he had emulated his entire life. The old man's once dark brown hair was now all silver, and lines fanned from the corners of his eyes, but otherwise in Drako's eyes this man would always be the powerful guardian leader he had respected and admired. His father's body was still heavily muscled, his mind sharp as a blade. Drako guessed retirement hadn't slowed him down a bit.

Only the deep shadow in the old man's eyes hinted at how close he was to passing from their world to the next.

"I miss her, son," their father said. "Your mother loved like nobody I've ever known. The last ten years have been so empty without her."

Drako touched the side of his neck. He could almost swear his tattoo, which had been, ironically, his mother's final gift to him before she died, was tingling. "I miss her too." Knowing somehow this would be the last time he'd see his father alive, Drako gave the old man a hug, then watched as his brothers did the same. It wouldn't be much longer, he guessed, before their father would be reunited with the woman he missed so dearly.

Their father left with a final wave and a smile, and Drako shoved aside the deep sorrow tugging at his heart and forced his mind to the next task he faced as leader of the Black Gryffons.

It was his duty to help his brothers find brides, women who would be willing to live with husbands who, in Malek's case, wouldn't be faithful. And, in his own, would accept his lifestyle. It had to be this way, even if it meant it would take longer to find the right brides.

He had to be honest with his future wife, and he expected his brothers to do the same. He would never be able to live with the guilt of hiding the truth. The pain those secrets would cause.

His wife. His bride. Who would she be?

It was a matter of choosing the right woman. A special woman.

A certain set of deep brown-black eyes and sculpted cheekbones flashed in his mind, and it was then that he remembered where he'd first seen his quiet little Rin.

It couldn't be. But it was.

The supposedly shy Rin wasn't who her friend believed. Quite the opposite.

His lips curled into a smile and his heavy heart lifted.

He knew exactly where to find his bride. Rin was one very special woman, and he had a good feeling she'd be willing to listen to his proposal.

In general, people tried too hard to simplify issues. Life wasn't comprised only of black, white, sane, insane, good, bad. There were an infinite number of shades of gray in between.

He had gone to great lengths to find people who saw a full spectrum of gray in the world. Only they could appreciate him, could share his vision.

Someday, every man, woman, and child on the earth would thank him. They would finally appreciate the truth he'd tried to share with them so many times. The simplemindedness that had blinded them wouldn't matter anymore. The truth would be too big and dazzling to deny.

That someday would be soon.

Smiling, he signed the document, ending his voluntary stay at the hospital. He gathered his prescriptions, medications, and personal possessions and stepped out into the warm, sunny day. The antipsychotic medication left his mind a little fogged and suppressed his emotions, but even with a full dose of Haldol still coursing through his bloodstream, he was ready.

So much work to do; so little time to do it.

A sleek black Mercedes-Benz crawled down the driveway and rolled to a stop in front of the hospital's entry. He waited, unsure whether it was his ride or not. The window rolled down, and a hand waved at him.

When he approached, the passenger handed him a card with no name, no phone number, only a gray-scale image of a chimera.

"Enter," the passenger said, his or her head turned, so he couldn't see the face.

Without questioning the passenger or driver, he got in the car.

2

"Fifty thousand."

Rin Mitchell's heart slammed to her toes.

Fifty thousand. Those two words echoed in her ears as she stared at the scumbag sitting across from her, sipping coffee in the cheerful Coney Island restaurant.

Why so much? Dammit!

She'd known the price would be high, maybe as much as ten thousand dollars. She'd managed to scrape together almost half that much by starving herself, living in a dump, working in a pit, and selling her car.

But fifty thousand? Why?

There hadn't been any of the normal expenses associated with smuggling a sex slave across an ocean or over international borders. Rin's sister Lei had been born and raised in the United States. And although Lei was pretty, and exotic—she was half-Japanese and therefore could work in brothels catering to men who liked Asian women—Rin saw no reason why she'd command such an unbelievable price.

Fifty thousand was unreasonable.

Impossible.

"Your price is too high." Rin shook her head, trying her best to hide the sense of defeat eating away at her confidence. The image of Lei's hollow-eyed stare flashed through Rin's mind. She had to buy Lei's freedom, whatever the price.

Five thousand. Ten thousand. Whatever. It was worth every penny if it meant her shy, innocent sister would be released. She could only imagine what kind of hell Lei had already lived through. Their mother had sold Lei into slavery over twelve months ago, then lied and told Rin she'd been kidnapped. When Rin had learned the truth, she'd vomited in the middle of the kitchen and then spit in their mother's face.

How could she do such a thing? To her own child? And who would have ever guessed that a young woman could be sold into slavery? In the twenty-first century. And in the United States.

What made it that much harder to swallow was the pittance the bastard had paid. No human being was worth so little. Not even the woman who'd sold her child into slavery.

"Too high?" The man poured some more cream into his coffee, stirred it, and lifted it to his mouth for another sip. "Name your price, and perhaps we can come to an agreement."

Holding her breath, she locked her gaze to his. "Ten thousand."

"You insult me." He set down his coffee cup and leaned closer. "She is priced fairly. That girl is very special, and you know it. For ten thousand, you can go buy yourself a common whore." He stood, turned away, and headed toward the door.

"No, wait!" Rin could hardly believe months of hard, disgusting, demeaning work had led to this. Months of starving herself. Sacrificing everything.

For what? Failure? No!

Trying not to cause a scene, she hurried to her feet and followed the man to the restaurant's exit. He pulled open the door, but she caught his wrist before he left the building. In her peripheral vision she watched the waitress dashing over to a coworker and thrusting a finger toward the door, no doubt thinking she was running out on the check.

"Please," she whispered, waving at the waitress. "Fifty thousand dollars is a lot of money. Give me a week."

"A day is all I can wait."

"Five days. Please. I'll get the money. Somehow."

His gaze slid down to her hand, still gripping his wrist. "Three days."

She unfurled her fingers. "Okay. Three."

"Call me when you have the money."

Defeated and desperate, Rin nodded and watched the bastard walk away. Calling him every name in the book, she rushed back to the table, slapped down a ten-dollar bill, and headed back outside. The second the door swung shut behind her, the dam broke loose and the pent-up tears burst from her throat in painful sobs.

This was so freaking unfair.

The average person would probably tell her to go to the police. But she'd done that the minute she'd learned her sister had been sold, and they'd given her no help.

A month later, she decided she'd have to search for her sister herself. Over the months, as she travelled through some of the most god-awful places in the United States, she'd learned a few things. First, that the sex slave industry was huge business. Second, that sex slave traders were slick and had more connections than she'd ever have guessed. And third, that they protected their property fiercely and hid their identities behind successful-business-owner masks.

Twice, she went to the police after she'd located her sister—in New York and Chicago—and twice her captors smuggled her away again.

Going to the police meant certain failure.

She was so close, once again, and now nothing.

No doubt, after this meeting, Lei would be moved again.

Fifty thousand dollars.

That was the price she would have to pay for her sister's freedom. Fifty freaking thousand. It might as well be a million. Ten million. Where could she get that kind of money? Where? How?

A scream of frustration sat at the back of her throat. Rin swallowed hard, over and over, struggling to keep it from sliding over her tongue and through her lips as she made the long walk home.

To think she had to work tonight too. Even though she wasn't a masseuse—thank God!—she was not in the mood to deal with a bunch of leering suburbanites buying sensual massages. Buying sex.

Call her jaded, but it seemed there was a price attached to everything nowadays. Sex. People. Morals. Power. Freedom. You name it.

Her pessimistic mood followed her home, accompanied her through her getting-ready-for-work ritual, and shadowed her as she walked to work, growing heavier and darker as she turned toward the massage parlor's grimy back door.

She'd hated every minute she'd spent in this building. Every second. But knowing she was getting closer to finding Lei, to freeing her, had made it at least tolerable. But now, she felt Lei slipping from her grasp, her hopes slowly evaporating. Her stomach turned at even the thought of spending five minutes in the filthy dump.

The men and their hungry eyes and grabby hands.

She shuddered and nearly gagged. There was no way she could do this. None.

Doing a one-eighty, she headed back outside, into the trash-strewn alley. Hoping no one inside had seen her yet, she hurried back around the side of the building, her head down, her gaze fixed on the littered sidewalk. Up ahead, a pair of men's feet were approaching. Probably a customer. Walking, she slowly lifted her gaze while stepping to the side so he could pass.

No. She halted midstride, and her heart practically jumped up her throat.

It was *him.* The guy from the bar. And the only man she'd ever seen at Magic Touch Massage that she might actually be tempted to do something with—other than rub his back.

Drako. Drako Alexandre. He was a man no girl could forget. Especially after that dance last night.

Instantly, memories of his hands gliding over her skin filled her mind. Her face burned hot. Her nerves sizzled and zapped. At the same time, a chill prickled her nape.

It couldn't be a coincidence that he was here now. He recognized her last night. Obviously, it had simply taken him a while to remember where he'd seen her.

He smiled as he moved closer. The expression was as friendly as it got, coming from a man so large and darkly sexy. "Hello, Rin." He stopped within reaching distance. "Are you heading into work? Or leaving?"

Nervous, she glanced over her shoulder. "Um, leaving."

"Good. Care to get some coffee with me?" His hand slid under her elbow, and his fingers curled around it, tugging gently.

"Actually, I . . ." *What? Need to get home to plan a bank robbery?*

"There's something important I want to talk to you about." He tipped his head and gave her arm another little pull.

Talk to me? Important?

She stood there for a second, until her curiosity got the better of her. *Important?*

She gave him a quick up-and-down glance, then concentrated on his face. Such a stunning face it was too. All sharp angles and hard planes. He wasn't a pretty man; he was magnificent. His features were formed like a man's should be, his body thick and hard and powerful.

And looking at his clothes, their fit, their quality. His shoes. If they were any indicator, he wasn't just financially comfortable, he was rich.

What did he want?

Unlike last night, the guy wasn't looking like 100 percent predator-on-the-prowl. More like 50 percent. The other half of him appeared to be just a man who wanted to talk to her. A man who wasn't out to hurt her, or take advantage of her, or throw some lame line at her to get into her pants. Only sit down and share a cup of coffee.

And talk. About *something important*.

"Okay, let's go talk." She let him lead her back down the street. They had to walk a couple blocks to find the nearest restaurant, past dilapidated brick buildings housing tattoo parlors and party stores. As she walked beside him, her curiosity grew. Her imagination ran wild, drumming up one bizarre scenario after another to explain why he'd tracked her down and what he wanted to talk about. Most of them revolved around her friend Andi.

Finally, they reached the restaurant, a greasy mom-and-pop diner. A cowbell clanked over her head as they entered. *Charming*. Her nose burned with the oily odor of fried meat and the cloying stench of cigarette smoke. Her escort led her to a booth in the back, resting a hand on the tattered, red vinyl-covered seat. "This isn't my first choice of places. I'd rather go somewhere else—"

"It's fine." She slid into the booth and watched him take a seat across from her.

The waitress, a tired-looking woman with her silver hair scraped flat against her skull and knotted into a tight ball at the back of her head, shuffled over, took their orders, and left.

"So . . . ?" Rin curled her paper napkin around her fork, wondering what a man like Drako could want with someone like her. This never happened—a rich, powerful man from the right side of the tracks hunting her down and asking her out on some kind of pseudodate.

Granted, she was decent to look at. And she was far from a dummy. And if things had been different, a guy like Drako might have been interested in dating her. But they weren't. Not yet.

Someday they would be, she hoped.

She'd had a very humble start in life, but she'd worked hard to drag herself out of the gutter. She'd waitressed and phone-solicited her way through four years of college and two years of grad school. But he didn't know that. All he knew was that she worked at the massage parlor his brother frequented. One that was known for illicit activity.

A couple of times, Drako had come inside with Malek. But he'd always declined a massage. Another reason to admire him.

Finally, when he didn't say anything, she glanced his way.

He was staring out the grime-streaked window, a muscle in his jaw clenched so tightly it looked like it might snap.

Was he angry? No. Couldn't be.

He visibly inhaled. Exhaled. His gaze jerked to her face. His ears reddened.

Ohmygod, was he nervous?

Now, more than ever, she wanted to know why he'd come looking for her.

He cleared his throat.

The waitress returned, carrying a cup of coffee for him and a glass of diet cola for her. He thanked the waitress, asked Rin if she wanted anything else, and then scooped up a handful of sugar packets and emptied them into his coffee.

"Like a little coffee with your sugar?" she teased, watching him tear open a couple more.

One side of his mouth lifted into a lopsided smile that nearly stopped her heart. "I have a sweet tooth."

"I see that."

He stirred, the spoon clanking against the ceramic. "Thanks for coming."

"Sure." She took a sip of her cola. Lukewarm and watered down, just the way she liked it—*not*. "You said you wanted to talk to me about something?"

"Yes, I did." He curled his hands around either side of his cup. He had nice hands. Long, tapered fingers. Neatly trimmed fingernails. A little spark of heat buzzed up her spine at the memory of those hands, touching, holding her. Arms pulling her close. Music thrumming. Bodies swaying. Nice memory. "I wanted to discuss a proposition with you."

Proposition. Her mood dimmed, all thoughts of dancing fled her mind. That word called one particular activity to mind—sex. He thought she was a whore, a semilogical deduction, considering where she worked. But if he wanted to buy sex, why was he going to so much trouble? Why not just head down to the massage parlor, like his brother did?

She wanted to get up and walk out, to let him know she was not for sale, and then suggest he take his *proposition* to Magic Touch and offer it to one of the girls who wouldn't be insulted. But something made her say, "What kind of 'proposition'?" instead.

His expression changed, and some emotion she couldn't name flashed in his eyes. "Actually, it's more of a proposal. One that involves marriage."

It took at least a heartbeat or two for his words to register in her head. Her hands flew to her mouth, slamming over it just as an expletive of disbelief tumbled over her tongue.

What the hell? Marriage? No. This was a joke. A bizarre, sick prank.

Finally, she trusted herself not to say something rude or embarrassing—for some reason, she wasn't ready to tell Drako to fuck off yet. "You're asking me to *marry* you?" she asked, exaggerating the disbelief in her voice. "Marry? As in church, flowers, dresses, veils. *Vows?*"

"Yes, marry. Vows, sure."

"You? A guy who could have any woman you want?"

Dammit, she thought he was an idiot. Or desperate. Or both. He wasn't either.

Before his intriguing Rin could shoot him down, he fought to explain, "Yes, me. I know this isn't the way things normally go between a man and a woman, but I just thought..." What? That she was desperate, since she fucked men for money. For very little money, as he had been told.

He couldn't say that. She'd probably cry.

"Thought what?" she shot back, scowling.

He sighed, shoved his fingers through his hair and looked at her. What an ass he was making of himself. It was easy hooking up with a woman. He had that routine down pat. But this was new territory. He wasn't looking for a quick fuck. This woman was going to be his wife. He couldn't be his usual guy-on-the-hunt self. Dammit, he didn't know how to be anything else with a woman. "Look. I'm the last guy who should judge anyone. I'll admit, I've fucked more women than I can count. But you and I both know what you so-called masseuses do in Magic Touch for your money. You're not giving therapeutic massages."

Her mouth tightened and she turned away from him.

Shit! He'd hurt her feelings.

He swallowed a growl of frustration. It wasn't supposed to go this way. She was supposed to be squealing with glee, her little arms wrapped around his neck, and those lovely eyes filled with tears of joy.

All the way into the city, he'd told himself how easy this

would be. Rin—as lovely as she was—was a sex worker. Thanks to his brother, who lacked principles and thus had friends in low places, he'd met many sex workers. Dancers. Prostitutes. Actresses in adult films. He may not know any of them intimately, but he knew one thing—to a sex worker, everything had a price, even her body. Especially her body.

Rin should be glad to walk away from the life she had now. She couldn't love it, right?

Right. Rin was just doing a job because she had to.

Like all the others, she'd found herself trapped in a life she despised. She didn't know how to get herself out. Whether she'd admit it or not, she needed the kind of opportunity he was about to offer. Yes, she did.

All he had to do to convince her to accept his proposal was tell her how great she'd have it with him—tell her about the money, the clothes, the shoes, the lifestyle—and she'd gladly kiss that life good-bye and scamper down the aisle with him.

He just had to determine what her price was. No problem. Cash talked, he reminded himself.

He reached into his pocket, pulled out his wallet, and lifted out a Grover Cleveland. Because he used cash only, for everything, he always had a pocket full of large-currency bills. He quietly laid the thousand-dollar bill on the table in front of her.

She glanced down. Her eyes narrowed to slits. Her pretty lips thinned even more. But she didn't shove the money away. Or cuss him out for making any presumptions. Nor did she snatch it up and stuff it in her pocket either. She didn't make any move.

Weighing her options.

Maybe he needed to sweeten the deal.

Dipping into his wallet again, he pulled out a second Cleveland. He set it on top of the first.

Still nothing from her.

He added a third, fourth, and fifth.

Finally, she looked at him. "Why do you need to buy a wife, Drako? Maybe years ago men like you would buy a wife. But anymore? Come on. Guys with money buy whores and collect trophy wives."

Drako slid his wallet back into his pocket. "I won't disagree with that—for the average guy like me." Hell, if it weren't for the fact that his duty as a Black Gryffon called for him taking a wife for more reasons than appearances, he would've found himself a woman who was content to call herself his wife in public while living separate lives in private. "But my situation is a little unique."

"Unique? How?"

They were straying from the topic at hand. And more than ever, he was determined to convince her to accept.

She was lovely. Delicate and small. Her voice was sweet and smooth. He sensed a spark of intelligence. And the memories of their dance made him hard and tight. He pulled out his wallet again, added another thousand dollar bill to the pile. On top of that, he placed a ring box and lifted the lid.

Her eyes flared with some unreadable emotion as they tracked his movements.

"You'll have a very good life. A nice home. Clothes. Jewelry. Art. A very generous sum of money to spend any way you like. As my wife, you'll have every comfort you can imagine."

After a beat she asked, "How generous?"

Yes, even this stubborn beauty had her price. Now, he felt like he was on solid footing. Negotiating a deal, he could handle. Tiptoeing through a woman's emotional minefield was an entirely different matter.

He measured her reaction to the money, the ring. She hadn't reacted as he'd hoped, leading him to believe she might have very high expectations. Her manner of speaking, the way she carried herself, and her cool demeanor spoke of culture and refinement she shouldn't possess. "Twenty thousand a month."

Her eyes revealed nothing. "What's the catch? There's always something. What do you expect from a wife you'd buy versus one you'd meet, fall in love with, and then marry?"

He felt the smile spread over his face, "See, that's just it. If I wanted love from a wife, I wouldn't need to buy one."

"No love?"

"No love."

"Can I ask, why?"

Shit, he'd hoped she wouldn't ask that question. "Well, because I'm trying to avoid some very serious complications in my life."

She set her elbows on the table and plunked her chin on her fists. "So, you've had some bad experiences?"

"Yes and no."

Rin placed one hand on his. "I'm not judging you. I'm just trying to understand."

Feeling like things weren't going the way he'd hoped, and anxious to get the conversation back on track, he searched for the right words. "I've watched men fall in love and then fall apart. I can't allow myself to be weak. Too many people count on me."

"I think I understand." She stared down at the ring. "Kind of." She touched the stone, a brief, hesitant contact with one fingertip. "Will there be sex?"

"Yes. That would be part of the marriage."

"Children?"

"Most definitely. That's the most important reason for my taking a wife."

"But no love. Not ever."

"Not ever. I can't let myself fall in love. I won't. I'm trying to be honest, lay everything on the table upfront." He slid the stack of bills closer to her. "And it may go without saying, but I don't want any misunderstandings. Divorce is not an option.

So, now you understand why I'd rather buy a wife than find one by more traditional methods. I want my wife to understand and accept my limitations ahead of time. It's my hope you can approach our marriage like a business partnership, or a friendship, rather than an emotion-driven relationship. That's not to say there won't be some tender feelings. Respect. Admiration. Loyalty. Even affection."

"I see. Will you be...?" She sipped her cola and set down her glass. "Will you still go to the dungeons? Do the bondage stuff?" After a beat, she added, "My friend Andi told me."

"Yes, I will," he answered, making sure to keep his voice free of any guilt or apology. "D/s is a part of who I am. But if it's not something you're interested in, I respect that. I would never ask you to do anything just for me, my pleasure."

"Then you'll do those things with someone else?"

"Yes. But I promise I won't have intercourse with another partner. I won't put your health or mine in jeopardy. My activities in the dungeon will be strictly nonsexual."

Again, he could read nothing in her eyes.

"I need time. To think. One day?"

He nodded. "One day. Should we meet here?"

"No. This is the worst dump ever. There's a nicer restaurant on Main and Seventh. Riley's. How about we meet there tomorrow at noon?"

"Tomorrow at twelve o'clock, at Riley's." As he watched her stand, he palmed the ring box, then pushed the money toward her. "This is yours to keep, regardless of your decision."

This time, as her eyes met his, he did read something in them, something that looked a lot like gratitude.

"Okay." She gathered the bills into her fist and tucked them into her purse.

Confident he'd found his bride, he smiled. "I hope next time you'll let me buy you a meal."

For the first time in a long, tense stretch, she returned his smile. "I'll think about it."

He'd just walked out. Nobody had stopped him; nobody had known they needed to. According to the United States Constitution John Dale Oram, head of a clandestine group called the Chimera, had every right to sign those papers, releasing himself from the hospital. For the past ten years, he'd been in and out of halfway houses and hospitals, but he'd never been violent, never hurt anyone. His diagnosis: hebephrenic schizophrenia. Just a month ago, he'd voluntarily committed himself again, but his "condition" was under control. And he was no longer viewed as a threat to himself or others.

Drako knew better.

Oram wasn't delusional and his thoughts were far from disorganized. He was calculating, intelligent, and his seeming preoccupation with religion and philosophy had a purpose.

Nobody suspected the truth.

Oram was a bigger danger than anyone had ever guessed—not to himself, not to a few people, but to millions.

Drako had put out a call to a few close friends, hoping he'd get a bead on the man, but Drako had found out too late that Oram had checked out. Within minutes of being released, the man, and the vehicle he'd left in, had vanished.

The timing of Oram's vanishing act was too convenient to be accidental.

Within moments of learning his father had taken his last breath, Drako had been told that the man his father had nearly executed was out walking the streets, the shroud of a fake psychiatric condition cast aside.

When his brothers entered the library, Drako didn't wait to tell them the news. He started with, "Father's dead," and ended with, "Oram's on the move and he already shook our tail."

Malek was the first of the two to find his tongue. "Damn."

Talen shook his head. "I knew it would be soon, but... shit. I'll miss him."

"Me too." Standing at his desk, Drako flattened his hands on the top and leaned forward. "Unfortunately, there's no time for grieving. It'll be a quick burial. Nothing complicated. And for obvious reasons, we can't attend. We've got to keep focused; it's our duty." Drako straightened. "Oram has had ten years to plan for today. We have to be ready, to be aware of everyone and everything around us. He doesn't know what we look like or our aliases. And he might not know how to find us yet, but already it's obvious he's been using the time wisely. If he launches an attack before we're ready, we're fucked."

"And so is most of humanity," Talen added.

"Yeah," Drako and Malek agreed.

The three shared a silent moment, a thought, a prayer, for their father's peace. None of them said it, but Drako imagined they all thought it, he was finally with their mother again, in a better place.

When his brothers both met his gaze, letting him know they were ready to move on, Drako pulled a file from his drawer. "We need eyes and ears. But we need to be careful who we hire. We don't want to risk tipping off the enemy." Drako pointed at Talen. "I'm thinking two good men should do it."

Talen nodded. "I'm on it."

"Malek, if Oram finds out who we are, we want to divert him to another location, not here. We need another house, somewhere far enough from here to keep us safe."

"Got it."

Satisfied they were on the right track, Drako sat. "I'm going to—"

"Get married," Malek interrupted. "As soon as possible. You can't put it off now. Not with father gone. There's nobody but us. Father's brothers died years ago, and they left no sons to take our places. If we die without sons, there isn't a man, woman, or child alive that won't suffer the consequences."

"You're right." Drako drew in a deep breath, released it. "A wedding is the last thing I want to think about right now, but it's my duty. It will be done."

3

"There's our Romeo." Chuckling, Malek pounded Drako on the back and sauntered into Drako's bedroom. "Oh, what's wrong, big brother? Are you *scared?*"

"No, I'm not scared." Drako stuffed the velvet jewelry box into his jacket pocket and sent his taunting brother a warning glare, wishing he could physically wipe that smirk off his face. "You laugh now, but your time's coming, little brother. Just wait." Sitting on the bed, he stuffed his feet into his shoes.

"Waiting is exactly what I plan on doing." The spark somewhat faded from Malek's eyes, he threw himself into the chair in the corner and stretched his arms over his head. "In the meantime, I'm enjoying every minute of my bachelorhood. Or what's left of it. Last night. Mmmm. Those Randall twins were something else. Let me tell you . . ."

Drako didn't bother interrupting Malek's story to tell him he was full of shit. Drako had had the Randall twins. A month ago. But his experience with them was a far cry from the erotic scene his brother was describing. They laid on their backs, legs spread, arms at their sides, stiff as blow-up dolls. He'd never have guessed. The gorgeous blondes looked the part of wildcats in heat, but in reality, they were as cold as corpses.

Just wasn't right.

Talen shoved open the door and strolled in. "Ready to go throw away your freedom and tether yourself to the old ball and chain?"

"Can't a guy get dressed in private anymore?" Drako grumbled, tying his shoelace.

Malek threw an arm over the chair's back. "Check it out, our bro's nervous. What's wrong, Drako? Afraid she'll say no?"

"She's not going to say no. Not a chance." Standing, he headed to the large mirror hanging over his dresser. His shirt collar wasn't lying right. The cleaner didn't use enough starch. Again. "I told you, I know how to pick them. You'll see." Still fighting with his collar, he grimaced at himself in the mirror. He wished he felt as sure as he sounded. If Rin changed her mind, after all the crowing he'd done, he'd look like a total ass.

Last night, he'd been so sure she wouldn't shoot him down. But this morning all that confidence evaporated as he'd checked into the details of getting married.

Hitched.

Tying the knot.

The old ball and chain.

Shit, the whole institution made him feel sick, let alone all the tedious details. Dresses. Flowers. Churches. Dinner menus. Licenses. It was enough to make a guy want to run as far and fast as he could. But, duty being duty, and his life being what it was, he had no choice. Neither did his brothers. And it was his responsibility as the oldest son to set an example, to step up first and accept this responsibility like a man.

"What kind of ring did you make her?" Talen asked. "I haven't seen it yet."

The ring. That was the only detail he didn't mind seeing to. "The kind any woman would be glad to have." As a jeweler who specialized in designing high-quality pieces crafted with rare stones, he knew a fine, quality gemstone when he saw one. And even more important, he knew how women reacted to one. A little chunk of carbon could turn the most furious hell-cat into a soft, sweet woman.

Ironically, he'd thought the ring he'd tucked into his pocket would have inspired his Rin to fall to her knees and propose to *him* when she'd first seen it. But it hadn't, and she didn't.

"Forget about my personal life for a minute. What's the news about Oram? Anything yet?"

"Still nothing." Talen shook his head. "The boys I hired have checked everywhere. The bastard is deep underground. And I'm beginning to wonder if maybe he's having a hard time trying to gather enough resources to lead another attack. After losing so many guys when father—"

"Right. And Malek's the perfect candidate for the priest-hood." Drako turned to face his brothers. "That's exactly what he wants us to think. The bastard wants us to think he's lost the Chimera's support, get careless and sloppy. But I won't be caught by surprise. He's been watching, waiting, planning for years. Once he knows who we are, he's going to look for any vulnerability he can find. And then, when we least expect it, he'll attack. Our father won the last battle, but the war's far from over." He headed toward the door. "As soon as I'm through with this marriage stuff, I'm getting back to work. No more distractions."

"Good luck, bro!" Malek shouted after him.

"I don't need luck." Drako hesitated at the door, catching sight of something glittering in Malek's hand. "Hey, what's that?"

"What? This?" Malek raised his hand, something small—a piece of jewelry?—pinched between his index finger and thumb. He shrugged. "Just an earring one of the twins left behind. It's worthless. Cubic zirconium, I think."

"Hey, you know the rules about keeping things left by visitors," Talen said, charging over to snatch it from Malek's hand. After a brief inspection, he handed it back. "Get rid of it."

"Yeah, yeah. I will." Malek shrugged his shoulders, giving the tiny piece another look. "Wouldn't want to find out it's a bomb, bug, or secret spy camera. It's too small to be any of those. You're getting paranoid."

"You can never be too careful." Still standing at the door, Drako gave his brothers one final wave. "Later, boys."

Rin dragged her sweat-slicked palms down her thighs and concentrated on taking slow, deep breaths. She straightened her skirt, tugged at her knit top, and checked her watch for the gazillionth time. Quarter to twelve.

Ohmygod.

Riley's was only two blocks away. She'd be seeing *him* soon. Him. Her future husband.

I'm making the right decision.

The irony wasn't lost to her—that she was selling herself into an arranged marriage in order to buy her sister's freedom. If anyone would have told her a year ago that this was where she'd be now, she would have laughed in their face.

Arranged marriages? In the twenty-first century? In Michigan? No way!

Yes, way.

Just like there wasn't slavery in the United States anymore. All the slaves were freed during the American Civil War.

Not even close.

The minute Rin had learned her sister had been sold, she'd hit the Internet for information. And she was shocked, appalled, and sickened by what she'd learned. Slave trade was big business. International business. And way more common than she'd ever have guessed.

She shoved those dark thoughts aside as she rounded a corner and checked her watch again. It was twelve minutes before noon. She could see the restaurant now. Her nerves were skittery, her heart thumping heavily in her chest.

What if he changed his mind? Or what if he refused the only condition she wanted to add to their agreement?

She wouldn't, couldn't, change her mind. It had taken her only a few hours to think this through, weigh her options (there weren't any), and get herself semi-used to the idea. She was going to be married. Married! Soon.

The air seeped from her lungs again, and she gulped in another breath.

It was going to be okay. Drako was an attractive man. Sex wouldn't be bad. In fact, it would probably be downright enjoyable. There was most definitely chemistry between them. She didn't know him very well, but she sensed he wasn't a psychopath. And—most important—she, her sister, and her future children would have the kind of stability she'd always dreamed of. Already, she'd formulated a rough plan of what she'd do after she had Lei safe.

The restaurant was less than fifty yards from her now. Her pace slowed.

Everything's going to be fine.

She repeated her mantra in her head a few dozen times. Took a few more deep breaths.

Better.

Her resolve reinforced, she clasped and unclasped her hands to work out the tension, hurried up to the door, yanked it open, and stepped inside. Semiblind after coming in from the glaring sunshiny day outside, she clacked up to the hostess. "Hi, I'm meeting someone, Drako Alexandre."

The hostess tucked a blond lock behind her ear as she checked her list. "Yes. He's already been seated. This way, please."

Feeling a smidge faint, Rin followed the pretty girl to a

wooden booth at the back of the restaurant. Drako—quite the gentleman, for a guy who was about to buy a wife—stood, flashing one of the most charming smiles she'd ever seen. That grin kicked all the fluttery butterflies in her stomach into frenzied action.

Ugh, like she was going to be able to eat a bite of food. Then again, she wasn't there to eat anyway.

"Hello, Rin."

"Hi."

"You look very nice." He waited for her to sit before he eased back down.

"Thanks. So do you. Nice . . . shirt."

The hostess placed a menu on the table and she stared blindly at it.

He cleared his throat. "A drink?"

"Oh! Um, it's a little early for the hard stuff." Although she could sure use a few shots of something. She directed her drink order to the hostess. "I'll just take a cola. Diet, please."

"Coke?" the hostess asked.

"That's fine. Thanks." Trying to hide how nervous she truly was—the butterflies in her stomach were doing cartwheels now—Rin sat on her hands and smiled. "Have you eaten here before?"

"No, I haven't."

"The burgers are good. Salads too." When he glanced down at his menu, her gaze skimmed down his neck, following the curve and curl of his tattoo before landing on a broad shoulder covered in crisp white cotton. "Then again, you probably don't eat much salad."

"Actually, I do."

"Oh."

He looked up, eyebrows pulled down. "Do you know what you're ordering already?"

"Um, no." She scooped up the menu sitting in front of her

and unfolded it, deciding it made really good cover. Her cheeks were so hot the cook could probably fry bacon on them. "The soup looks good." Shoot, her hands were shaking. Just a little. But she wondered if he could tell.

Calm down, Mitchell! Why are you so freaking nervous? You never get this wound up.

A set of familiar fingers curled over the top edge of her menu, and then she felt it being slowly pushed down, gradually uncovering Drako's handsome face.

He tipped his head to the side. "The waitress is waiting."

Had the waitress spoken? Was she so out of it that she hadn't heard her? Knowing she wouldn't eat, regardless of what she ordered, she just rattled off, "I'll take your house burger with fries."

"I'll take the same." Drako watched the waitress retreat for a split second before turning those haunting eyes her way again.

So dark. And mysterious. She could seriously get lost in them. And then there was that mouth. When the corners quirked up, she got warm all over. He'd almost kissed her when they'd been dancing. That moment was burned into her memory forever. Her lips still tingled.

"Can we talk now?" she blurted, anxious to just get the business end of the conversation over and done with. Before she passed out.

"Sure." He clasped his hands together on the table. "I take it you've made a decision, then?"

"I have." *Deep breath.* "I'll accept your offer. But on one condition."

He didn't seem surprised by her acceptance or the fact that she wished to add a condition to the arrangement. "Which is?"

"I need fifty thousand dollars right away."

"For?"

"A personal debt." She added quickly, "This is a one-time thing. I promise I'm not a gambling addict, druggie, or shopaholic. I won't have a problem living within my budget from this point forward." She held her breath.

"How soon?"

"Today. Or tomorrow at the latest."

Gaze sharp, almost to the point of being intrusive, he bent his elbows and leaned forward. "And how do I know you won't take my money and disappear?"

Good question.

If she were he and he were she, she wouldn't trust him. Herself. Whatever. Bottom line, it was a lot of money to risk. "I wonder how long it takes to get a marriage license in Michigan," she thought aloud.

"Three days," he answered.

"You've done your homework, then." *Three days? Shit.* Plan A was out. "Okay, how about we go ahead, get the license, and then you give me the money? I'll stay at your place for the next two nights, so you know I won't run off." She held her breath again.

After a couple of heartbeats, he shook his head. "No. You'll wait for the money."

Noooooo, I can't!

She scrambled to come up with a Plan C.

Where could they get married today? Vegas popped into her head. But it was too far to travel. It was after noon already. By the time they got to the airport it would be late afternoon. And then who knew what kind of flight they'd get, if they could even get one. Anywhere else? Closer. Where they could drive?

Ohio, of course.

She'd have to get on the phone pronto, make some calls, see if she could find someone to officiate. It was doable. Maybe. "Any chance you'd be willing to take a road trip today?"

God, this was awful, throwing together her wedding like this. As the oldest daughter of a single mother, she'd never expected to have a fancy wedding. But she certainly hadn't thought it would be this pathetic. Married in a courthouse—hopefully. In her regular clothes. In a rush. To a stranger who was into kinky stuff she didn't fully understand.

Yet the only part about her plan she really hated was having to leave the state without Lei. It was risky, but waiting three days would be even riskier.

"Road trip? Where?" he asked.

"My home state, Ohio."

He nodded. "Did you want your family to attend?"

"Oh, no." Outside of her sister, she had no family. Their grandmother had died several years ago, and as far as she was concerned, their mother was dead too. "It's just that there's no waiting period in Ohio. I remember some friends from school got married on a whim once. And I'm assuming you're just as anxious to get this..." *Over with.* "...rather, anxious to move on to other things as I am."

Say yes. Please!

He frowned, eyebrows bunching, lips curling down. Even with his features all puckered, he was attractive. "Wouldn't you rather have a nice ceremony? You know, with all those things you talked about yesterday? Dress, veil, church—"

"Oh, no. Not me!" she lied. "I'm a very practical person."

"Or very desperate for money."

No use denying it. "As the case may be." For the third time since arriving, she held her breath. This was it. Her cards were on the table. She'd either walk away a winner or lose everything. Her insides twisted into a knot.

She'd never had the stomach for gambling.

4

He had learned from the best. He'd learned to hunt, to kill, to outsmart the enemy and to find a weakness and use it to his advantage.

He'd also learned to avoid vulnerability.

Now, after years of planning, of hating, and of living with nerves strung so tight with anticipation he'd thought they'd snap, he was free. And he was ready.

The first step: to set the trap.

The Black Gryffons had been created by Augustus, emperor of the Roman Empire, two thousand years ago. They served only one purpose—to guard The Secret, an ancient power source some ignorant son of a bitch a couple of thousand years ago had misused, almost wiping out the entire human population. It had taken the Chimera two thousand years to track down the Black Gryffons, to learn who they were and where they were hiding.

The Secret had been within their grasp.

And then they'd fucked up.

But now the Chimera had a new leader, a man who had vision, devotion, and determination. He would give humankind the gift that had been stolen from them. No action was too bold or price too high.

Shades of gray.

With the power source under his control, humanity's reliance upon all other forms of power would be eliminated. No emissions from burning coal. No destruction of wetlands by oil drilling. No production of dangerous radioactive by-products. Man would have all the power he would need.

And he, The Serpent, as he'd been dubbed by the other members of the Chimera, would rule all the nations.

What was it going to take to lure the Black Gryffons from their hole? How would he defeat the Lion, the Eagle, and the Dragon?

The three brothers who were the Black Gryffons were mortal, but it wouldn't be easy to defeat them. They were well trained, educated, and as determined to protect The Secret as he was to find it. The brothers would have to be subdued, separated, and then manipulated into revealing the location of his possession. There were a lot of details to work out yet. Practice runs. Unlike his predecessor, he would be prepared.

He figured by the end a few innocents would die. But if they could understand what cause they were about to die for, surely they would agree their life was a small price to pay.

The view outside the window, of acre upon acre of cornfield, was not even remotely as intriguing as the one inside the sleek black Mercedes they were riding in, but Rin was too lily-livered to turn and look at the man sitting beside her.

In a little over one hour, sixty-some-odd short minutes from now, she would be that man's wife. Mrs. Drako Alexandre. And all her dreams, of falling head over heels in love with a dashing man, Mr. Perfect, and joyfully trouncing down the aisle in a white, frothy wedding gown, would be nothing but a silly childhood fantasy.

It won't be that bad.

How many marriages between starry-eyed lovers started in bliss but ended in bitter, ugly divorce? At least she'd be spared the shock of discovering her husband spanking another woman; she knew from the start he'd be doing that and more. And wouldn't it be easier to make a commitment last decades if it was built upon something more stable, more enduring than passion?

Mutual dependence, respect, and friendship had to be a more solid base for a relationship.

Her soon-to-be husband was still and silent as he drove, his eyes focused on the road, hands resting on the steering wheel, fingers curled loosely around it. When she stole a glance at his profile, she saw his expression hadn't changed since they'd left to make the all-too-brief trip to Toledo. The Ohio–Michigan border was less than ten miles up ahead. Her heartbeat was speeding up a smidge with every mile that passed, not just because of what was to come but also the heavy, tense silence hanging over their heads like churning storm clouds.

She wouldn't listen to the quiet voice in her mind, the one that kept whispering, "You're making a big mistake." That voice had been wrong before; it could be wrong now.

Another mile passed and one itty-bitty nerve, pulled too taut, snapped, and she blurted, "Tell me you won't be a jerk and make me regret this. Tell me something, anything, that'll give me some hope that we won't make each other miserable for the rest of our lives."

He looked at her, smiled, then turned his attention back to the road ahead. "I put the toilet seat down. And I do my own laundry. I wash windows. Oh, plus I don't watch sports."

She wasn't buying it, but she was relieved to have finally broken the quiet. "Liar. No man is that perfect."

"I'm not saying I'm perfect. But I'm telling the truth. I don't watch football, baseball, hockey, basketball, or even the sports roundup on the news."

She couldn't help it. She laughed. And it felt good to release some of the pent-up energy crawling through her system. "You sound like a dream-husband, then."

He shrugged. "Maybe to a woman who doesn't like putting the toilet seat down, washing windows, or watching football."

"Wouldn't you know it, but that would be me. I guess we were made for each other." She took the first full lungful of air since they'd left. "Thank you," she said to his profile. "For making me feel a little better about this."

The corner of his mouth curled up, and the skin around his right eye crinkled. "That's not to say I'm not without my faults. You might want to know about those before you say 'I do.' "

She was almost 100 percent sure she didn't want to know what his faults were yet, but that didn't stop her from asking, "And those would be . . . ?"

"Well, I've been told by one or two people that I'm as stubborn as a mule. I'm the oldest son of a demanding, disciplined, distant father. As such, I've learned to work hard and accept no less than perfection from everyone around me. I'm a perfectionist, so everything I do, I do flawlessly, or at least to the best of my ability. That works to my advantage sometimes, but not always. I don't accept my own failings well."

"You're Type A. Me too. I'm the oldest of two. I have a younger sister, who is the typical second-born, attention-seeking, rebellious . . ." She cleared her throat, a feeble attempt at disguising the catch in her voice. "Our mother wasn't much of a parent, and so I sort of stepped in at an early age and tried to take care of Lei. I can't say I did a good job, but I tried my best."

He glanced at her before responding, "Lei is very lucky to have had a sister who was willing to do that for her."

"I don't know. If you said that to her, she might disagree."

After a semilong stretch of silence, he asked, "Why didn't you invite your sister? To the wedding?"

"I would've liked to. But she's...she's sort of busy right now. There's no chance she could make it, even if we waited a few days. But I'm hoping she'll come to see us after the wedding, maybe stay with us...?"

"She's more than welcome to stay as long as she likes. My home—our home—is large. There's plenty of room." He flipped the turn signal, and Rin, realizing it had been a few minutes since she'd looked out the window, turned her head to read the sign approaching.

It was their exit.

Her life was about to change, and it wasn't going to be a minor adjustment. It was going to be a major transformation. She would have a new home, new responsibilities, and a very different lifestyle. Her heart did a little fluttery hop in her chest. Her palms were instantly coated with sweat, making them itchy and warm. She dragged them down her thighs and tried to pretend like she wasn't petrified.

The conversation they'd shared in the last few minutes had erased some of her worries, not that they were completely eradicated. No single five-minute chat would do that, especially not one as strained as that one had been. But at least her future husband wasn't a complete stranger any longer. She knew a little about him, and he knew a little about her. So far, she'd neither heard nor seen anything—beyond the obvious, asking a stranger to marry him—to make her think he was anything but a decent, hard-working man who had a very realistic, if cynical, view of marriage.

"I think we'll understand each other okay," he said.

"I hope so too."

He met her gaze again. It was probably only for a brief moment, less than a second, but his eyes really focused on her. "We both want the same thing—to make this work as best as we can."

She nodded. "Yes, we do." She didn't say anything for the rest of the drive. There wasn't anything to say, even though there probably should have been. After all, they were about to say vows in front of a judge, and enter into a binding lifelong contract.

After Drako put the vehicle into park, he turned to look at her. The tension between them was so strong, the air between them crackled. "If you don't want to go through with this, all you have to do is tell me now. I'll take you home, no hard feelings."

"No, I'm ready." As ready as she'd ever be.

"Are you sure, Rin?"

"Absolutely. What about you? Any doubts?"

"One."

"Oh?" She hadn't realized she'd looked away until he caught her chin in his hand and moved it to the left. Her eyes followed a fraction of a second later.

"I'm not convinced you'll make it through the ceremony without passing out or throwing up."

Her laugh was a nervous titter. "You might be right about that." She patted her belly, which she had to admit seemed to be home to a whole swarm of wildly flittering butterflies, overdosed on super-heavy-duty flower nectar. "I'm hoping my stomach'll settle down by the time we get into the courthouse."

"Can I get you something before we go in?"

"No." She felt her cheeks flushing and wondered if the heat gathering under her skin was from overwrought nerves or the embarrassment of being so freaking nervous in front of this man that she felt she might throw up.

Please, God, let me get through this without making a fool of myself.

When he released her chin, he gave her jaw the lightest brush of his fingertips. Then, while she sat there tingling, her face flaming and her hands trembling in her lap, he opened his door, exited the vehicle, and as she fumbled with the lever, he opened her door and helped her out of the car.

Standing next to him, she was very grateful for the fact that he was much bigger than she, strong and stable and capable. She looped one of her arms around his and held on, surprised and mortally humiliated by how wobbly her knees were.

She wasn't about to face a firing squad. She was just going into a courthouse, for crying out loud.

The next bit of time seemed to rush past in a hazy blur. Her mind focused on Drako, his quiet strength a welcome comfort during the ceremony. They signed in, took a seat in a waiting area and, when they were called into the courtroom, took their places in front of the cheerful judge. The vows were over before she had fully comprehended what she'd promised, rings exchanged, papers signed, and congratulations given by the employees serving as witnesses.

She didn't faint.

She didn't throw up.

As they were about to leave the courtroom, as Mr. and Mrs. Drako Alexandre, the judge stopped them with an unexpected, "Wait a minute. We forgot the most important part."

They'd said the "I do" 's. Signed on the dotted lines. Mr. Judge had stamped and Ms. Notary had sealed and signed... and what important part was left?

"You may now kiss the bride," the judge said, grinning.

Rin's stomach slid to her toes, and the butterflies in her belly, the ones that had finally stopped flapping around like headless chickens, went back to doing dives and swoops and spins. She looked up into her husband's face. Her brain registered his I'm-only-doing-this-because-I-have-to expression just before he tipped his head.

She slammed her eyelids closed, curled her fingers around his forearms, and waited.

His lips were warm, moist but not soggy, soft but also not timid. They slid across hers smoothly, like satin. The brief contact was enough to make her head spin . . . and a few parts of her anatomy blaze. He didn't stop there, evidently deciding he needed to put on a believable show. His hands cupped her face, thumbs grazing across her cheekbones, and he kissed her more earnestly. His mouth tormented and teased hers until she parted her lips to drag in a deeper breath, which only opened her up to even greater torment. And pleasure.

When his tongue dipped inside to fill her mouth with his sweet, intoxicating flavor, she actually whimpered. Raw, unexpected desire flared in her body, igniting little simmering blazes along all her nerves. Driven by that desire, she slid her tongue along his, enjoying the taste of him, the scent that had filled her nostrils, and the gentle pressure of his hands as he held her head still, captured, so that he could taste and take and possess at his leisure. She was powerless to move away.

She didn't want to move away.

But then that silly judge, the one who'd made a point of suggesting the kiss in the first place, cleared his throat, putting an end to what had no doubt been the most amazing kiss of her life.

At the moment, she was mighty happy she'd married Drako Alexandre. If that glorious kiss was a sign of things to come, then she was going to enjoy the more intimate parts of their arrangement a whole lot.

The world seemed to be rocking under her feet, necessitating her wrapping her arm around his waist and smooshing her body against his side. She gave the judge a self-conscious smile, muttered, "Thank you," and with her husband's help, walked out to the car.

No sooner were they on the road than her thoughts were back where they should be, on getting the money to the jerk who was selling her sister, and getting Lei safely under her roof, or rather, Drako's.

It was done. He had accepted his duty and taken a wife. There was only one thing left to do now, and after that kiss, he was sort of looking forward to it.

She wasn't anything like his typical lover, seeking dark carnal pleasures through D/s, looking for him to play a role, take control, lead him or her on a journey into themselves. Drako hadn't taken every one of his play partners into his bed, but he couldn't remember the last time he'd had sex without scening with the partner first. Power play was his foreplay. It warmed his blood. But it did more than that. It turned his mind away from obligations, duty, responsibility.

Tonight would be a different experience for him, one he had been anticipating with less enthusiasm than a trip to the dentist. Vanilla sex had never been fulfilling for him. It had been too mechanical, robotic, detached from the rest of him—soul, mind. Insert Rod A into Slot B, slide it around for a few minutes, and that was it. Done.

But that was before that kiss.

Was it hopeful thinking on his part, or had he sensed a level of submission in his new bride's response?

Then again, did he dare take their marriage to that level and allow himself to be that vulnerable?

What if he learned to need her?

Love her?

The thought terrified him.

He couldn't let it go that far. The price they would pay, not only he and his bride, but his brothers, and others too....

Nonono.

It was far better to be safe. To protect himself, his brothers, and the many other people who depended upon them, he would have to keep things under control. That was, after all, the reason for his buying a bride in the first place. She would understand. She'd accepted his proposal. They'd both made their choice, freely, and were facing the consequences as adults. There was nothing more to think about.

He pulled the envelope from his pocket and handed it to her, assuming she was anxious to get the money now.

She accepted it with a soft, "Thank you," and slipped it into her purse, turning her head away again to stare out the window.

Anxiety was etched into her expression, her tight lips and taut jaw, the slender column of her neck and slight tremble in her hands. Long tapered fingers were curled tightly around the leather straps of her purse, her knuckles white from the pressure.

"I hope you don't mind....I have a quick errand to run when we get home," she muttered as she toyed with her ring. "It's important."

"I'll drive you."

"No. Please." She looked at him. "I mean, thanks for offering, but I hate to drag you along, make you waste more time—"

"I don't mind." He enunciated the words clearly, hoping she'd get the message without him having to say it. There weren't a lot of good reasons—ones that didn't involve assholes with guns—for a person to need as much cash as she did all at one time. He might not be striving to be Husband of the Year, but he would protect his wife, whether she was willing to let him or not.

She chewed on her lip. "I don't know."

"I'll wait in the car if you want," he lied.

It took her a minute or two, but she finally acquiesced with a breathy, "Okay."

"Where to?"

"Magic Touch. I need to make a phone call."

He reached for her, wanting her to listen closely, to hear his words, and to believe them. "Tell me why you need so much money. What could possibly be worth selling yourself, your future, for? Rin, you can trust me."

5

You can trust me.

Rin had heard those words so many times before, and from so many untrustworthy people, they were like a red blinking light, a signal. *Warning: Danger Ahead, Do Not Enter.*

Yet, despite her instinct, she had a gut feeling she needed Drako's help. He'd be her backup, in case the bastard who had Lei decided his original price had been too low.

But did that mean she had to tell him *everything?*

"My sister," she blurted. "It's for her."

"Your sister," he echoed, glancing at her with those dark, probing eyes.

"She's worth it. Any price."

"You sold yourself to help your sister?"

She shrugged. "Yes. I needed the money for her."

"I see." His puzzled expression said exactly the opposite. "Did she borrow more than she could pay back? Or did she build up a gambling debt?"

"No, it's nothing like that." Rin stared down at her wedding ring. It was going to take some time getting used to wearing it.

Sure, it was beautiful, the prettiest ring she'd ever seen. The center stone was a brilliant blue shade. Absolutely gorgeous. Regardless, it felt heavy, strange.

It was going to take some time getting used to something else—having someone else care what happened to her, what she was doing and where she was going. If there was going to be any hope of trust developing between them someday, she had to tell him more.

She said, "I won't lie, we'll be dealing with somebody who's just as dangerous and slimy as a loan shark. I'm . . . I met with him once, and I'm not sure he's going to give me what I want, even after I hand over the money."

The car came to a sudden stop.

"Who?"

She knew he was staring at her, shocked, angry, bewildered, which was why she couldn't stop looking down at her hands, tightly gripped in her lap. "A man named Campioni. He's a local contact for an international sex slave smuggling ring. I'm . . . buying my sister."

Her husband visibly gritted his teeth. "The police should be involved—"

Panic set in. "No!" She threw her hands forward, catching the front of his shirt in her fists. "Please." Within a single stuttering heartbeat, her eyes filled with hot tears. "Please," she repeated, the words choking her, clogged in a throat that was closing in on itself. "You don't know how long I've been searching. How many times—" Despite trying to swallow it down, a sob tore through the blockage and slipped between her lips. "They'll send her away again." It was no use now, months of desperation, of pain and longing and frustration had taken their toll and all the emotions she'd been squelching broke through the barrier she'd fought so long to hold up. Tears ran from her eyes in hard gushes, and sobbing, retching noises thundered from her chest. Her head dropped forward, her forehead striking something hard. Her hands went to her face, catching hot, salty tears and somewhat muffling her sniffles and sobs.

She wanted to stop, but she couldn't. Tried to, but failed. Fought to, but eventually surrendered. It was only then, when she finally accepted that she couldn't control the outburst, that it eased a little. A little more. Finally, she was breathless and dizzy and exhausted, but the worst was over.

When her vision cleared, she realized her face was buried in his shirt and he was touching her. On the head. His hand wasn't moving; it was just resting there. But the gesture was so patient and kind it almost made her start crying again.

"I'll handle this," he said.

"But I never expected you to," she said to his chest. "She's *my* sister. My responsibility."

"It's dangerous." When she looked up, he explained, "What makes you think a man who sells human beings is going to keep his end of any bargain, especially with a woman who is—no offense—the size of the average twelve year old? It's more likely you'd end up becoming his next victim. Then where will you both be?"

"You're right." Sitting upright, she crossed her arms over her chest and tried to subdue the shudders still quaking through her body. "I thought of that, and I wasn't going to assume fifty thousand dollars was going to be enough to appease his greed. I was hoping..." What? That'd he'd give her Lei anyway?

"You said your sister's name is Lei?"

"Yes." She grabbed her purse, unzipped it, and pulled out the worn photograph she always carried. She handed it to him. "This was taken just before..."

"...she was kidnapped?" he finished.

Unable to tell him the ugly truth, she simply nodded. "I still feel guilty making you do this."

"You aren't *making* me do anything." He placed Lei's picture in his wallet, shifted the car into drive, and pulled back out into traffic. "After you call Campioni, I'll take you home. I don't want you there when the deal goes down. Just in case things go bad."

Those words hung in the heavy air for several moments until she couldn't help herself, and she had to apologize. "I'm sorry. For dragging you into something I'm sure you don't want to get into. I feel awful."

"Don't."

"But I'm not used to this, to letting somebody else handle something I should be doing—"

"I just wish you'd trusted me before." When he stopped the car at a red light, he gave her a long, hard look.

She lifted her chin, making sure he saw the determination in her eyes. "I wouldn't have accepted the money without marrying you, if that's what you're thinking."

"What about a loan?" he asked, turning when the light changed.

"I couldn't pay that much money back." She shook her head, more convinced than ever that she'd made the only choice she could have. "There was nothing you could have said or done to make me take money I couldn't repay."

At the next red light, Drako commented, "You're stubborn."

She crossed her arms over her chest. "When it comes to some things, like matters of honor, I guess I am."

"That makes two of us."

They shared a smile, a moment, and in that magical second or two, as they gazed into each other's eyes, Rin wondered if she hadn't, by some bizarre twist of fate, found the man of her dreams.

Of course, it was way too soon to tell. In her current state, she certainly couldn't trust her intuition or gut feeling, not when her emotions were so stirred up. She was anxious, petrified something would go wrong with Lei, confused and worried about her new marriage, and unsure whether she'd made the worst mistake of her life.

But there was something in her heart now that hadn't been there for a long, long time. Hope.

Drako hid his thoughts from his bride as he drove down familiar streets, knowing what he was thinking would make Rin even more upset, feel guiltier. He wasn't happy about this situation, but he couldn't blame anybody but himself, certainly not Rin. He hadn't known the details, but that didn't mean he had been taken by complete surprise by her story either. Women didn't marry men for fifty thousand dollars, cash, every day. There was a very good reason why she'd done something so odd, so desperate.

Her sister was a sex slave? That wasn't something he'd exposed himself to in a while. There'd been a time or two—he'd been at his worst—when he'd resorted to paying for some female company. He hadn't asked, but one girl told him, after she'd serviced him, that she had been kidnapped from her home, shipped out of her country, and forced into prostitution. He'd briefly considered helping her, had in fact planned to hire her again and ask her some questions, but when he'd called the call girl agency, he was told she was gone and nobody knew what had happened to her.

Much later, he learned she'd been found dead, the supposed victim of a mass murderer who had been killing local, high-priced prostitutes.

After that experience, Drako never hired another prostitute again. He also decided, after the fact, that getting involved in smuggling a sex slave out of the country wasn't something he needed to be doing, for a lot of reasons. How ironic that he was facing a similar situation now, so many years later.

At least he had learned something useful. He knew that one small mistake could cost Rin's sister her life.

He'd have to use a fake name. No doubt about that. Above all else, he had to protect his family and the secret they were charged to keep. He wouldn't ask his brothers to help, even if it was a temptation. He'd have to go alone.

He parked the car in the lot next to the massage parlor where Rin had been working, and as she jumped out of the passenger seat with a quick, "I'll be right back," he stared at the little piece of his face that was reflected in the rearview mirror. How could he disguise himself?

Sunglasses and a hat would have to do. He'd make a quick stop somewhere to pick some up.

When she returned to the car, she turned a nervous smile his way. "He'll meet you in a half hour. Here." A little reluctantly, she handed him the envelope of cash.

"Perfect. That gives me enough time to take you home." As he shifted the car into gear, he warned her, "You can't tell my brothers anything. No matter what happens. Promise me."

Her eyes widened. "I promise."

He gave her one final look and then, figuring he had a fifty-fifty chance of her keeping his secret, and wishing his chances were better, he decided he couldn't take her back to his house yet. His brothers were taking up temporary residences to give them some privacy, but they wouldn't be gone yet. "I think we'd better go with Plan B."

"Plan B?"

"Where do—did—you live?"

"Oh! That Plan B. Take a left at the next light." She pointed up ahead.

"Can I get there and back in fifteen?"

"Ten, and that's if you hit every light."

"Excellent. I need to make a quick stop and I'd like to be there before Campioni does. Don't want to risk walking into an ambush. He isn't expecting me, right? That'll work to my benefit."

"Actually, I told him it wouldn't be me. I was afraid..."

"It's okay." He left her at the curb, looking small and terrified, and an uneasy sensation washed over him.

Earlier, when she'd been crying, he'd blamed his weakness on that awful sobbing. Even he, who was normally impervious to the majority of human emotions, had a hard time remaining stoic when a woman was crying. But there'd been no tears since, and still, at this moment, a part of him wanted to hold his new bride, to protect her and take care of her. Badly. Not because it was his duty, like he had told her, or like he had tried to convince himself.

But just... because.

This was not the way he'd thought his wedding day would go.

This wasn't the way Rin had imagined her wedding day would go. There'd been no formal ceremony. No church. No altar. No flowers. No reception or maid of honor.

No love.

No stolen kisses in the back of a limo.

No being carried in strong arms over the threshold.

Not even a giddy, happy anticipation of things to come. Tonight. Tomorrow. Next month or year. Nope.

Instead, here she was, married but alone. With nothing, not even the money she'd basically sold herself for. And she was clinging to a promise from a man she barely knew and the miniscule shred of hope he had sparked in her heart, that she hadn't made the mistake of a lifetime.

Hardly the wedding day of her dreams.

Even so, she was sitting in what she'd always expected would be her temporary home, feeling some sense of optimism. Drako was nobody to mess with. She could see it in his every movement, the flinty black depth of his eyes and the firm set of his jaw. If her sister hadn't been smuggled off already, to another pimp somewhere, he would convince Campioni to sell her to him. He would buy her freedom.

Rin just hoped Drako or Lei wouldn't be hurt.

She burned off some nervous energy by packing what few personal possessions she'd accumulated in the tiny apartment over the past few months, stuffing the items she didn't want to throw away into cardboard boxes and suitcases. She checked the clock often—about every fifteen minutes—as she worked.

This was absolute torture.

A half hour passed.

An hour dragged.

An hour and a half crawled.

Two hours crept at a sloth's pace.

Just as Rin was contemplating calling the police to report her new husband missing, a knock on the door sent her heart racing. She didn't walk, or even jog, to the door; she raced. Without bothering to check the peephole or ask who it was, she unlocked it and threw it open.

Her sister's face was a deep scarlet, stained with tears, and her almond-shaped eyes were rimmed in bright red. Lei lurched forward, throwing her thin frame into Rin's arms, and overwhelmed with relief—it was over, finally over!—Rin cried into the slick black sheet of her hair.

No matter what, the sacrifice she'd made had been worth it.

Together, the two sisters unleashed the tears they'd held back, the sorrow and fear and frustration escaping them in shivers and sobs. It was only after the shaking eased to slight tremors and her eyes had cleared that Rin looked in the narrow, dingy corridor for her husband.

"He's outside waiting," Lei answered as she dragged the back of her hand across her face. "He said he wanted to give us some time. Privacy. Who is he? A detective?"

"Not exactly." Uneasy about Lei's line of questioning, and hoping her sister wouldn't be upset once she found out exactly how Rin had managed to free her, Rin admitted, "He's my husband."

Lei's gaze dropped to Rin's left hand. Her expression sobered. She took Rin's fingertips in hers and lifted to get a closer look at the ring. "You're married? Really? I've missed so much. Your wedding."

"You won't miss anything else. I promise."

Lei glanced up, rewarded her with a small smile, no doubt the best she could produce after living in hell for twelve months. "Then whose apartment is this?"

"It was mine. I was just... moving some last-minute things."

Lei stepped into the dinky, sparsely furnished living room. "How long ago were you married?"

"Not long." She avoided Lei's gaze.

"What are you keeping from me?" Lei turned slowly. "You're here in Detroit, not back home. Living in this dump... why?"

"I had to find you. I'd do anything for you."

"Anything? How long have you known him? Where did you meet him? How long were you dating?" Lei strolled around the living room, checking tabletops, bookshelves. "Where are the pictures of you two together?"

"Um..."

"You were just married—when, today? Where's your dress? Your flowers?"

"Well..."

"Rin, what's going on?" Lei glared at her and stomped back across the living room, halting directly in front of Rin.

Rin wanted to lie, but she knew it would be no use. If Lei was going to live with her, she'd figure it out soon enough. "We sort of struck an agreement."

"Rin!" Lei smacked her hands over her face.

Rin grabbed her sister's wrists and tried to pull her hands away from her face. "It's no different from what grandmother did so many years ago. And her mother before her."

"It's no different from what mother did to me." Lei's shoulders shook as she began crying again.

"No, no, no, Lei! Oh, God, please don't be upset. It's not the same." Rin dragged one of Lei's hands down and stared into the one eye that was uncovered. "That man out there is a good, honest person. He's nothing like the bastard mother sold you to. He's not going to hurt me, sell me to someone else, or abuse me. And I went into the deal willingly. I had a choice."

Lei murmured something, her voice so soft, Rin couldn't make out the words. Lei lifted a shaking hand, pressing fingertips to her lips. "I can't believe this. You bought my freedom by selling yours."

"I got you away from criminals. I saved you from what had to be a living hell. And I did it by agreeing to become a man's *wife,* not his slave."

"I don't know. . . ." Lei dragged the back of her hand across her face.

"There's no going back now. What's done is done," Rin said, for both their sakes.

"If he were such a good person, would he keep you to your promise after learning why you did it?"

That was a good point, but one Rin couldn't allow herself to dwell on. "Look, Lei, I don't think it's going to be hard to make the best of the situation. You saw him. He's a very handsome man. He's wealthy. And he was kind enough to walk into what might have been a dangerous situation to free you. That right there tells you something important about him."

Lei chewed on her lip while Rin went to her room to get the last box of her belongings and set it on the floor next to the door. "How long have you known him?"

"Long enough."

"I hope so."

Rin gave her visibly troubled sister another hug. "I'll be okay. We'll be okay. Now that we're together, and you're free from that horrible life"—she tightened her hold on her baby sister—"we have each other now, and that's all that matters."

The leader of the Chimera tossed the car keys into the air and smiling, caught them. He pointed at the wall of hunting trophies. "The old man taught me a thing or two about hunting, most of it illegal but damn practical. Being a practical man, I listened. I learned. And now I'm going to put what I learned to use."

"What's hunting got to do with anything?" For a smart guy, his second in command, Leonard Clancy, was very stupid sometimes.

"Didn't I tell you to stop taking that shit? It's rotting your brain." He smacked the joint out of Clancy's mouth. It sailed across the room, hit the wall, and landed on the floor. "If you're hunting deer and you want to draw it out so you can get a clear shot, what do you do?"

"Ummm. Use a call?"

"Yes. Exactly!" He smacked Clancy on the back. "Now you're thinking."

Clancy's face screwed into a mask of confusion. "But what kind of call do you use for a griffin?"

"Well, it's not a call so much as bait. We're fishin', not hunting." He extended his arms. "You're looking at it."

"You're the bait?"

"Yes. And you know who the hunter is?"

Clancy's grin was disturbing enough to make the Chimera's leader second-guess himself. Could he really trust this moron? Sadly, he was the only man among the Chimera members he'd even think to trust.

"Don't get yourself too worked up. You've got to stay in control. Can you do what I say?"

Clancy nodded. "Sure. I can. What do we do first? You've got to know where to drop the bait if you want the prey to find it."

"Now that's the most intelligent thing you've said all day." He turned to the map he'd hung on the wall. Years ago, he'd pasted a big red star on the spot where his predecessor had been defeated. "All animals are creatures of habit, even humans," he said, thinking aloud. "We should go there." He pointed at the red star. "Back where the bastards made their last kill. They can't resist going back. But this time it'll be different. We'll win."

6

Rin had always possessed a very vivid imagination. As a child, she'd learned to escape into fictional worlds, magical places where parents were always nurturing and gentle, food was plentiful, and there was nothing to fear. But even after employing her wildest imaginings as she'd ridden to her new home, she hadn't visualized this.

This couldn't be his house. It was too freaking enormous. No, it had to be a museum, an office building, or something. As the car rolled to a stop on the side of the contemporary building, a long span of windows glistening in the waning sunlight, she twisted to exchange a questioning look with Lei over her shoulder.

"What an interesting building. What is it, your office?" Rin asked.

Drako cut the engine and opened his door. "My—your home. Our home. Wait here."

"Home?" She shot Lei another look. And as he strolled around the front of the car, she mouthed the word "home," eliciting a shrug from her sister. Her door opened, and she swiveled around to give Drako a thank-you smile. Looking serious and maybe a little distant, he offered his hand. "My things?" She motioned toward the trunk as she stepped out of the vehicle.

Drako unlatched Lei's door. "Don't worry. I'll get your stuff later, after I've shown you and your sister around."

"Okay." With her sister following, she let Drako lead her up to what would be, from this day forward, her home. She whispered a little "Wow," when they stepped inside. Her voice echoed louder than she'd expected, and she clamped her mouth shut.

This was where she would live? It was hard to fathom.

They'd entered into what she'd describe as an atrium. They were at the back of the house. Straight ahead was a walkway that led deeper inside, and to the right was a gorgeous room with a swimming pool. The tang of chlorine hung heavy in the air. The walls that weren't glass were gleaming wood. Her shoes made sharp clack-clack sounds on the stone-tiled floor. Under the bank of windows facing the driveway stretched a long planter filled with cactuses and flowering plants.

"Do you swim?" Drako ushered them deeper into the house.

A vivid image of Drako, his wavy hair wet, droplets glistening off his sun-burnished skin, played through her mind. Her face warmed. "No, I sink."

He pointed over his left shoulder. "Maybe it would be safer if you read instead?"

Safer, but a lot less fun. "Much." She peered through the door they were passing, finding a library-slash-bar featuring tall white bookcases filled with volumes. Smack-dab in the room's center was a full service bar with a loaded glass rack. At one end of the bar stood a high, round table with padded benches pushed up to it. The light from hanging pendulum fixtures reflected off the gray and silver flecks in the glossy black granite top, flashing silver.

Reading and drinking. Interesting combination.

"Such a large home for one person," she commented.

"I don't live alone. I share the house with my brothers."

"Oh."

"They're out," he said quickly. "Won't be back for a while."

She had to assume that was intentional, so they could have some privacy their first few days or so. Once again, her cheeks burned.

On they traveled, through one room after another. Living room. Den-slash-media room. Kitchen. Dining room. Game room. As they walked, Rin tried to push aside the one thought that kept slipping into her mind, the one that kept making her flush like a kid on her first date.

The one that kept making her heart race and hands tremble ever so slightly.

It was hell trying to hide her jittery nerves from her sister, someone who knew her inside and out. Especially when Drako was close enough for her to feel the heat of his body, catch the scent of the spicy cologne he was wearing. And ohmygod, when he accidentally brushed against her back—or more specifically, her butt—she could swear she stopped breathing for at least ten seconds. She tried to mask the worst of it under friendly chatter. Her sister didn't need to know how anxious she was about tonight.

Her wedding night.

The house was nicely furnished, its style contemporary but not so industrial it was uncomfortable. Up a short flight of wide steps, the bedrooms were spacious, tidy, and airy, each featuring a wide wall of windows that looked out upon what had become heavily shadowed grounds as the sun had slipped below the western horizon.

When Drako showed Rin a room and told her it was hers,

not *theirs,* Lei gave her a pointed look. Rin ignored it. She also tried to ignore the fact that Drako didn't show them the rooms farther down the hall but instead turned back toward the stairs, leading them down to the ground floor again.

The grand tour ended in the kitchen, where her husband opened the steel refrigerator door. "Are you hungry?"

"Starved." She pressed a hand to her hollow stomach.

"Feel free to help yourself to anything in here." He inspected a plastic container with a wrinkled nose. "Everything *should* be safe to eat." He tossed the container into the sink. "If you'll make a list of what you like, I can have the kitchen fully stocked by tomorrow."

"Thank you." Standing close enough to Drako to smell that intoxicating cologne, Rin rubbed her belly. "Do you have any deli meat? Cheese? A sandwich will do for now."

"I don't know." Drako pulled open several refrigerator drawers before shaking his head. "How about I order some takeout? What would you like?"

She moved a smidge closer to him, telling herself it was so she could see inside the open appliance. "It doesn't have to be anything fancy. In fact, I'd rather eat something simple but solid. I guess I'm not in the mood to experiment today." Reaching around him, she grabbed a bottle of water. "Lei, what about you?" She handed her sister the bottle, then reached in for another one.

Lei twisted off the bottle's cap. "A sandwich sounds good to me."

"I'll get some sandwiches then." Drako closed the refrigerator, stepped aside, and pulled his cell phone from his pocket. While he placed the order, he handed Rin the remote that had been sitting on the counter and pointed toward the enormous wide-screen television in the media room, set off from the kitchen. By the time he had ended the call, she'd settled down with her sister on a comfortable couch, an episode of *CSI* playing. But even with her favorite show playing bigger than life, her gaze continued to wander back to him again and again.

That was her husband. Husband. A week ago, she couldn't have imagined herself married. Nor had she dared to hope she'd have her sister back, safe, at her side.

He was staring out the window, his jaw set, gaze locked on something in the darkness beyond the walls of glass. She had to wonder, was this him, his true personality? Brooding and quiet. Mysterious and inscrutable. Or was he as uneasy and nervous as she was about what would happen next?

Even though she knew logically the worst was over, her sister was safe, Rin couldn't help feeling squirmy and on edge. It felt as if every nerve in her body prickled. Every muscle was pulled just a tiny bit tighter than normal. The sensation was making her warm and twitchy.

Unable to focus, she positioned herself in front of him, closer to the window. She peered through the ceiling-to-floor glass, into a still world full of thick shadows. The sky was cloaked in heavy clouds, masking any starlight or moonlight that might have lent a little illumination to the nightscape. She could see the smudgy outline of the treetops against the sky. Nothing more.

"The house has one of the best views in town." Drako had moved closer; she could tell by the proximity of his voice. A slight quiver of awareness shimmied up her spine. "We're on riverfront property here. The water's down the hill about a hundred yards. I hope you'll enjoy it."

Without turning around, she nodded. "I'm sure I will." She pressed her fingertips to the glass pane, thankful for the chill as it seeped into her skin. The man behind her was her husband, and he would exercise his marital rights. Tonight? Tomorrow night? Every night? A low vibration hummed in her center. "I just love sitting and watching wildlife. Birds. Animals. . . ."

"Very good, then." Drako's voice sounded far away. The

change in his location inspired her to turn around. When she did, she found he'd walked all the way to the opposite end of the kitchen. "I have some work to do. And unfortunately, it can't wait. Today's road trip wasn't planned, so I had to set aside some important obligations. You won't be upset if I don't keep you company while you eat, I hope? I'm guessing you and your sister have a lot to talk about."

She leaned back against the window. The glass was cool against her shoulder blades, her buttocks. "Oh. No, not upset at all."

"Okay." He looked uncertain, eyebrows pulled, mouth tight. "You'll listen for the door?"

She nodded and forced a smile she didn't feel. "Sure."

"The bill's been paid."

"Okay."

He shifted his weight from one foot to the other. "And... you can find your bedrooms on your own?"

On her own? Was he going to avoid the obvious tonight? The wedding night?

She felt a little relieved but also let down. Maybe she wasn't ready to be intimate with Drako. They were, after all, strangers. But wouldn't he give her some time alone with him tonight? To get to know him? She blinked, hoping he couldn't see the emotions playing through her at the moment. "Not a problem. I have internal GPS."

"Okay. Then, good night."

Lei barely waited until after he was out of earshot before heaving a highly exaggerated sigh. "Rin, what are you doing?"

Rin flopped into a nearby chair and pretended to be carefree. "I'm waiting for our food."

"That's not what I'm talking about, and you know it."

"Fine." Because she'd missed most of the episode of *CSI* that had been playing, and couldn't follow it, she scooped up the television remote and started clicking through channels. "I'm keeping my end of the bargain."

Now it was her sister's turn to pace the floor. "You're going to be so sorry you did this, and it sucks because you did it for me."

Rin shook the remote at her sister. "I'm not convinced yet that it's the huge mistake you seem to think it is. Look at this place." She did a Vanna White, standing up and sweeping her arm in a wide arc. "We're living in a freaking mansion. Not that what happened to you was in any way good, but if I hadn't been in this town looking for you, and willing to listen to Drako's proposal, I would never have married a man like him. What were my prospects back at home? Honestly? This isn't bad. I'll be getting money every week to spend any way I like—"

"An allowance."

She shot her sister a grumpy-faced scowl. "No, it's not an allowance. I deserve every penny that man will be paying me."

"Then you see yourself as a whore."

"No! No." How would she make her sister understand? She went to her sister and made sure she was really listening. "This is no different from an arranged marriage, or a marriage of convenience, like you've read in those romance novels you're so fond of. And before you tell me they were set in the nineteenth century, that marriages of convenience don't exist anymore, I say bullshit. You and I both know women who've married men they didn't love, just so they could have financial security."

Her sister blinked, drawing Rin's attention to her eyes, which were growing red and watery again. "I never thought you'd do it though. You had so much more going for you."

Rin hugged her weepy sister, suspecting some of her tears were more about the hell she'd been through than what Rin had done to get her out of it. "Who says I have to give up all my dreams just because I'm married? If anything, this marriage should allow me to pursue what I want. I won't have to work some menial job to pay the rent. That frees up all kinds of time for other things."

Lei stepped away from Rin, crossed her arms over her chest, her body language telling Rin she still wasn't listening. "I can see where you're going with this. But still, Rin, I see that look in your eye. I know you're scared, uncertain."

"Things will get better with time. It's all very new. Drako and I both need time to adjust, to understand each other." The doorbell rang, and Rin, after waving her sister to follow her, headed toward the front of the house. "I don't want you to feel guilty. In fact, it'll kill me if you don't support me in this. Please, Lei. Please. . . ." She stopped at the front door, turning to her sister. "Forget why I got married. For both our sakes." Before her sister could respond, she pasted on a happy face and opened the door, greeting the delivery guy with a friendly, "Hello."

She hoped, as she accepted the food from the teenager on the porch, that she wouldn't need to hone her acting skills, or that she wouldn't spend the rest of her days living a lie. It would be hell trying to hide the truth from Lei.

But if that was what it took to make her sister happy, then that was what she'd do.

"An unexplained illness has brought at least a dozen people to a local emergency room—"

Drako hit the power button on the remote, cutting off the news broadcast. He needed quiet, to think, to remind himself what was important, and what would happen if he forgot. A knock interrupted his thoughts before he'd gotten past remembering the disappointment he'd seen in his new bride's eyes earlier, and how good she'd looked, smelled, tasted during the ceremony. . . .

Talen entered without being invited, but that was nothing

new. Both of Drako's brothers knew his door was always open. They kept very little from each other. There wasn't much need for closed doors and absolutely no room for secrets between them. Talen flopped into the chair opposite Drako's desk and snatched the book Drako had been trying to read off the desktop. Without reading a word, Talen thumbed through the pages. "Somebody's been in the old Chimera hangout since Oram was released, digging through some old files and stuff."

Drako sat a little taller. This was news. There hadn't been any movement in the old headquarters in months. Drako and his brothers had all basically agreed the place and everything in it—mostly rusted steel desks, broken chairs, and file cabinets stuffed full of worthless documents—had been abandoned. "How do you know?"

Talen glanced at the book's cover, then returned it to its place. "The boys saw a car parked out back when they were reviewing some of the security camera footage. They went out there and took a look."

Drako put the book in his desk drawer and shut it. "I don't know why Oram would go back there. There's nothing left that's worth anything. We combed through every piece of paper, searched every corner. It's all garbage."

Talen shrugged. "Evidently, he disagrees."

"Are you sure it's Oram?"

"Not yet. Could be anyone—curious teenagers, indigents looking for something to sell for a quick buck—but the timing's interesting."

Drako agreed with a nod. "Probably not a coincidence." He ran his fingertip over the trackpad on his laptop, waking it from sleep mode.

"The boys are going through some of the older security tapes to see if we can make an ID. I guess it's a good thing we didn't disconnect the cameras yet. I'll let you know what we find, once we get through them all."

Staring at his computer screen, but too distracted to really see it, Drako drummed his fingertips on his desk. "Something feels off. It doesn't make sense."

"What do you mean?"

"I mean, Oram's been sitting in plain view all these years, until the day our father dies, and next thing we know, he's disappeared."

"The timing makes sense to me. Or at least, it doesn't strike me as illogical. The old guard's gone for good, and now Oram is ready to slide under the radar and prepare to test the replacements."

Drako set his elbows on the desktop and steepled his fingers under his chin. Thinking aloud, he asked, "So why go skulking around empty warehouses? Especially ones he has to know we're keeping an eye on?"

Talen, restless as usual, got up and started pacing the office. "There's gotta be something important in there."

"Why wouldn't he send somebody else?"

"Maybe he knows what he's looking for but nobody else does?"

That was possible. If Oram hadn't fully trusted the other members of the Chimera, he might have felt he needed to hide some things to protect them, or to secure his place within the Chimera while he was in the hospital. Still, Drako couldn't shake the feeling they were looking at only half the picture. "I don't know."

"Don't worry. I'll send Wilkerson and Dobbs over there to check things out. If there's anything to find, they'll find it." Talen walked with his usual loose-hipped saunter toward Drako's desk. "You've got other things to think about now anyway." He gave Drako a little slug on the shoulder. "How was the wedding?"

"Fast," Drako answered, still distracted as he opened a file on John Dale Oram on his computer. Oram had a gift for deceit and manipulation. His criminal record went back to his childhood, when at the tender age of eight he'd talked some other kids into stealing some equipment from their elementary school. His take, about a thousand dollars worth of electronics. From there, he'd graduated to bigger crimes, more profitable, including embezzlement and fraud. Yet he hadn't spent a single day in jail, thanks to a convenient, well-documented defense.

"Fast is good, at least when it comes to weddings."

Drako wouldn't argue that one. "Yeah."

Talen strolled over to the bar in the corner and helped himself to a glass of scotch. "I didn't expect to see you here tonight. Tomorrow night, yeah. But you're working on your wedding night?"

Drako gave his brother a glance, then went back to skimming the Oram file. "I'm not ready...."

"Not ready for what?" When Drako didn't answer right away, Talen shook his head. "Damn, is it that bad?"

"No." Drako scrolled to the bottom of the page as he listened to the clank of ice in Talen's glass, the thunk of the bottle striking the glass as he refilled it. "She's a decent woman. Knows what to expect."

His brother grunted. "Sounds like hell to me."

"Not at all. It's just going to take some time for her to get used to everything." Drako stole a quick glance at his brother, emptying his glass again. "That'll be easier with you two staying at your condos."

"Are you worried at all about her being at the house by herself, with Oram out?"

"No. He doesn't know who we are, let alone where we live. That'll change, of course, if we learn Oram's snooping too close to home."

Talen filled his glass a third time, and drained it just as quickly. "It's been years. If our old man and his brothers had left any trail for him to follow, it's long gone by now."

Drako clicked the X, closing the file on Oram. "I hope you're right."

"You've always been overly cautious. That's not a bad thing. As long as it doesn't work against us somehow." Talen set his dirty glass on Drako's desk.

Drako snatched it off and set it on a surface that wouldn't be marked for all eternity. "I don't see that happening."

"Me either." His brother's head jerked down. He pulled his cell from his pocket. It vibrated with a deep humming sound. "There's my baby. Gonna head down to the suite for some fun. Maybe you need to unwind a little too."

Drako shut down his computer. "Yeah, unwind. Good idea."

7

Her skin was like fine alabaster, smooth and clear, not even the smallest imperfection marring its surface. Even though Rin's skin wasn't the color of ivory, he could easily imagine it was her kneeling before him now, waiting eagerly for his touch, his commands, his rewards.

Drako's gaze traveled the bony ridge of the submissive's spine from nape to the crease of her exposed buttocks. Lovely. His canvas. He would paint a masterpiece, and in the process, he would provide for her every need.

And deny his own.

This wasn't going to be pleasant, but it was what they both needed—no, they all needed: himself, his submissive, and his new bride as well. If he didn't exorcise his darker urges, using them as a prolonged foreplay, he would be tempted to try to pull Rin into this world of pleasure-pain and power play. It wasn't what she wanted; he only played with submissives who came to him, willingly, eyes wide open, knowing it was what they needed. Not to mention, he would become too vulnerable if he scened with Rin. During the exchange of power and control, the submissive wasn't the only one tested, challenged. The dom's defenses could just as easily be stripped away.

No, he could not, would not scene with Rin. Not ever.

Focus on the present, on the submissive kneeling before you now.

The first thing this submissive craved was pain. Only a mild burn, just enough to prepare the nerves, to get the blood pumping a little. He selected a hairbrush with metal bristles, the sharp tips coated in plastic. He squatted, leaned over her, inhaled her scent, feminine and clean, no sharp, cloying cologne to burn his nostrils or mask the smells he hungered for. He blew a soft stream of air across her nape. When her skin puckered with goose bumps, he dragged the hairbrush down the center of her back and watched the muscles under that smooth surface tighten ever so slightly.

Ah, yes, she was so responsive. Already, his blood was warming, his body responding to the minute signals hers was sending.

A slight increase in heat emanating from her skin.

A tiny change in her breathing.

The almost-imperceptible spice of a woman's arousal perfuming the air.

He inhaled again, exhaled, closed his eyes, imagined it was Rin's shallow breaths he heard as he gently tapped the brush down the canvas, her aroma he was pulling into his lungs.

"Master." The word, a sweet gift, hadn't so much been spoken as sighed.

She needed more; he would give her more. More pain. More pleasure.

This submissive had been broken long ago, her defenses stripped away. She freely submitted to him now, eagerly accepting every morsel of pleasure he gave her, and in return, she offered her gratitude in the form of sighs, shudders, and, later, orgasms.

"Tell me what you want," he commanded. "Not with your words. With your body."

Her shoulders quivered. Her spine arched prettily, pushing her round buttocks out. He stood, set the brush down on the table nearby, and made his next choice—a little whip with a bouquet of smooth satin tails that would make his submissive shiver with expectation at the sound of those ribbons sailing through the air. Its bite, however, was not what she would expect. Instead of sharp nips, she'd feel a soft cascade of taps that would prepare her for what would come next.

He drew his arm back high and brought it down quickly, maximizing the speed of the tails as they rained down upon her upper back. She flinched, relaxed, then tightened up again. Again, he struck her, and, again, her body responded. Over and over. He didn't stop until he could tell she couldn't handle any more torment.

As her body coiled with pent-up tension, so did his. Every shallow gasp, every shiver, every swallowed moan did he mirror. His response was completely involuntary, totally out of his control. He was in awe. Enraptured by her surrender. She held back nothing, not a shiver or sigh or moan. By the time he had set aside the satin flogger to take up the leather one, his cock was thick and hard, his blood simmering, his muscles tied into taut knots, his senses hyperalert.

His submissive responded to each strike of the leather flogger as if it were a thrust of his cock. She moaned. She sighed. She tightened until the svelte lines of her torso and arms looked as taut as a runner's during a marathon. Her skin grew flushed, the dusky rose tinting her back, her cheeks, her chest. Tiny droplets of perspiration coated her shoulders, back, breasts.

He saw her face, knew she was lost in a cloud of pain and pleasure, and loving every excruciating second. He wasn't with her, and yet he was. This was a journey she would make alone. But he was within reach, her guide. Her escort. Showing her the way to that place deep inside where thoughts couldn't dull the sensation, smother them like a heavy blanket thrown over a flickering flame.

Many new submissives had asked him why he was a dom, what pleasure he received. He'd tried to tell them, but words could only reveal so much, a tiny fraction. This exquisite moment was what it was all about for him. His reward was in watching a submissive succumb to such deeply satisfying pleasure that every cell in her body vibrated on the perfect frequency. It was music one couldn't hear with the ears, could only feel with the soul.

As he whispered the words, "Come now," he knew he was ready to go to his bride, to give her what she needed.

Rin always had a hard time falling asleep. She assumed it was her body's way of protecting itself, an unconscious response shaped by events she'd long ago pushed out of her mind. Unfortunately, her insomnia only got worse when she was in a new place, a new bed.

It was her brain. It simply wouldn't slow down. Thoughts bounced around inside her skull like superballs dropped from the Sears Tower. She'd learned a long time ago that only one thing helped. Books. Reading.

Unfortunately, she hadn't brought any books with her. In her rush to pack, she'd left them all. Stupid, stupid, stupid. Then again, she'd assumed she wouldn't need a book tonight.

Ack. This was awful. Even if she had read them cover to cover, several times, rereading an old book was better than lying in bed listening to all her doubts and fears echo in her ears over and over and over.

Drako had left hours ago. Where was he?

She sat up, flung her bare feet over the edge of the bed, and listened to the quiet stillness of her new home. It sounded like everyone was asleep. Good. She could go down to Drako's bar-slash-library and take a gander, see if anything looked interesting.

Sporting a T-shirt and cropped sweats, her hair in a messy ponytail, she padded down the stairs, around the corner, and down the hall. She got about ten feet from her destination when she heard his voice. Drako? He was home? He was speaking in a low, sultry tone that made several of her body parts warm up. Even muffled and distant, his voice didn't lose its ability to spark a reaction in her body.

Where was he?

She slowly pivoted on the balls of her feet to take a look behind her. His voice was ever so slightly louder. He had to be in one of the rooms she'd passed. Which one? Several closed doors lined both sides of the corridor.

He stopped speaking, leaving her to stand there in the dark, wondering who he might have been talking with. It was late. Very late. Or early, depending upon how you looked at it. Right before she'd left her room, she'd checked the clock... again. The red glaring numbers had told her it was just after three-thirty in the morning.

What did it say about her new husband that he was awake, just like she, and talking to somebody in the middle of the night? Was he a workaholic? Was he talking to a girlfriend? His brothers? A family member?

Those weren't the kinds of questions she'd get answers to tonight.

Press on.

She did a one-eighty, crept quietly into the library. Just in case he came out into the hallway, she shut the library door before turning on a light. At the flip of one of the switches on the wall, the pendulum lights over the bar illuminated, providing just enough of a glow for her to read the books' spines while not completely blinding her. She started at the closest shelf, skimming titles. *The Catcher in the Rye. Fahrenheit 451. The Color Purple. Ivanhoe.*

Classics.

She moved to the next shelf.

Emma. Jane Austen. Now, that was more like it, something light and fun and diverting.

She pulled the book off and flipped to the first page.

> Emma Woodhouse, handsome, clever, and rich, with a comfortable home and happy disposition, seemed to unite some of the best blessings of existence; and had lived nearly twenty-one years in the world with very little to distress or vex her....

"I'm happy to see someone making use of the library." His baritone voice vibrated through the stark silence, making her heart lurch for a fraction of a second. "I went as far as putting in the bar, thinking it would draw my brothers in here. It worked. Though the books still sit, collecting dust."

Clutching the hardback to her chest, Rin turned to face her husband. He was standing at the door, his button-down shirt unfastened, revealing a glorious stripe of suntanned and chiseled torso. One arm was bent, supporting his weight as he leaned casually against the door frame. His other hand was balled into a fist and resting on his hip. The overall picture he painted was of a man who was relaxed. Comfortable in his skin, and in his surroundings. A tiny glint sparkled in his eye. Ah, was the predator from the bar coming out to play?

She ran her fingertips across the spines of the books sitting on the closest shelf. "I'm a chronic insomniac. This library is going to be my salvation."

"Good. I'm glad to hear that." He reached forward, fingers

hooking beneath the back cover of the book that was still pressed against her breastbone. He gently pulled until she released her hold on the volume. "What do you have here?"

"*Emma*. Jane Austen."

"Excellent book." He opened the cover, the spine cracking from disuse and age. The air filled once again with the scent of dust and old paper. The corners of his mouth lifted into the hint of a smile as he read the first page.

"You've read it?" she asked.

"I've read every book in this room." He closed the novel but didn't hand it back to her. Instead, he swung his arm behind his back, hiding it from her. His gaze focused on her face, and something a little bit wicked and a tiny bit evil played over his features.

Her face instantly flamed, and she was grateful she was standing with her back to the light now, knowing the shadows would probably hide the deep red staining her cheeks. "Really? Every single one?"

"I have no reason to lie to you."

"Of course you don't."

A silent moment passed between them. Their gazes locked. Rin's heart rate doubled, or maybe tripled.

"I can be honest with you about everything." He took a step closer, and she could feel the heat emanating from his body.

"Yes, everything," she said, her voice taking on a breathy, raspy quality. With him so near, she had to tip her head back to look into those dark, shadowed eyes of his. She felt small and vulnerable like this, but it wasn't wholly a bad thing. No, quite the opposite, it was a very good thing.

Although she knew so little about the man standing before her—the man calling her his wife, the man looking down at her with a hungry, feral expression—she still trusted he wouldn't hurt her.

She watched his gaze flick down to her mouth and then

jump back to her eyes, and out of reflex, she moistened her lips with her tongue.

Would he kiss her again like he had in the courtroom? Would he make her forget for one magical moment that this whole thing had been a business deal and spark an even greater hope that there might, someday, be more between them?

"My book?" she asked between shallow inhalations that weren't delivering nearly enough oxygen to her brain.

"I'll give it to you, once I have what I want."

"Which is . . . ?"

"We can start with a kiss."

"Start?"

His expression darkened, making him look even more like the predator she'd met a few nights ago at the bar. This Drako, big and dangerous and sexy, made her blood pump hot and fast through her veins.

And his kiss . . .

Just like the one in the courtroom, this kiss started out soft, fleeting, teasing, but it quickly grew more demanding. Welcomed with a parting of her lips, his tongue slipped inside her mouth. He tasted rich and sweet, like expensive brandy and chocolate and man. It was an intoxicating combination, making her head spin so fast, she had no choice but to throw her arms around his neck and cling to him.

She returned every stab and stroke of his tongue with one of hers. Hungry for more, for something deeper, a touch, a caress, a possession, she pressed her body to his. His heat seeped through the thin cotton of her T-shirt within seconds, the warmth making her blood burn hotter, pump faster.

Between her legs, a deep throbbing need had been set off, and with every excruciating second he kissed her, that wanting doubled. She told him how much she ached for him the only way she could. Fingers curling into his hair at the nape. Tugging desperately. Soft sighs filling their joined mouths. Tongue dancing with his.

She heard a soft thump a split second before he hauled her into his arms. The book. Dropped on the floor.

The kiss had ended, but something much better was about to begin. She shuddered with expectation as he carried her up the stairs.

8

He barely set her on her feet before he gave her a hungry look and dragged her against him for another kiss. It wasn't a tender meeting of mouths or gentle exchange of breath, but a hard possession, full of raw emotion. Her head spun. Her heart lurched in her chest, then settled into a wildly racing pace that made her breathless. She curled her fingers around starched cotton and held on, as he unleashed his fury on her mouth.

If she'd hoped for a slow seduction, she knew she wouldn't receive it. Instead, it seemed she would be getting something much more primal. He kissed her like a man should. He touched her like a man should.

She found herself being half carried, half dragged across her bedroom, only to be pinned against the wall. He held her there, motionless, as he ripped her shirt off. Her bra was next, torn off her body and tossed away, and she was bare and vulnerable and trembling all over.

This wasn't like anything she'd ever experienced, and it certainly wasn't what she'd expected, but she wasn't afraid or shocked. Quite the opposite. She liked the way he was taking command of her body while acting like he was just a little out of control.

He laid a hand over one of her breasts, and she dragged in a shuddering gasp and arched her back, pushing her breast into his palm. Her nipple hardened, the peak becoming supersensitive. His palm was a little rough, the skin grazing over the turgid tip, and her eyelids fluttered and fell, closing her into a world of swirling colors and building need.

She reached for him, but he knocked her hands away, bent down, and laved one nipple with his tongue while he rolled the other one between his finger and thumb. She hovered in some magical place, between heaven and hell. She didn't want him to stop and yet she did. A warm, wet, pulsing need was throbbing between her legs, and she longed to be touched there. No, she needed more than that. She needed him to drive his cock into her and take her until she was sweaty and writhing and quaking.

"Drako," she whispered. "Oh, God."

He lurched back so fast, he stumbled. "I'm sorry." His face was tinted a deep scarlet and his eyes were wild.

"No. Don't apologize."

"I should be gentle. You deserve better than this." He looked down at the torn remains of her shirt, scooped them up, and balled them into his fist. "I'll replace your clothes."

"It's okay." She reached for him again, but once more, he flinched, jerking just out of her reach. Why wouldn't he let her touch him? What was the problem?

He set her shirt on the dresser and turned to face her, his gaze fixed on some point beyond her.

Not knowing what to do next, she quietly stripped off the rest of her clothes and slid under the covers. "Drako."

He gave his head a little shake, as if he was trying to wake himself up. He combed his fingers through his hair, then, expression unreadable, shrugged out of his shirt.

That was one glorious chest.

Next, he unzipped his pants and pushed them down to his ankles, kicked them off.

He wore boxer briefs. And that was one mighty promising bulge front and center.

The underwear was next. He didn't hesitate, just pushed them down his muscular legs and kicked them away. Of course, with a body that perfect, toned and sculpted and beautiful, he had no reason to hesitate.

She tried not to think about the other women who had seen him unclothed, or would see him in the future. For now, the next hour or so, he was hers. And she was his. And nobody else mattered.

What the hell am I doing? This isn't one of your slaves, who expect it rough. She's your wife, you fuckup.

Did he even know how to be with a woman without getting rough?

Drako had to admit, playing with his hot little submissive while denying his own pleasure had done the job. He was hot and tight all over. His balls felt like lead. His cock was so hard he could bust concrete with it. And his blood was searing every cell in his body. He needed release and he wanted this woman, his wife, so badly his teeth ached from his clenched jaw. Instead of having to force himself to carry out an act he was sure he would dread, he was struggling to hold it together long enough to give her a little pleasure.

Breathe, asshole. You're going to scare her right out of that bed, out of your house. Then what?

He took a few slow, deep breaths. They didn't help much, but the burning in his blood eased a fraction of a degree. In some respect, this was no different than a scene with a new submissive. It was his responsibility to serve her needs first. She needed patience, tenderness, gentle kisses, and no matter how fucking bad his balls hurt, he was going to give her that.

One step at a time.

He hesitated at the side of the bed for a heartbeat, or two, or three, then peeled the covers back and climbed in, throwing them over himself.

Rin tensed.

Drako was warm. And the hair on his leg tickled when his calf grazed against hers. She settled on her back as he rolled onto his side and propped his head on a fist, his bent arm displaying a flexed bicep to full advantage. "I won't hurt you."

"I know."

"Are you afraid?"

"Of you? No. There's no reason to be."

He cupped her cheek and rolled toward her, staring into her eyes so deeply she felt a little vulnerable and uneasy. He moistened his lower lip with his tongue and kissed her again.

This time, it was like she was kissing a different man.

His mouth was soft, his touches fleeting, almost too timid. It tickled, but at the same time, those tickles made her squirm. Shivers made the skin of her arms prickle.

They kissed for a while, like two teenagers, hands shyly exploring each other's shoulders, arms. He didn't touch her breasts again, and that made the aching between her legs even more pronounced. He cupped her cheeks, he touched her neck, he caressed her arms. She did the same. It went on so long, she began to wonder if he intended things to go any further. She tried to relax and enjoy, appreciate the simple pleasure of their breaths blended, bodies pressed together, tongues exploring the decadent flavor of each other's mouths. She'd forgotten how good this felt and how frustrating it could be.

When he turned her head and nipped on her earlobe, she

moaned. The warmth between her legs was a pounding ache now, and she needed something there, pressing against her flesh.

"I can't..." she mumbled as she arched her neck to give him access to the most tender spot, just below her ear.

He shifted off her, exactly what she didn't want, and caught her chin in his fingers, pulling it down. When she opened her eyes, she found his gaze troubled, full of uncertainty.

"No, don't stop." She curled her fingers around his wrist and pulled, coaxing his hand down lower, lower still. She left it on her breast and once again, arched her spine, pressing the burning flesh into his palm.

His nostrils flared a tiny bit, enough to barely be noticed. A wash of pink tinted his cheeks. "I don't want to rush you."

"I don't know what you define as 'rushing,' but I can tell you this—I was ready after the first kiss." To show him exactly how hot and wet he'd made her, she took his hand and placed it between her thighs.

The pressure was oh so good. She actually groaned, parted her legs a little wider, and prayed he wouldn't make her wait another second.

The pink stain on his skin darkened a few shades.

He pulled the covers off her, the sensation of the slick cotton dragging across her burning skin only making things worse. She couldn't remember ever wanting a man so badly. It was almost bad enough to make her weep. Or beg. Or throw him onto his back and climb on top of him.

What was he waiting for? Did he dread it so much he was trying to put it off? No hot-blooded male would do that.

When the covers had finally been removed completely, he sat up and eased her legs apart. His teeth bit into his lower lip.

She locked her jaw and stared at his face, watching, breathless, as his eyes took in the sight of her nude body. Her stomach was contracting, making her hips rock forward and back, the motion timed to the thrumming pulse beating through her body.

Seeing him look at her, at all of her, was more powerful than any touch, any stroke. But he wasn't moving, wasn't making good on the dark promise she saw in those eyes. This was too much. She wasn't going to lie there and wait, beg. She wasn't one of his playthings.

She opened her legs wide and, eyes locked on his, parted her labia and touched her clit. The first stroke produced a blade of stabbing, almost unbearable heat. It knocked the air out of her lungs and left her gasping and shaking.

The muscle in his jaw ticced. His mouth thinned. He knocked her hand away, shoved her legs even wider apart, and bent over her pussy.

She held her breath.

His tongue found her clit and she saw stars. He used just the right pressure, the right motion, and the right pace. She raced to the verge of climax and tumbled over the edge. An electric charge buzzed through every single cell in her body and then she quaked and spasmed and locked her knees against the sides of his head. When the sensation dulled, she realized she'd grabbed two fists full of silky hair. She unfurled her fingers and threw her hands up, over her head.

He stopped tormenting her hypersensitive bud, but, thank God, he didn't leave her. She had come. Hard. But she still was missing something, and marriage of convenience or not, she'd been anticipating this for days, since the first time he'd touched her.

When he lay next to her, she thought he might be finished for the night. But as she was rolling onto her side to face him, he eased her onto the opposite side, took her hips in his hands, and entered her from behind. She arched her spine to change the angle of penetration and grabbed onto the sheet to try to hold her position.

He fucked her slowly, his thick cock sliding all the way in and then dragging almost all the way out. The friction was absolutely delicious and, coupled with her own hand on her clit, produced wave upon wave of pure ecstasy.

She'd never had sex in this position. It was relaxing, comfortable, and yet at the same time a little frustrating, much like the entire experience with her new husband was proving to be. It was unbelievably wonderful finally having a hard cock inside her, and when she clenched her inner walls around him, she quivered. But it also left her mildly frustrated that she couldn't take him deeper and she couldn't watch him as he drove them both stroke after stroke toward ecstasy.

He was a beautiful man; why wouldn't she want to see him?

She lifted her outer leg up and rolled slightly back, so she could hook her bent knee over his leg. He grabbed her inner thigh and held it up, pulling it toward her shoulder. Yes, that was better. Then, releasing her leg, he wrapped a strong arm around her waist and held her still. Even better yet. Meeting the pace of his thrusts, she stroked her clit, round circles, until her muscles were all tight again and she was trembling with the need to climax.

Was he close? His thrusts were becoming jerky, his hold on her tighter, his breath sharp little puffs against her shoulder. She was so close. Hot. Tight. Shaking all over. She could feel that tingling electrical current building stronger, stronger.

He growled and began pounding into her pussy in a frenzy, and that was all it took. Over she tumbled, into the abyss. Caught up in a torrent of sensation, she held onto whatever she could reach and let herself go. Wave upon wave of pleasure pulsed through her, washed over her. So good. So right. She didn't want it to end. Not ever. But the spasms slowly eased to twitches, then to tingles.

With a little grunt, he withdrew from her and flopped onto his back. Having lost the support of his body, she rolled onto her back too. Next to her husband and still flying high on endorphins, she waited for her racing heartbeat to slow and her breathing to regulate. When she opened her eyes, she realized she was smiling. Not at anyone or anything. Just because.

"Are you okay?" he asked.

"Sure. I'm fine. Better than fine."

He didn't say anything else.

It got quiet and she thought he'd fallen asleep. But a little while later, before she'd drifted off, he slid out of bed and crept out of the room.

9

"Wilkerson's in the hospital."

Talen's announcement was enough to immediately yank Drako out of his thoughts. He realized, as he jerked his head up, that he'd been staring at his desk for who-knows-how-long. He'd been thinking about Rin, about last night. Again. He'd been doing that all morning.

This had to stop.

Drako waved his brother into his office. "What happened?"

Talen, followed by Malek, rushed into the room and plunked down into the closest chair after dragging it up to the desk. "We don't know yet. He's still in the E.R. The doctor's running some tests. Dobbs called me to let me know. He's with him now. Said he'd call as soon as he knew something."

Drako's phone rang. He checked the caller ID. Dobbs. He hit the speakerphone. "Dobbs?"

"Yeah. I'm here."

Talen leaned closer to the phone. "I'm here too. And Malek. What's up?"

"Don't know much yet," Dobbs said. "We went to the old Chimera place, did a little looking around. That building's big, so we split up. I went one way, Wilkerson the other. An hour or two later, I went to find him, but he was gone."

"Why didn't you call us?" Talen asked.

"I was about to when I got a call from Wilkerson. Or rather, his phone. It was a nurse calling from the hospital, looking for a family member to answer some questions about his medical history. I headed right over to the hospital, learned someone had dropped Wilkerson off and left. Don't know who it was."

Drako asked, "What's Wilkerson saying?"

"Nothing. He's out of it."

Talen shook his head. "Okay, let us know what happens."

"Will do."

Drako's finger hovered over the button, but he didn't end the call yet. "Before you go, Dobbs, did you find anything?"

"Nothing. But it would take a lot longer than a couple of hours to go through that place, inch by inch."

"And you're feeling okay?" Drako asked, wondering if they'd been exposed to some kind of poison while searching. Considering the state of the place, it was a distinct possibility.

"I'm fine."

"All right." Talen, looking at Drako, shrugged. "Let us know if you hear anything, or if Wilkerson's condition changes."

"Will do."

The call ended, and Drako, Talen, and Malek gave each other a look.

"There was something on the news last night," Malek mentioned. "Some kind of mysterious illness."

"I heard something about that." Drako nodded, recalling what little of the broadcast he'd watched last night. "I missed the report. Did you catch it?"

"No." Malek shook his head. "But I can check the station's Web site. I'm sure there'll be a report."

"Good." Drako pointed at Talen. "T, pull the surveillance tapes. See if you can find anything suspicious."

"Okay." Talen's expression turned grim. "Do you think Wilkerson's illness is somehow related to his work with us?"

"Maybe. But most likely it isn't. Dobbs is fine, but then again, he was searching a different part of the building. We need to check it out thoroughly, just in case." Drako's gut told him it might be. "Could be he came into contact with something in the warehouse, rat poison, or maybe some kind of industrial solvent. I don't want any more men in there until we know if it's safe."

His brothers both stood, nodded, and left. And Drako, feeling like he was no closer to finding Oram, or, more important, anticipating his next move, went back to Oram's file, hoping something would click this time. The man had something going for him that Drako lacked, and it was pissing him off. That something: the kind of genius that teetered on the line between intelligence and insanity. If Drako couldn't outsmart him, he'd have to find another way to stop him.

But what way would that be?

Someone was here. Drako?

Lounging on the couch in the den, her sister next to her, Rin felt her heart do a little pitter and then a little patter.

Lei's eyes narrowed. "What's wrong?"

"Nothing." Breathing a little faster than normal, Rin tried to pretend she was reading. In truth, she couldn't tell anyone what had happened the last three or four pages.

She loved reading, but today she'd been living in the world between her ears long enough. For hours upon hours. It didn't help that it had rained all day long. This kind of steady rain was rare at this time of the year when showers generally blew in and out in a matter of hours, if not minutes. Thus she and her sister had been forced to stay indoors.

Outside of a few television shows, she wasn't much of a TV watcher. She swam like a rock. She had no hobbies. Didn't sew, knit, crochet, paint, scrapbook, or make jewelry. Oddly, after only one day, she missed having a job, a reason for waking up, taking a shower, and putting on makeup in the morning. From the look of it, so did Lei.

She had to talk to Drako. Until they had their first child, she would need to do something to make the time pass, or Lei was right, she was going to deeply regret her decision. The house was absolutely spotless. There hadn't even been anything to clean.

This was no way to live.

Heavy footsteps approached at a casual pace. She counted each one until he was there, her husband, looking more gorgeous than last night—how was that possible?

"Hi," she greeted him, not trying to disguise the sparkles in her eyes.

Lei stood. "I think I'm going to jump in the shower."

Drako slid into a chair, swung one thick arm over the back, and propped one ankle on top of the opposite knee. He looked at her for a moment, his expression unreadable and noticeably lacking the sexy glimmer of last night.

She was sort of relieved. At least she would have a chance to talk to him about her concerns without being distracted.

"Did you have a good day?" he asked.

"Sure. . . ."

"But?"

She smiled. "You're very perceptive."

"It's not hard to be with you. You're very transparent."

Her face warmed. She fiddled with the pages of the book, now lying in her lap. "Is that a good thing or a bad thing?"

"It depends. For me, it's a good thing." After a beat, he asked, "What's wrong?"

"Nothing's wrong." She set the book aside and leaned forward, resting her elbows on her knees. "The house is great. The groceries arrived this morning, so we had plenty to eat."

"But?"

"But . . . don't take this wrong, I'm not used to living like this. I had nothing to accomplish today, no job, no deadlines, no goals. I guess I didn't expect it to be like this—you leaving home before dawn and not returning until late in the evening. . . ." She checked the clock. It was after eight. "Me sitting around doing nothing."

He didn't respond right away. "What do you want?"

"You think I'm a whiner. Already. Don't you?"

"No."

Everything—face, voice, body language—reinforced Drako's words. Still, she couldn't help explaining herself. "I suppose some women would love to live like this. Everything is done for me. The house is cleaned. The groceries delivered. The phone answered. The grass cut. The flowers watered. All I have to do is sleep, eat, and make myself pretty."

"So tell me what you want."

"I was thinking I could volunteer, do some charity work. Or get a part-time job. Or take a class."

"You can do any or all of those things. I won't stop you." He leaned forward too, mirroring her position. "I'll make sure you have a set of car keys tomorrow morning. I will ask, however, that you stay away from Magic Touch and places like it."

"Oh, absolutely. Believe me, I hated working there. I wouldn't dream of going back."

"Very good."

She smiled, relieved he seemed to understand. At the same time, she was semi-excited about all the possibilities she could explore. "Thank you for understanding."

"Um-hm." When she didn't say anything else right away, he picked up a newspaper lying on the coffee table and sat back to read.

She talked to the front page of the business section. "I think I'll check into volunteering first. I've never been in a position such as this, where I didn't need to make money. Quite the opposite, since I was fifteen, I've been working and needing every penny I earned."

He nodded but didn't say anything, not that she needed him to. She wasn't talking about volunteering to impress him, to try to make herself look better in his eyes. She didn't need to.

Or did she?

He folded the paper and returned it to the table, then scooped up the television remote and hit the power button. She studied him as he stared at the enormous high-definition screen, channel surfing in silence. Outside of an intimate knowledge of the glories hidden behind his well-fitting clothes, she knew so little about the man who had just last night explored every inch of her body.

"What kind of work do you do?" she asked, the question popping up out of nowhere.

"I design jewelry."

Her gaze slid to her hand first, to the beautiful ring on her finger. Then it slipped to his hands, and memories of last night—more specifically, the way he had touched her—flooded her mind. In the midst of that out-of-this-world experience, she'd noticed how deft and clever his fingers had been.

A jeweler.

"Did you make my ring?"

"Sure did."

She shifted the ring, watching the way the light played in the stone's depth. "It's beautiful. I've never seen anything like it."

"Thank you." His smile was genuine, sweet. "I didn't tell you before. The center stone is a blue diamond. They're fairly rare. I like using rare, fancy-colored diamonds in my work."

"It's absolutely amazing. Will you show me more of your work sometime?" she asked.

"Yes." He finally looked at her, but she wasn't able to read him. Tonight, everything was different than last night, the energy between them, his body language, the way he looked at her. She wondered why. "I will. Soon."

"I'm looking forward to it."

He gave her another smile, then turned his attention back to the television screen. "What types of programs do you like to watch?"

She scooted back on the couch and, turning sideways, kicked her feet up on the cushions, stretching her legs out in front of her. "I don't watch much TV. What about you?"

"I don't either." He started going through the program guide. "Hmmm, how about a movie? Do you like movies?"

"Sometimes. When I'm in the mood."

He glanced at her. "You aren't in the mood now?"

She shrugged. "I'd rather talk, get to know you."

He hit the power button and the screen went dark. His gaze turned to her again, but this time his expression wasn't so impossible to read. His brows were furrowed, his mouth pulled taut, the muscle along his jaw tight. "Do I need to worry?"

Was he upset? "About what?" she asked.

"Have you forgotten the terms of our agreement?"

"No, of course I haven't." She grabbed the book she'd been reading and set it in her lap, flipping open the cover. "I was just trying to get to know you a little bit better."

"No emotional entanglements." He enunciated every word. Every syllable. It wasn't necessary.

"No worries, Drako." Feeling jittery and uneasy, she turned to face him fully, dropping her feet back to the floor. "I remember every detail of our agreement—at least, I'm pretty sure I do. I'm not looking for love. Or even affection. But you never said we had to remain strangers. In fact, as I recall you said we could become friends."

"Of course I did." He chewed his lip.

Now, on top of everything else, she was frustrated. She pulled the elastic out of her hair and shoved her fingers through the waves. "This is awkward, Drako. Uncomfortable. For both of us. Don't you agree it would be better if we became friends sooner rather than later... at least?"

"At least?"

Whoops, he caught that slipup quickly enough.

She inhaled a deep breath and let it out slowly, using those few seconds to plan what she would say next. Clearly, she had to watch every word, at least when they were talking about their marriage. "I'm not going to renege on our agreement."

"I'm glad to hear that."

She stood, went to the window, and leaned a shoulder against the cool glass. Once again, she was staring out into the dark world beyond, just like last night. "Why is it being in your bed feels so good, so natural and easy, but being in any other room with you feels so strained, awkward?"

"I don't know. But I won't stay if it makes you uncomfortable. I'm not trying to make things harder on you. I swear it."

Something inside her pinched, and she felt herself stiffen a little. She turned around, catching him striding toward the kitchen. "No. Please. Don't go." When he hesitated, she added, "I'll eventually get used to this. It's a lot to adjust to all at once. A new marriage, a new home, a new lifestyle...."

He lifted his hands in the universal sign of surrender. "I know. I'm trying to make it easier. Tell me what you want me to do."

"Open up just a little. Let your guard down a tiny bit. Am I asking for too much?"

He didn't respond right away; he made her wait five excruciating seconds before finally saying, "No, you're not." As he visibly tracked her returning to her seat, he asked, "The book. How are you liking it?"

"Very much." Breathing a little easier, she lifted the novel in question, pointing the top toward him. "I had a lot of time to read today. I'm almost a quarter of the way through it."

"I see that."

"Are you reading anything right now?"

"No."

An idea popped into her head, but she shoved it aside. It was silly. Or was it?

It seemed books, worlds of fiction, were going to be the thin strand that would link them, at least until they had a child.

"Can I read to you?" she asked.

His brows rose to the top of his forehead, now lined with surprise. Quickly, though, they settled back in place, and with that change came an even more welcome one. His smile, granted, not a beaming grin, returned. "Yes. Please."

She leaned back, getting comfortable and began, " 'Perfect happiness, even in memory, is not common; and there were two points on which she was not quite easy. . . .' "

The next morning, Rin discovered a set of car keys, a credit card, and some cash had been left for her on the marble-topped table next to the front door. Correction—Lei had discovered them, and she'd let Rin know about them with a bouncy enthusiasm Rin had rarely seen in her sister.

Their days of living confined to a house were over.

"What're you going to do first?" Lei dropped the key ring into Rin's hands.

Rin took one up-and-down look at her sister and knew immediately where they needed to go. "The nearest clothing store. To buy you something decent to wear."

Lei's smile was wider than Rin had seen it in ages, and Rin's heart swelled at the sight. Her eyes burned. Blinking, she laughed. "Don't look so depressed, Lei."

"I know I'm being totally self-centered, but I can't remember the last time I got new clothes. Growing up... well, you know."

"Yes, I do." When they were young, her mother gave Rin hand-me-downs—one of the neighbors in their shabby apartment building had had a daughter one year younger but one size bigger than Rin. Lei got the garments after Rin couldn't wear them anymore. Most of the clothes were in rough shape when Rin got them; they were in even worse shape by the time Lei did. "Now, do you understand why I made this decision? At least we'll always have what we need. And the children I have someday won't grow up hungry like we did, scared and alone and always wondering where our next meal would come from."

"Yes, Rin. I do. The truth is, I did from the very first moment you told me. But I was scared. I want to make sure you're okay with your decision, and not because you want me to be happy for you. So, I let you see how upset I was. I know you." She shook an index finger at Rin. "You would have tried to convince yourself you were happy if you thought I was glad."

"That's some very convoluted logic." Rin chuckled. "But you're probably right."

"No, I know I am."

Rin fingered the car keys. "So you don't think I made a huge mistake?"

"Not if you walked into this with your eyes wide open and with realistic expectations. And not if you know for a fact that you aren't going to wish you could change the agreement you made with him later. Then, I'd say you didn't make a mistake."

"Got it." There were a lot of ifs in there. Rin couldn't be sure, though she wanted to be, that she could agree 100 percent with all of them. Not yet, at least. Like in all things, time would tell.

She had to admit, though, she was feeling fairly good about her marriage at the moment, and it had nothing to do with the credit card or the brief note from Drako sitting beside it: *Buy whatever you need, anything you want. No limit. Drako.* No, she was hopeful because of last night, the simple pleasure they'd found together as she'd read to him.

They hadn't confessed any dark secrets or made any promises of enduring love. Those were never going to happen. Yet, their bond had strengthened. She'd felt it, like translucent silk threads being wound between them.

The air hadn't crackled with sensual electricity.

They hadn't touched, or kissed.

But they had shared something precious: seconds. Minutes. Hours. During those moments, they had set out on a journey together with Emma as their guide and no expectation of where it would lead them.

She knew the power, the magic, of the written word. Stories had been one of her favorite escapes during her darkest days.

"I'm going to grab something to eat. Have you eaten yet?" she asked her sister.

"Not yet. I'm going to run up and do something with my hair first. Oh, and I need some makeup...." Lei gave her a pleading look.

"Of course, you can use mine." Rin set the car keys back on the table. "What do you want for breakfast?"

"I'm good with just a banana and some coffee."

"I'll get a pot going."

Lei extended her arms. “Rin, I owe you so much.”

“Don’t even think about it.” Rin closed her eyes and returned her sister’s hug. It felt so good to have her back. Better than good.

“You’re the best sister in the world. I don’t know what I’d do without you.”

“You forget. I’m the one who should be thanking you.”

10

"Don't class us together, Harriet. My playing is no more like hers than a lamp is like sunshine."

A lamp is like sunshine...

Jane Austen's words, spoken in Rin's sweet voice, played through Drako's mind all day as he worked on a ring that he hoped would make his client's soon-to-be fiancée happier than she had probably ever been. It was an engagement ring, platinum, almost but not quite as special as the one he'd made for his wife. Whereas Rin's ring had one of the most unusual diamonds set in the center, vivid blue, cushion cut, this one had a flawless three-carat green-blue diamond. Around the center stone he was setting a frame of tiny perfect diamonds, the brilliance a gorgeous contrast to the center stone's deep hue.

As he looked at that stone, he couldn't help thinking about his wife. Just like the stone, Rin was a rarity, something pure and glorious and organic. He couldn't wait to see her tonight. Listen to that soft voice as she read to him.

Only one stone remained when Malek entered his workshop, taking a seat on the bench next to him.

Drako set down his tools and looked at his brother.

Malek cleared his throat. "I found the report about the 'Mystery Illness.' The original report didn't give much in the way of details, but thanks to the fact that Wilkerson was brought into the same emergency room, with similar symptoms, we were able to find out what the nature of the illness was."

"Which was?" Drako checked his work through the loupe.

"Poisoning. There were a few substances found in the patients' bloodstreams, including LSD and a drug commonly prescribed for insomnia, midazolam. Wilkerson's blood tested positive for the same substances."

"He was dosed?"

"Yep." Malek picked up one of Drako's pliers, weighed it in his hand.

"Do we know when or where the other patients were exposed to the drugs?" At this point, Drako didn't know what to think about Wilkerson's poisoning. Because there had been other victims, he wanted to believe Wilkerson's sickness was a matter of being at the wrong place at the wrong time.

"No, that hasn't been determined yet. But I was told the FBI is investigating. One victim died."

"That's unfortunate." As much as Drako hated to hear someone had died, he was semirelieved to know that Wilkerson's condition was probably not caused by the work he'd done for them. "Any word on Wilkerson's recovery?"

Malek set down the pliers and picked up a pendant Drako had just finished. Inspecting the piece, Malek said, "The doctor told me Wilkerson will be fine. I talked to Dobbs after I talked to the doctor. There's a huge hole in Wilkerson's memory of that day, but it sounds like he's feeling better."

"Good."

Malek set down the pendant and stood, his hip resting against Drako's work table. "I guess Wilkerson has some Good

Samaritan out there to thank, for taking him to the hospital. If he was hallucinating, there's no saying what might've happened to him if he'd continued to wander the streets. Especially in that neighborhood."

At least that was one less problem to worry about. Drako was tired of chasing shadows. He wanted to find Oram, and he wanted to know what the Chimera were up to next. Whether it was intentional or not, the day that Oram vanished, Drako had interpreted it as a message.

The Chimera were ready to make their move.

But damn if Drako knew what move they were about to make. It was like trying to play a game of chess without being able to see the board or the pieces.

"We've gotta find the Chimera, instead of waiting for them to find us," he said, more to himself than to his brother.

"The Black Gryffons have been guarding The Secret for two thousand years. But, Drako, we've never been the aggressor. We keep quiet, hide in plain sight, and live like we have nothing to hide. It's worked all this time. Why change it now?"

Drako leaned back, away from his work, and crossed his arms. "Because if we don't stop the Chimera once and for all, our children, and our children's children, and their children are going to spend all their days looking over their shoulders, just like we are, fearing the Chimera's next attack. This is no way to live."

Malek didn't look convinced as he shook his head. "But do you think they can be stopped forever? As long as someone knows about The Secret, there's going to be somebody else who wants it."

Malek had a point. There'd always be someone looking for The Secret, because traces of its power lingered in mankind's history—how the Egyptian pyramids and Stonehenge were constructed to name a couple. The Chimera were their primary concern, but there had been others who'd come close to discovering the truth. There was the occasional UFO enthusiast who put two and two together, the archeologist who'd find something in a dig, and the scientist researching new power sources. Every now and then, Drako would find an article in a scientific journal or on the Internet describing The Secret, using one of its many aliases, but nobody ever got too close. The Chimera silenced anyone who was almost there, either by making them a member of their organization or by bullet.

Drako shoved his fingers through his hair. "If there was a way to destroy it, I'd do it."

"But would that be fair to future generations? To the people who will someday use it the way it was meant to be used, and benefit from its power?"

Drako stood, putting himself eye-to-eye with his brother. "We all know history has a tendency to repeat itself. So, what's worse, risking the destruction of everything mankind has managed to accomplish up to this point or taking away what he might have someday?"

Malek looked defeated and confused as he studied Drako for a cold, silent moment. "Okay."

"We can't wait for them to come to us, like our father and his brothers did. Because of Father's one mistake, the Chimera found them, and they were almost successful in stealing The Secret."

"But you're not going to make the same mistake Father did." Malek gave him a squinty look.

"Of course I'm not," Drako said. "I loved that man more than anyone, but when he fell in love with Mother . . . he wasn't the same. He lost his focus. His commitment to his duty." He shook his head. "Doesn't matter. I won't repeat our father's mistake. But we've got to be proactive anyway."

"What's your plan?"

Drako stared past his brother. "I don't have one yet. We've got to put our heads together, the three of us. Oram's too fucking smart. And crazy enough to not care about risks. Exactly the kind of enemy we don't need."

Malek nodded. "You know what they say, you've got to think like a criminal to catch one."

"Excellent point." Drako paced back and forth in the tight space of his workshop. "So, if I were Oram, trying to track down an enemy I'd never seen or met, what would I do?"

Malek stepped back, giving Drako more space to move. "I'd make him come to me."

"Yes." Drako smiled and clapped his brother on the back. For the first time in a long time, he felt like he wouldn't be running from an invisible enemy for the rest of his life. "That's exactly what we need to do. Make him come to us. Call Talen. Have him meet us here. We have work to do."

That evening when Drako came home, Rin had plenty to talk about. While he sat in the den and listened, looking moderately interested—bless him—she chattered on and on—about the great deals she'd found while shopping; the horrible car accident she'd witnessed; the lunch she'd shared with her sister at the mall; the work she did at the local Salvation Army, helping organize the food pantry and hang items in the store; and the trip she'd made to the local community college campus, where she'd enrolled Lei in a few classes for the summer semester, starting in a few days.

It had been a busy day, and she was genuinely happy. In fact, she told him that as she wrapped up the Tale of Two Sisters. "If you were worried," she said, "about me being unhappy, worry no more. You've given me everything I need to live a full, productive life, and that's all I've ever wanted."

"Good." He stretched his arms over his head, and she watched, ever aware of the latent strength of his limbs. He was a powerful man, his body beautifully formed. Every time she closed her eyes, she saw him as she did their first night together as husband and wife, nude, standing next to the bed, his skin gleaming in the soft lamp light.

When would they be together again?

After a long yawn, he said, "My brothers will be returning home at the end of the month."

That was going to be interesting. She'd never lived with a house full of men. "Okay," she said, hoping she sounded cheery.

"They won't bother you." There was an edge to his voice she hadn't heard before.

Was he the jealous sort or was she reading his tone all wrong?

"How many brothers do you have?" She pulled the soft throw off the back of the couch and wrapped it around herself. She had no clue what the house's thermostat was set at, but it seemed to be perpetually cold. In every room. Here it was, June, and she was wearing a long-sleeved shirt and a hoodie, and she was still freezing.

"I have two brothers."

This was a conversation Rin had anticipated. After all, she'd been told about the brothers the moment she'd stepped foot in the place. It was the perfect lead-in to a question she'd been waiting to ask. "The house is going to get more crowded then. We'll have less privacy. Would you prefer Lei found her own place to live? I'd be willing to pay—"

"No. She can stay here as long as she wants."

If her husband truly didn't want her sister to stay, and was just saying what he thought she wanted to hear, he was one of the most convincing liars she'd ever met.

She decided she'd rather believe he wasn't a liar. The smile she gave him was genuine and heartfelt, as were the words she said, "Thank you."

"Don't. This is your home now, and your family is as welcome here as mine."

She nodded. Picked up the book lying on the coffee table and showed it to him. "I haven't read any more since last night. I thought...we'd read it together. The whole thing. A little each evening?"

"Sure. That's fine."

She opened to the next chapter and began, " 'Emma continued to entertain no doubt of her being in love....' "

An hour later, after she'd read three chapters to him, Drako stopped her with a soft touch on her arm. "I have to go now."

"Go?"

"Please, don't ask questions you don't want the answers to." Sweetly, he cupped her cheeks and pressed a kiss to her forehead. "Good night." Before her next inhalation, he turned and walked away, leaving her standing there alone, whispering good night to his retreating back.

Struggling to tamp down an emotion she didn't dare explore, she listened as Drako left the house. A soft thump echoed when he closed the door behind him.

Her sister's arms wrapped around her from behind.

Doing her damnedest to hide her true feelings, Rin turned to give her sister an empty smile. "He had work to do."

"Sure." Hair still dripping from the shower she had just taken, Lei flopped onto the couch and picked up *Emma.*

Rin sat beside Lei, swiveling to face her. She rested one arm on the couch back, and with the other, she pulled a throw pillow onto her lap and hugged it to her chest. The pillow was tall enough for her to rest her chin on it without bending over. "We had a nice time together, reading, talking."

"I'm glad." Her sister gave her a faux look of pity.

"Don't give me that fake pity pout."

"What's there to pity, right?" Lei thumbed through the

pages of the book, then set it aside. "You have the world's perfect marriage."

"Exactly." Rin lifted the book and set it in her lap. She ran her flattened hands over the cover. "I'm happy, Lei."

"Good. So am I. I want to forget everything that happened, but I can't. But in a way, that's okay. It makes me appreciate this more. Being here with you. Living a simple life. Going back to school." Lei yawned, stretched. The brand-new tank top she was wearing lifted, showing a slice of stomach. "All that shopping today wore me out. I think I'm going to go to bed. What about you?"

"I'll be up in a bit," she told her sister, already having made the decision to stay up awhile and wait for Drako.

"Okay. See you in the morning." Lei blew her an air kiss, which Rin returned.

"G-night." Rin watched Lei pad barefooted into the kitchen, grab an apple, and after taking a bite, head toward the back of the house. After Lei was out of her line of sight, Rin jumped into action. First thing, she started some coffee. While the coffeemaker was doing its thing, she headed to her room to put on the hot little baby doll nightgown she'd bought today. After fussing with her hair and makeup, she headed downstairs again, to the den, and settled down with a steaming mug of crème brûlée–flavored indulgence and a book, hoping the caffeine would help her stay awake.

An hour later—early by Drako's standards—she heard a key slide into the back door's lock. It disengaged with a metallic snick, and the door swung open with a creak. Rin fluffed her hair, took a pose that she hoped was more sex kitten than street whore, and quickly slicked on some lip gloss.

His footsteps signaled his approach. Closer, closer. It was hell trying to pretend to be completely engrossed in the book she held in her slightly trembling fingers.

"You're still awake?" His voice was a little deeper than normal, rougher.

"I . . . couldn't sleep. This book"—she looked up—"is riveting." He looked different too, but she couldn't say what exactly had changed. His hair was maybe a little messier, his clothes not quite so crisply starched anymore.

Or was it his eyes?

Yes, that was it.

A little shiver swept up her spine. There, in the darkest part of his eyes, was that spark, the one she'd seen the first time they'd met, and then again the first night they'd made love.

"Riveting, you say?" His gaze traveled her full length, from her head down to her feet and back up again. "Nice pajamas."

"They're new."

"Mmmm."

Oooh, she liked how he'd said that. The low vibrations seemed to travel through her body, making her feel bold and sexy. She also liked how he was devouring her with his eyes. Slowly, she set the book aside and stood, relishing the rising color in his face and neck.

Earlier, she'd felt distanced from him, almost powerless to change things, but not anymore. How many times had she read or heard that women had the upper hand over men? She'd never believed it—until this moment. Right now, she watched her husband struggle to maintain the cool, semidetached mien he clung to with such fierce determination.

Make him lose control with desire. You did it once. You can do it again.

When one shoulder of the frothy white gown slipped down her shoulder, she didn't catch it up and move it back into place. Instead, she shifted her shoulders to let the lace strap move lower, so that a good part of one breast was exposed to her husband's increasingly feral gaze.

"I'm your wife," she reminded him. "Yours to take. Whenever you want. I'm not going to stop you."

"I didn't think you would."

"You did make it clear you want children."

"Yes, I did." He didn't move closer.

"Then why—?"

She didn't get the chance to finish her question. One second, he was standing in the center of the den, the next he was dragging her to her feet. His lips claimed hers with fiery, heated hunger. His tongue swept into her mouth, filling it with his sweet flavor. And his hands found her hips, pulling them snuggly against him.

At the feel of the rigid rod pressing against her stomach, and the passion of his kiss, Rin melted. Her thoughts became liquid, thin and unsubstantial, impossible to hold on to. They flowed from her mind in pulsing waves as carnal heat pounded through her body.

Yes, this was right.

More.

She crushed herself against him, hungry for his heat, his touch. There were too many clothes between them. She needed to feel the heated satin of his skin beneath her fingertips. The torturously decadent abrasion of his chest hair over her nipples.

Between her legs, heat had gathered. Pulsing, tingling need. It was growing, building, moving out from her center like a churning storm cloud.

"Drako," she whispered against his lips as she rocked her hips forward, pressing her aching pussy against his leg.

He answered with a low, rumbling growl, lifted her off her feet, only to set her back on the couch. With eyes glimmering, he unfastened his pants and shoved them down, exposing slender hips and that full, thick erection. A droplet of precum glistened on the ruddy head, a bead of sweet temptation she didn't have the strength to ignore. Sitting upright, she took his rod in her hands and coaxed him closer until her nose filled with the scent of male hunger and soap. When she took him in her mouth, she was rewarded with another of those deep, growling moans.

He curled his fingers in her hair, taking two fists full. And he tugged, not too hard, just hard enough, pulling her away from him. His cock slid out of her mouth. But she was hungry for another taste and leaned forward again, taking him deeper, relishing his flavor as his skin glided over her tongue. Ambrosia.

Again, he pulled her back, and again she rocked forward, over and over in a steady rhythm, her tongue a cushion for his length.

Although she was burning inside, her blood simmering, her muscles—every single one—pulled taut as piano wires, she didn't have the strength of will to stop herself. Her husband did. She whimpered when he moved out of her reach, dropping on his knees. Before she could bend down and fist his cock, he forced her knees apart and cupped her pussy in his palm.

"Ohhhhh," she murmured as she fell backward. The pressure was divine, but it was only a tease, and she was beyond the point of enduring the torture.

Thankfully, he seemed to have read her mind. No sooner had she dragged in a shallow gulp of air than his fingers filled her pussy. Now, she teetered on the border between heaven and hell. She needed more. More kisses. Caresses. Strong arms enfolding her. A thick, hard cock filling the pounding emptiness.

She received the last. His cock breached her entry in a hard, quick thrust, and she shuddered at the sudden pleasure. Desperate to take him deeper, she wrapped her legs around his hips, changing the angle of his entry so that every stroke, out, in, out again, produced a shock wave through her whole body.

A fingertip pressed against her clit, and she clenched her inner muscles around him. A shuddering, tingling, whole-body orgasm was only a few thrusts away. With every thrust, every flick of his finger, her body tightened, heated, until she was trembling, her skin slick with sweat, her pussy clamped tight around his invading member.

His cock thickened, and she could hold back no longer. She relinquished with a moan and a sigh, and let his quickening pace extend the tingling pleasure of her orgasm. He caught her hips between strong hands, fingers curled, and lifted them, driving into her fiercely, until he too found his release. He came with a shuddering, throaty cry, drove into her a few more times and then lowered himself onto her, leaving his cock buried deep inside.

Now, that was the way a quickie should feel.

When he wrapped her in his arms, she smiled to herself, closed her eyes, and enjoyed the moment, knowing it would end too soon and they would become what they had been.

Husband and wife in name.

Partners in bed.

Acquaintances in life.

She wasn't sorry. She wasn't sad. As he kissed her forehead, stood, pulled up his pants, and left her, she told herself this was enough. She had everything she had ever hoped for.

Absolutely everything.

The next morning, she found a box sitting on her nightstand—the kind that came from a jewelry store. The top of the box was embossed with a swirling, interwoven D and A.

Drako's logo.

Inside, Rin discovered a small velvet box, and inside that a pair of gorgeous diamond drop earrings. The bigger stones, a perfectly matched pair, were an intense yellow; the smaller stones that sat on the earlobe were clear, colorless. The combination was breathtaking.

She'd never owned anything so precious, beautiful.

She smiled at the irony. Where would she wear them? A party? The club? A date?

An idea came to her, and she smiled.

She'd plan a special surprise for Drako tomorrow night.

Yes, it would be perfect.

11

Rin could feel the shadows as they swept over her bared skin. They were cool, satiny, not at all unpleasant like she'd expected. This quiet, secluded place, bordering still, deep waters, was the perfect setting. She just hoped Drako would find her earlier than later. She was counting on Lei to give him the note.

They'd fallen into a routine already, after only a few days. Routines were good, when it came to certain things. Dressing for work. Paying the bills.

But not marriage. Not sex.

Tonight, instead of finding her in the den, her book in her lap, he'd find her here, at the very back of the property where the river scented the air and fireflies danced in the inky night. And instead of finding her wearing a frothy concoction of lace and satin, she was wearing nothing but the gift he'd given her.

Earrings and a smile.

Thankful it wasn't a cold night, she stretched out on the soft throw she'd spread on the ground and plumped the pillows she'd brought to make things comfy.

The snap of a twig up the hill told her someone was on his

way down. Moving quickly, she lit the single lantern she'd brought—ambient lighting was always good. The moon was nothing but a mere sliver tonight, but she looked forward to doing this again, maybe in the fall, and seeing Drako's beautiful body illuminated by nothing but the light of a fat harvest moon.

"Rin?" He was close now, near enough for her to make out his shape in the still shadows. "What's this?"

"A surprise."

"A surprise, you say?" When he stepped into the soft lantern light, she swallowed a sigh. The weak illumination cut shadows across his face and over his body, but instead of looking strange or scary, he looked even more gorgeous. "Hmmm, this is a surprise."

"Well, I figured I owed you." She tucked her hair behind her ears and fingered her earlobes, hoping the light would reflect off the diamonds. A million tiny stars flickered around them.

"You don't owe me anything."

"Thank you. They're beautiful." Since he was still standing, she patted the ground beside her. "Will you join me? It's such a lovely night, so clear. I discovered something while I was waiting for you to come home."

"What's that?" He sat beside her, allowing her a good, close look at his eyes. She was quite ecstatic to see the glimmer she was so fond of in their depth, the one that promised all kinds of carnal pleasure.

"If you lie down and look up, you can see thousands, maybe millions of stars." She reclined onto her back and looked up. "I've never seen so many."

He lay down beside her. "You can see even more if you get farther from the city."

So glad she'd come out here, she inhaled the sweetly scented air and smiled. "Will you take me away from here someday? To see the stars?"

"Maybe. I don't get away very often. But it's possible." He rolled onto his side and propped himself up on a bent arm. With one index finger, he drew a tingly line from the base of her throat, down between her breasts, to her belly button. "Rin, you are full of surprises, aren't you?"

"I try."

He cupped her cheek and bent down to kiss her. The kiss was as impossibly beautiful as the heavenly show above them, and she let herself savor every brush of his lips before welcoming his tongue into her mouth.

His sweet flavor danced on her taste buds. His intoxicating scent teased her nostrils, and his heat warmed her skin.

A silly thought popped into her head but just as swiftly popped out, and once again, she was adrift in a current of sensation. Scents of earth, water, flowers, grass, and man. Sounds of insects whirring, birds calling, water lapping at the bank, and her own shallow gasps as Drako kissed her collarbone, her shoulder. The feel of his clothes grazing against her heated skin, his thumb teasing her nipple to an aching, tingling peak, the warm tightness coiling deep inside her body.

She reached up, pushed her hands under his shirt, and traced the lines cutting the muscles of his abdomen into a series of sloping planes. Up, she moved her hands, to his broad chest. When a fingertip found a tight little nipple, he growled softly and nipped her, sending a blade of pleasure-pain slicing through her system.

"When I saw you that first night," he whispered, his voice breathy, "I thought I knew what you were like. I was wrong."

"Is that a bad thing?"

"No, not at all." One of his hands skimmed down her body, finding the heated juncture of her thighs.

"Tell me what did you think I was like?"

"Two-dimensional. Predictable." He parted her labia and flicked her clit softly.

She quivered as a heated chill swept up her spine. "Mmmm. So glad you believe you were wrong."

"So am I." He pushed two fingers inside her, and she arched her back and bent her knees, sliding her feet apart. When he withdrew his fingers, she rocked her hips back, and when he plunged them deep inside for a second time, she thrust them forward. He hooked them, applying just the right amount of friction against that spot inside, and sparks lit up behind her closed eyelids.

This time, she didn't want a quickie. She wanted the pleasure to last.

"Will you take your clothes off? All of them?" she asked.

As torturous as it was, having him stop fucking her with those fingers, she was glad when he stopped. Off came his shirt, revealing the glory of broad shoulders, arms that looked strong enough to lift her with ease, and that unbelievable stomach. Down came his pants, and she was gifted with the lovely sight of thick legs. Finally, off came his boxer briefs, and she was staring at the thick cock she was desperate to feel filling her.

She wanted to open her legs wide and take him, but she knew the minute she did that, she'd become lost in her own need and too soon she'd be soaring over the crest of orgasm. And then he'd leave her.

They had little time together, and every moment, every second, was precious. She wanted to make the best of whatever time she had with him.

She sat up, and before he could get her back down on the ground, she cupped his testicles in one hand, curled the fingers of her other hand around his cock, and took him in her mouth.

Just as he had last night, he grabbed her hair, trying to use it to control her. But this time, she didn't let him. When he pulled, she pushed forward, taking his cock deeper into her throat. And when he pushed, she pulled back until the flared ridge circling the head slipped between her lips and only the tip of him remained in her mouth. It wasn't easy, fighting against the laws of physics, but thankfully, he quickly gave up, dropping his hands to her shoulders. His fingertips curled, his nails pressing into her skin, but the slight sting only amplified her satisfaction.

This time, she'd have him quivering, on the verge of losing control.

She realized, though, what a foolish notion that was all too soon. Just as she was certain she was setting the pace, he yanked away from her. In the next breath, she was flat on her back, her legs pushed wide apart, her bent knees forced up toward her shoulders.

If she had been in control of him a moment ago, she wasn't anymore. Now he was in control of her. And the first time his tongue flicked over her clit, she was both oh so glad and oh so frustrated by that fact.

Things only went from bad to worse when he continued to perform magic with that mouth. With tiny nips and flicks of his tongue, he made every cell in her body vibrate. She tried to touch him, caress him, but he made it close to impossible. All she could do was dig her fingernails into his hard shoulders and shiver, quiver, and sigh through his assault.

When he added a couple of fingers sliding in and out of her burning pussy, she all but cried out for mercy. The senses that had once been keen became clouded. Smells didn't matter. Sounds. Tastes. She was being pulled deeper and deeper into the throbbing pleasure he was churning inside her, and like a swimmer caught in a strong undertow, she couldn't find a way to the surface.

She couldn't speak, but if she could, she would have pleaded with him to release her. Especially when the torment continued on and on, to the point she thought she couldn't endure another second... and then beyond that. It seemed he read her body somehow, knew when the heat was getting too great and how much to back off. She tumbled through the darkness, completely at his mercy, until, finally, he stopped.

In that instant, she felt as if she was floating up, to the surface, but before she'd caught her breath, he wedged his hips between her spread thighs and entered her slowly. One fraction of an inch at a time.

All thoughts of prolonging the pleasure were banished from her mind. Now, as he began to thrust in and out in a steady rhythm, everything she felt and thought revolved around one thing—release. The tension inside was building so quickly, she trembled all over.

This time, she would hold him tightly to her as she came. He was supporting his upper body with straight arms. She looped her arms around his neck and pulled, coaxing him to rest on top of her. It felt so right, having his weight settled on top of her, his heat searing her skin, his breath caressing her face. As she rocked her hips in time to his thrusts, she kissed his shoulder, savored the salty taste of his skin.

So close. Almost there.

Eyes shut, she dragged her fingernails down his back, and his rib cage vibrated beneath her fingertips as he growled. This was one feral, powerful man, and she ached to see him at his wildest, all of his dark fury unleashed. Would he ever strip away the restraints and let her see him as he truly was?

That was the last thought she had before her brain shut down entirely. Her orgasm started as a tiny tingling spark, but it didn't stay that way for long. In a heartbeat, her entire body was shaking, her pussy spasming. Pure carnal bliss coursed up and down, up and down, buzzing from the soles of her feet to the roots of her hair. Those zapping charges increased when Drako found release, and his hot cum filled her pussy. She clung to him, arms wrapped around his neck, legs around his hips. For one glorious moment, she was one with him.

She had no idea how long it took for the after-sex glow to

cool. She was only grateful for the fact that Drako didn't hurry away like he had the last two times. Instead, after he pulled his softening rod out of her, he rolled onto his back and lay beside her, eyes closed, arms resting at his sides.

They didn't speak for a few minutes. It was nice, a simple pleasure she'd never shared with anyone.

"I made an engagement ring today," he said. "For a customer."

"I bet it was beautiful."

"Sure. They always are."

She heard something in his voice. What was it? Cynicism? "But...?"

He rocked his head from side to side. "When I saw them together the first time, I could tell it wasn't going to last."

"Really?"

"His fiancée isn't marrying him, she's marrying his bank account. That's what most of them do."

"Does it bother you? Selling jewelry to men who are marrying women who don't love them?" She didn't want to point out the obvious because she knew there was a point to this conversation and she wanted to hear what it was.

"Yes and no. I don't feel sorry for either of them. Most of the time they're using each other. They get what they deserve. But it's hard to watch people make that kind of mistake, over and over, when they could have so much more."

"What could they have, Drako?"

He sat up and looked down at her. The lantern's soft glow gently caressed his features, giving them a softness they didn't normally possess. "Are you sorry you married me?"

"No, Drako."

"Are you certain what we have is enough?"

She wanted to tell him yes, absolutely, but she couldn't. She wasn't certain, though she was trying damn hard to convince herself it was. Instead, she said, "I think it is." When he didn't respond, she continued, "If I hadn't married you, who's to say I would have found the perfect man and had the perfect life? I'm convinced perfection doesn't exist. And I think you're saying the same thing. What marriage is perfect? Human beings have strengths and weaknesses, failings and triumphs, and so does everything created by man." She curled her fingers, fisting the soft material beneath her.

"Yes, but..." He didn't finish the sentence, instead leaving Rin wondering what he was thinking.

She sat up, looked down at him. "Drako, I made a promise to you, and I am going to keep it. I don't know you very well yet, but I believe you are the kind of man who keeps his promises too."

"Yes." He sat up, shoved his fingers through his hair. The action made him look confused or frustrated.

"Are you sorry you married me, Drako?"

"No, as long as you tell me you're happy."

"I'm happy." She hoped she sounded sincere.

"You don't wish you could have more?"

Her fingers moved to her earlobes. She touched the earrings and smiled. "More? You've done so much for me already."

"I'm not talking about things. I'm talking about...I can't love you."

"I know, Drako." She rested a hand on his arm and looked him in the eye. "You were honest with me from the start. I went into this knowing what to expect."

"Then it's good enough." He stood, lifted his shirt, but instead of putting it back on, he wrapped it around Rin, after helping her to her feet. Then he snatched the throw they'd been lying on; gave it a good, hard shake to remove the leaves, grass, and twigs; and wrapped it around her too, leaving the lower half of her legs free so she wouldn't trip. He took one look at her bare feet and grimaced. "Didn't you wear shoes?"

"No. It's okay. My feet are tough."

He scooped her up in his arms like a gallant prince and carried her, cradled to his chest, up the stone pathway, into the house, and all the way into her bedroom.

She wouldn't tell him how amazing it felt, having him take care of her like this. He treated her like she was delicate, fragile.

He treated her like he loved her.

She touched her earlobe as he turned away. "Drako." When he glanced over his shoulder, she said, "Thank you for the gift. They're lovely."

He looked at her for a handful of tense seconds, then nodded. "You're welcome."

12

Everything was in place.

Sitting in a white van that would blend into the surroundings and was packed with surveillance equipment, Drako motioned to his brother and said into the microphone, "Okay, let's send them in. Are you sure there's no risk of poisoning?"

Malek sat next to him, turning to face the equipment on the opposite side of the van. "The FBI's being very tight-lipped about their investigation, but Wilkerson told me they think someone spiked some pastries at a coffee shop he frequents downtown. An agent took some donuts from his house and is sending them to the lab for testing."

"Okay, then." Satisfied there would be no danger of the two men becoming sick, Drako ordered them to move in.

Down the street, the two men—their stand-ins—exited a black SUV and walked into the Chimera's abandoned headquarters, their conversation carried from hidden microphones to Drako and Malek's headphones wirelessly.

This had to work. Drako was sure of it.

After talking with his brother, Drako had concluded that Oram had paid a visit to this place for a very different reason than he'd first thought. Oram hadn't been looking for something; he was trying to draw them there, into a trap.

What Oram wanted, he would get.

Intentionally, to capture Oram's attention, the men talked about the Chimera and the Black Gryffons, revealing a bit of information here and there that only a Black Gryffon would know.

Drako, hoping their enemy would fall into their trap instead, watched the video displayed on the computer screens in front of him.

"I don't know about this." Spinning around to face Drako, Malek scowled. "Oram's too smart to fall for such an obvious ploy."

"He may be smart, but he's also highly motivated. After what happened the last time they tried to steal The Secret, he's got a lot to prove to the rest of the Chimera. They're going to be watching every move he makes. A guy like that isn't going to let anyone see him fail. He's going to want to believe we're stupid enough to stroll in there. That's all it takes, to give someone what they think they want."

"Are we still talking about Oram, here?" Malek gave Drako a nudge in the rib cage.

"Yes, of course we are." Drako pointed at the computer monitors. "Just keep watching."

"What exactly are we expecting Oram to do? You don't think he's going to jump out of a corner and start shooting."

"No, of course not. If he kills us, he won't know where we've hidden The Secret. That's what he's after."

"So, he'll... take one of us hostage and demand a ransom?"

"That's one possibility."

Malek studied him with sharp eyes. "You actually sent two

men in that building, knowing they may be taken hostage? I didn't think you could do something like that—let another man put his life in jeopardy for us."

"You're right." His nerves wound so tight, he could barely sit, Drako leaned forward, staring at the monitor. "I'm not happy about it. Exactly the opposite. I tried to come up with another idea, one that wouldn't put anyone in danger, but this was the only plan I could come up with. We want to stop the Chimera, but we can't be stupid about it. We have to protect our identities, no matter what." He pushed his hands through his hair, the movement barely burning off some of the excess energy charging through his system. "Believe me, I'd much rather be in there, putting my ass on the line than hiding in this goddamn van."

Malek patted Drako's shoulder, a sign of support. His expression, once assessing, had softened. "Of all people, I can appreciate how hard this is for you."

"Thanks." Drako gave his brother a grateful smile over his shoulder before turning back around. "By the way, I think it's time for you and Talen to move back home."

"Why? I thought you wanted us to wait a month or so. Are you worried about something?"

"No, not really. Nothing specific. But with our change in strategy, I'd feel better if we were all under one roof. Until Oram's stopped."

"Okay. Do you want me to tell Talen or will you?"

"I'll tell him."

That settled, Drako sat back and watched the monitors in silence. Because he was expecting something to happen at any moment, time dragged. Minutes felt like hours, hours like days. The two men who were pretending to be him and Malek took the opportunity to do some searching of the massive building, just in case Drako was wrong about Oram's reason for coming there a few days ago. By nightfall, they'd found nothing, and nobody had found them. No suspicious vehicles had come anywhere close either.

If Oram had cameras in the building, he was suspicious and waiting to see what would happen next, was pulling together a team to launch an attack, or wasn't monitoring the cameras on a real-time basis.

Drako hit the button on the mic, transmitting to the earpieces the men inside were wearing. "Let's call it a night. We'll come back later."

"Copy that," came one response.

"Copy," said the other.

Malek gave him a what-now look.

"We'll give it a couple of days and come back. I think Oram's waiting for the right time to make his move." Drako settled himself behind the van's steering wheel, started the vehicle, and, after his brother moved into the passenger seat, pulled the van out onto the street.

Today might not have been The Day. But Drako knew in his gut, it would come soon.

"I think I'm gonna head to the dungeon," Malek said, clicking his seat belt into place. "I need to burn off some energy, after sitting in that cramped space so long."

That sounded like a damn fine idea. Drako would give anything to get his mind off things. Oram.

Rin.

As Drako had sat in that stuffy van, staring at grainy video images, he'd been remembering the last time he'd seen her, touched her, tasted her. He didn't like how much she monopolized his thoughts. Images of her smile, her eyes, her body, played through his mind all day, all night. He wasn't ready to admit this to anyone, but she genuinely captivated him.

"You've been quiet today," Malek said, breaking the silence between them.

"I always am." Drako flipped on the turn signal and checked

the rearview mirror, watching for vehicles tailing him as he turned right. No cars turned. But unwilling to take the risk, he made several more turns before heading to the storage unit where the van would be kept until they needed it again.

"Sure, but you're quieter than usual. And you haven't said anything about your wife. Not a word. How are you two getting along?"

"Fine." Drako stole a glance at his brother, and realizing Malek was worried not about his oldest brother's marriage but his own upcoming nuptials, Drako gave Malek's shoulder a thump with his fist. "It isn't as bad as I thought. You've just gotta pick your wife carefully. Be upfront, honest. Don't make her think it's going to be a fairy tale."

Malek nodded. "Thanks."

"Sure."

After Drako parked the van and locked it up, the brothers each got into their cars and gave each other a parting wave. From the direction Malek had driven, Drako assumed Malek was headed to his favorite dungeon, a twenty-minute drive north from there. He opted for another one, a fifteen-minute drive west, and closer to home.

He didn't lease a private suite at Black Orchid. He'd have to scene in the main dungeon, but that didn't bother him. He'd done that plenty, and tonight he wasn't in the mood for intimacy anyway. Submissives weren't generally jealous or possessive, at least not his regulars, but that didn't mean there wasn't drama occasionally.

If he wasn't in the mood for intimacy, he was in even less of a mood for drama.

Maybe he'd find a new submissive, a stranger who knew nothing about him and had absolutely no expectations outside of one scene and a little aftercare.

By the time he'd pulled up to Black Orchid's valet entry, his mind was made up. He'd find a submissive who knew her limits—not a newbie—but wanted to test them.

It took him almost an hour to find her.

He'd noticed her right away, the minute he'd stepped into the dungeon. But he didn't approach her right away. Physically, she was the exact opposite of his wife. Rin was petite and delicate, with midnight hair that flashed blue in certain light. And her eyes were a deep brown, warm and comforting. The submissive's hair was a cool blond shade and her eyes gray. She was tall with heavy breasts and full hips and long legs.

He knew she'd seen him too. Their gazes met as he'd strolled past her, heading toward the rear of the open space where a scene that intrigued him was playing out. He paused for a moment, and something interesting passed between them. Her lips, painted a brilliant red that would have looked gaudy on most women, curled into a shy smile.

Very good. Not too timid, and not too pushy.

The scene he'd wanted to watch was growing more intense. A domme was flogging her male submissive, legs and arms bound to a free-standing Saint Andrew's Cross. From his breathing, visible to Drako's eye, trembling and taut muscles, Drako sensed the male submissive was close to breaking. It was a powerful moment, one Drako loved to witness, when he wasn't busy with a submissive of his own.

The blonde would wait for him. He was sure of it.

He went around to the back of the cross so he could see the male submissive's face. The man's expression, as the domme's leather whip struck him again, was one of absolute ecstasy.

Drako couldn't budge, he was so fascinated by the submissive's response. To surrender everything like that, to let it all go, it had to be wonderful, beyond his full understanding.

Drako didn't move from that place. He didn't look away, didn't think about anything or anyone until the final stroke of the lash. Only then could he pull himself away to go look for the blonde with the cool gray eyes.

She'd moved while he'd been watching that scene, but she hadn't gone far. In fact, she'd stayed where he could see her, and she could see him. He guessed she'd been studying him the whole time he'd been watching the scene. That pleased him.

So did the barely perceptible tip of her head she gave him when their eyes met again.

She was wearing a short dress that showed off her legs. The material, soft rose, almost but not quite transparent, moved as she shifted her weight from one hip to the other. The garment's movement drew his eyes to her pelvis. She was wearing underwear. Black, he guessed, from the deep shadow there.

She curled her fingers around the hem and lifted it a couple of inches. Not all the way. Just high enough for him to get a glance at the vee of black lace covering her mound.

This woman knew what power she wielded, and she used it well.

Unfortunately, that wasn't the type of submissive he was in the frame of mind to deal with tonight. He didn't want a battle over power. He wanted a submissive—male or female, gender made little difference when sex wasn't involved—who would eagerly serve him.

A little less enthusiastic than he had been a few moments earlier, he went to her, caged her head between his outstretched arms.

"Hello," she said, that temptress smile in place.

He inhaled her scent. It was nice, but he didn't care for citrusy perfumes, like the one she wore. He much preferred jasmine. "Are you really a submissive, or do you just like to pretend to be one?"

She didn't answer right away. Her smile didn't waver. Nor did her gaze. She licked her lips. "Are you really a dom or do you just pretend to be one?"

"What do you think?"

"I think if you're dominant, I'll be submissive. But if you're not..." She shrugged, letting the rest of her sentence trail off.

Didn't matter. He knew what she meant. There were the doms and dommes who played the role and then there were the ones who were dominant to their core. In their marrow. The latter were the ones a submissive could truly trust. Especially a submissive like this.

He was standing so close to this attractive woman he could practically taste her scent on the air. She was saying all the right things. Normally, he'd be charged up to take her to the edge of her limits.

But not tonight. He just wasn't feeling it. And even though it shouldn't, it pissed him off.

Muttering, "Maybe another time," he turned around and headed for the door. There wasn't any reason for him to be here. It wasn't happening.

He tried not to think about the reason why his blood remained cold as he stopped at the valet's station to get his car.

13

It was nine o'clock at night, and Rin had a good idea where her husband was. She knew she had no right to be upset. He'd made it clear he would be going to the dungeon after they were married. He wouldn't be giving up D/s. He'd also told her he wouldn't have sex with his partners.

Still, there was this awful feeling, a churning sensation, in her gut.

Why couldn't he give it up? And if it truly was impossible, why couldn't he do those things with her? Didn't other people in D/s play with their wives and husbands?

Maybe if she understood it all better, maybe if she went to one of those places and saw what happened there, she wouldn't feel so icky inside. Then again, maybe she'd feel worse.

It's worth the risk.

Sitting on her bed, in comfy sweats and a tank top, she powered up her cell phone and dialed an old acquaintance's phone number. Andi had hooked up with Drako that first night, when they'd met him at the bar. Rin hadn't talked to her since. It was going to be awkward. Rin couldn't stop imagining the two of them together, Drako touching Andi, kissing her, fucking her. Unfortunately, Andi was the only person she knew that was into D/s, and Rin was motivated enough to shove aside her discomfort to go to her.

Andi answered on the third ring. "Hey, girl, where have you been? I haven't seen you at the club, at work. I thought you'd fallen off the face of the earth."

"Some things have happened lately." Rin looked down, at the copy of *Emma,* sitting on her pillow and smiled. "A lot has changed."

"Oooh, sounds juicy. Tell me everything."

She felt her face paling. "I think I'd rather give you the Reader's Digest version."

Andi's exaggerated sigh was plenty loud enough to hear, even over the semicrappy connection. "I guess that's better than nothing."

"I'm married." Like she found herself doing a lot, she toyed with her ring.

"What? Married? When? Who? Why didn't you ask me to be your maid of honor?"

Maid of honor. Andi? Wouldn't that have been awkward. "We sort of... eloped. It was a spur-of-the-moment thing."

"Ohmygosh, I would have never pegged you for the eloping type. You're so... what's the word? Traditional. Where'd you go? Vegas?"

"Toledo."

"Not my first choice, but hey, if you're happy, who am I to judge? Do I know Mr. Right?"

"Yes. Um, you do." A lump the size of her bed congealed in her throat.

"Who is it?"

She swallowed hard. Once, twice, three times. "Drako Alexandre."

"No kidding? You and Drako? Holy shit! I had no idea. Well, actually, I could tell he was into you at the bar. But I kinda figured he was a little too much man for you, if you know what I mean. I mean..."

"This is awkward, I know. But he was single then. He could do whatever he wanted."

"Sure."

There was a long stretch of silence. Rin squeezed her pillow tighter. Was this worth it? Really? Wasn't there another way to find out about bondage? Couldn't she go by herself? Or maybe try to convince Drako to take her?

"Rin, I hate to tell you this, but you're my friend.... He's still coming to the dungeon."

"I know."

More silence.

"What made you decide to marry Drako Alexandre?" Andi sounded genuinely bewildered.

"I have my reasons. But don't feel bad for me, Andi. When I married him, I knew about the D/s, and I was okay with it. We talked about it."

"But...?"

"I just want to understand that side of him. He knows I'm not into it, so he doesn't want to force me."

"Ah, I see. Rin, he's compartmentalizing his life, for your benefit. If it makes you feel any better, a lot of people do that, you know. They don't necessarily want or need D/s in their marriage, so they'll scene with partners outside of their relationships."

"Yes, I figured as much." Rin stood, walked to the window. She opened it and peered out, into the deepening shadows. Here and there, fireflies twinkled. And the song of a bird floated on a sweet-scented breeze. "I still want to understand it."

"Do you know exactly what he does at the dungeon?"

"No. I haven't a clue. But he did tell me there would be no sex involved." Rin went back to the bed, plopped on her butt. "I'd like to go with you to a dungeon. I want to see what happens."

"Are you sure about this? It may be hard for you."

Rin nodded, even though Andi couldn't see her. "I'm sure." She waited. One, two, three . . . ten seconds. "Andi?"

"All right. I'll take you to a play party. You'll see what goes on. And no, I won't take you somewhere your husband will be. I'm not that cold-hearted."

"Thank you." Rin felt like a huge weight had been lifted off her shoulders. She hadn't even realized it had been there. She pulled in a slow, deep breath, let it out.

"I'd say you're welcome, Rin, if I felt I was doing you a favor. But I don't know. I may regret this." She already sounded like she was, but Rin wasn't going to point that out to her.

"Don't worry about me. I can handle it."

"I hope so."

"Just tell me when and where, and I'll be there."

"Fine. Tomorrow night. Be here at eight. If you have doubts, even the slightest, don't do it."

"I'm not going to change my mind."

"Then I guess I'll see you tomorrow night."

"Yes, you will."

She laid back, closed her eyes, and tried to imagine what a bondage dungeon might look like. Dimly lit. Screams and the snap of a whip echoing off the walls. Nude men and women bound in all kinds of positions, gagged. They were disturbing images. She hoped reality wouldn't be as bad as that.

Deciding she needed to do something else, other than make herself crazy, she checked on Lei. Sleeping. She headed down to the den and turned on the TV. Nothing worth watching. She pressed an ear to the door to Drako's home office. Not a sound. She went to the library, helped herself to a wine cooler she found in the bar's minifridge, then after taking a swig or two, found a mystery novel that looked interesting and headed back up to her room.

With the help of a little alcohol coursing through her veins, she was able to turn off her brain and enjoy the book. One hour passed. Two. Her eyelids were heavy and her vision blurry.

Drako still wasn't home. Where was he?

She set the book on the nightstand on top of *Emma,* turned off the light, and settled in, hoping if she dozed off, she'd wake when Drako came home.

She didn't.

Either she didn't hear him come in or Drako didn't come home at all. She peeked into his room the next morning. His bed was made. She headed down to the kitchen. No Drako. She checked his home office. Not there either.

She felt a little ill.

She went to the kitchen for her usual morning dose of caffeine and sugar. There was a box of cinnamon rolls on the counter. They hadn't been there yesterday. She helped herself, washing it down with a glass of cola.

Now what?

Where should she go today? Lei had classes all day. She wouldn't be home until dinnertime. Putting her glass in the dishwasher, Rin sighed. The sound echoed through the still house.

It was too freaking quiet. She couldn't sit in this empty house. Not another minute.

She'd go nuts.

Good thing there was always a need for volunteers at the

Salvation Army. She had a feeling she'd be spending a whole lot of time there, organizing canned foods and sorting through donations in the upcoming months.

"Number one rule—no matter what you see, or what you think you see, don't interrupt a scene." Andi flipped on the turn signal and maneuvered her car around a corner.

"Got it." Riding shotgun, Rin had one hand wrapped around the handle of her purse, the other her seat belt. The car was headed west, and the sinking sun glared so brightly in her eyes, she had to squint as she rooted through the things in her purse, looking for the sunglasses that had sunk to the bottom. She couldn't help noticing her hand was shaking a little. She was probably more nervous tonight than she'd been on her wedding day.

"Number two—don't touch anyone without permission."

Finally finding her glasses, she slid them on. That was better. "Okay. That should be easy enough to remember."

The car turned again, heading north. When they were stopped at a traffic light, Andi glanced at her. "It isn't too late to change your mind."

"I'm not going to, no matter what. I can't be afraid of what I'll see, what I'll learn. Domination and submission is important to Drako. It shapes all of his intimate relationships." She glanced down at her ring. She ran her fingertip over the smooth face of the stone. "As his wife, I need to have some understanding of what it means to him. I want to know what needs D/s fulfils. Maybe I never will get it, but I want to try."

The light turned green. Andi gave her a sympathetic pat on the knee, then hit the gas. "The significant others I've met—which are few, I admit—don't know and don't want to know."

"Sure. It's safer that way. It's like knowing there's something under the bed but being too scared to look and see what it is.

Maybe it's a monster. Maybe it's a sweet little kitten. I won't know until I take a look, right?

"Sure." Andi turned onto a single-laned, winding drive that led to a large brick home squatting at the back of a nicely landscaped lot. Off to one side was a small parking area, filled with maybe ten or fifteen cars. Drako's car wasn't among them. Andi cut off the engine, turned to Rin. "It's now or never."

"I'm ready." Rin slid her purse's strap up over her shoulder and opened the door.

Andi flipped down the visor to check her makeup in the mirror. "Okay. Let's go." After Andi walked around the back of the car, meeting Rin there, she said, "Remember the rules, Rin."

"No touching, no interrupting. You'll stay with me, right?"

Andi nodded, her long drop earrings flashing in the fading sunlight as they swung back and forth. "I won't leave your side."

Rin walked, Andi glided toward the building. Wearing a simple skirt, blouse, and pumps, Rin wondered if she'd stick out in the crowd. If the place was full of people like Andi she most certainly would. Andi's pearl-hued, floor-length gown was more fitting for the red carpet than a "simple" play party.

At the door, Rin hesitated. "Drako won't be here, right? You know for sure?"

"He shouldn't be. For the most part, the same people come here every week. Drako isn't one of them." Andi pushed open the door, holding it for Rin. "But I think you need to understand something." She let the door swing shut. "In this area, the D/s world is tight. I rarely go to a club or party without seeing some familiar faces. Even if Drako isn't here, there's still a pretty good chance someone who knows him will be."

Rin's heart rate doubled. "That's why I'm Kathy for the night."

"Yes, Kathy. Are you ready?" Andi gave her a tense smile. "You look great."

"Thanks." Rin clenched and unclenched her hands. She took a deep breath, let it out. "Okay. Let's go."

Rin followed her friend inside the house that wasn't much smaller than her own. As she walked across the marble-tiled foyer, she realized the home's owner had to be just as wealthy as her husband. All around her were signs of wealth. Original art on the walls. Fine furniture. Beautiful light fixtures dripping with crystals. Sweeping staircases. She wondered if it was any coincidence that the party's host was affluent.

A man met them at the rear of the room, checked the invitation Andi had in her purse, and offered to take any garments they wished to leave in the coatroom. Andi declined his offer, and when they both looked at Rin, she did the same. Together they headed down the wide hallway, passing quite a few people as they walked. Whether it was the cut of Andi's gown—bias, to fall over her curvy form in flattering drapes—or something else, Andi gathered appreciative looks from men and women alike. She was the belle of the ball.

Andi slid a hand around Rin's waist and pulled her forward. Rin hadn't realized she'd stopped. "I've been to a party here before. Let's head into the main dungeon. It's up ahead, on the left."

Trying to avoid eye contact with anyone she passed, Rin followed Andi's lead farther down the hallway. As they got closer to the dungeon, the space became more crowded with people. Many were dressed in elegant evening wear like Andi, but others were wearing clothing more in line with what Rin had imagined—leather and latex and lace. Still others were wearing little or nothing at all. She caught sight of one man dressed head to toe in black. Nicely fitting dress pants, equally nicely fitting sweater. Behind him, a beautiful brunette woman followed, wearing an itty-bitty G-string and a glittery chain hanging from her nipples. That chain caught her eye, and Rin had to consciously move her gaze. She glanced up, to the woman's pretty face. The woman's full lips curved ever so slightly, forming a ghost of a smile.

"Kathy." Someone tapped her shoulder, and she realized Andi had been trying to get her attention. It wasn't easy getting used to a new name.

"Yeah? Sorry."

"This way." Andi stepped through a wide doorway, pointed at the marble-tiled floor. "Remember what I said. And look down. There's tape marking out the area for onlookers. Stay behind it."

Rin, hesitant to look up, stared down at the blue painter's tape. "Got it."

Andi gently pulled her into the large room set up as a bondage dungeon. At a cursory glance, Rin counted eight scenes playing out simultaneously, each at a different piece of bondage furniture. Andi walked her to the scene closest to the door.

Rin didn't know the proper name for the big wooden structure the woman was chained to. She didn't know the proper name for the whip thing the man was hitting the woman with either. She only knew one thing—what she saw was shocking. Disturbing.

If that woman was really hurting as bad as she appeared to be, why would she ask for this? Why would she want it? This was painful to watch.

She looked at the man, specifically at his face. Right away, she noticed he didn't look angry. If she had to label his expression, she'd call it serious, concentrated, focused. "Why do they do it?" she whispered to Andi.

"Every person has their own unique reason, I guess. Just like every person has their own reason for any other choice they make."

"That doesn't help me." Unable to watch anymore, Rin focused on something safer, Andi's shoulder.

"There's only so much understanding you're going to gain about Drako by watching other doms play with their subs."

"Are you saying I'd need to watch my husband?" Rin couldn't imagine doing that. What would she think of him afterward? Would she feel the same way about him? She glanced at the dom again, tried to imagine Drako snapping his wrist like that, sending the whip sailing through the air.

"No, I'm saying you'd need to talk to him about it."

"I don't think he will." When the dom glanced her way, his eyes meeting hers, Rin quickly looked down at the floor.

"Have you tried?"

"No. I didn't want him to feel I was prying or judging him," Rin said to her feet.

Andi tapped her on the shoulder. "You never know, Rin, he may be relieved you want to talk about it."

Rin looked Andi in the eye. "Or he may not."

Andi shrugged.

Rin motioned to the dom with a slight tip of her head. "Does that one know Drako?"

"I can't say for sure. It's possible. I don't think I've ever seen him at Drako's favorite dungeon. Why?" Andi tapped her bottom lip with an index finger. "What if I asked him to talk to you? Privately, of course."

"I don't know."

"They're used to people asking questions. He'll think nothing of it."

Rin stole another glance at him. Would that stranger be able to help her understand Drako's need for D/s? Maybe. After a brief internal debate, she decided it wouldn't hurt to talk to him. "Okay."

"I'll ask him when he's done."

"Thanks." Rin's heart pounded hard against her breastbone as she watched the rest of the "scene." After the dom whipped the woman, he turned her around, making her face out, and brought her to orgasm at least a half-dozen times with several different devices.

After he released the woman, he held her tenderly and stroked her hair, and for the first time, Rin got a glimpse of what appeared to be genuine emotion.

Not long after that, Andi whispered, "Okay, I'm gonna go talk to him. Stay here."

Rin nodded and turned her attention to another scene. She couldn't have been watching long before she felt someone watching *her*. Trying to appear casual, she glanced over her shoulder, but there were so many people crowded into the space around the open dungeon area, she had no way of knowing who might have been watching her. Or if anyone had been. She didn't see anyone staring at her now.

She went back to watching the dom and sub.

Again, that feeling came back.

Once more, she glanced around, hoping this time she'd catch somebody looking at her.

No such luck.

She thought about moving but vetoed that idea right away. Andi had told her to stay put, and she wasn't in an adventurous mood. So she did the only thing she could—pretend that prickly feeling at her nape wasn't there.

"She's over here." Andi said from somewhere behind her.

Relieved to finally have her friend, her bodyguard, back with her, Rin spun around.

The dom, his submissive following, was headed her way. He

stopped a healthy distance away and gave her a quick up-and-down glance.

Andi motioned toward Rin. "Like I mentioned, my friend has some questions about D/s, and she was hoping you'd be kind enough to answer them."

The dom crossed his arms over his chest. Up close, this man was much more intimidating. He was not only a very handsome man, with spikey platinum blond hair, chiseled cheekbones, and very defined arm muscles, but he was also very intense. He gave off a vibe that made her feel twitchy, uneasy. "That depends upon the questions."

Rin cleared her throat. "If I wanted to encourage a dom I know personally to talk with me about D/s, what should I say?"

"Nothing," the dom responded. "If he wants to talk to you about it, he will. If he doesn't, he won't."

That was no help. Rin was beginning to feel this was a mistake. "So, you're saying there's no way to encourage him to open up to me?"

The dom's gaze sharpened. "Why is it so important to you that he does?"

Rin fiddled with her earring, chewed her lip. "He's... my husband."

The dom shook his head, turned, and walked away, leaving Rin confused and frustrated. "Did I say something wrong?"

Andi gave Rin an apologetic smile. "I guess he doesn't want to get in the middle of another dom's business. It's a courtesy thing."

"You could've warned me about that."

"Hey, I didn't know how he'd react. Everyone's different, though there is this thing among the doms here. Maybe it's because this group is so small."

"And that leaves me... ?"

"On your own, I guess. Unless you want me to take you to the bigger dungeon. But there you're more likely to run into Drako." Andi looped her arm around Rin's and started walking toward the door. "Come on. You don't belong here. If you ask me, the answers you need aren't here, or in any other dungeon. They're at home."

Rin glanced over her shoulder. "I was really hoping to get some advice."

"Yeah, I know." Outside, Andi stopped before they headed to the car. "You want some advice, I'll give you some. Talk to Drako. Tell him you'd like to understand that side of him, even if he doesn't want you to be a part of it. Ask him all those questions you wanted to ask that dom in there. His answers are the only ones that matter. Nobody else's."

Rin had to admit, what Andi said made sense. "I hear you. Thanks for bringing me here anyway."

"You're welcome."

Drako wasn't ready to admit it to Malek or Talen yet, but he was having serious doubts about his strategy. It wasn't working.

They'd wasted hours, make that days, waiting for Oram to make a move. Yesterday. All last night. And now they were ready to head out again today.

So far, their visits to the Chimera's old headquarters had produced absolutely no leads.

How did a guy get ahead of an enemy who had pulled a vanishing act?

Standing in the storage unit, leaning back against the van, Drako watched his brothers rib each other about women. He hated to admit it, but they were out of their element. Not that they hadn't been prepared for their duty as Black Gryffons. They'd been trained by their father and his two brothers in weaponry, defensive strategy, and martial arts. But their training had definitely been off-balance. When it came to offensive tactics, they'd been taught not a goddamn thing.

This would be the last time they'd go. If they didn't get something—either from the ongoing search of the building or from an unplanned visit—they'd go back to the drawing board and try to come up with another plan.

Dammit, he wanted this to work.

Talen, who seemed to have keyed into Drako's dark thoughts, turned to him. "What're you thinking?"

Drako let his head fall back, his skull resting against cold steel. "I'm thinking I wished our father had taught us offensive strategies, not just defensive."

"Why would he? The Black Gryffons have existed for centuries, but how many people know about us?"

"Only the Chimera."

Talen pulled the vehicle's passenger side door open. "And that's because the Black Gryffons are a defensive unit. We're guardians. We protect The Secret. We're not out there running willy-nilly hunting down bad guys like some comic book hero. We don't want to draw attention to ourselves, because in the end that'll only draw attention to The Secret."

"So what do you think has stopped the Chimera from outing us?" Drako asked, watching Talen load some bottled water into the cooler sitting between the passenger and driver's seat.

"The fact that they don't want to share The Secret with anyone."

"What's up?" Malek asked, strolling into the storage unit at least fifteen minutes late.

"Just having a little chat." Talen shut the cooler and turned to face Malek.

"Let me ask you both this, then." Drako gave each of his brothers a pointed look. "You've gone along with my plan so far. But do you agree it's the best course of action?" Neither brother spoke. But that didn't mean they didn't respond. The guilty looks they exchanged with each other told Drako everything he needed to know. "You don't agree, then."

"You know we respect you." Talen crossed his arms over his chest.

"But you think I'm nuts?" Drako finished for him.

This time, Malek spoke up. "Not nuts, just..."

"An idiot?" Drako offered.

His brothers shook their heads.

"What, then?"

"I don't think either of us knows at this point." Malek again. "We kind of get why you're doing this. But not really. Obviously, Oram doesn't know anything. He's vanished. The Chimera's quiet."

"So why am I stirring shit up?" Drako asked.

Malek nodded. "Yeah. Why? It's not like you. We've been the Black Gryffons for ten years. What we've been doing has worked all this time."

He'd asked himself that question—why?—a lot since they started doing this stakeout thing. He thought he knew the answer. They'd talked about it once already. He still felt the same way, didn't he?

Drako pulled the van's keys out of his pocket, stared down at them for a second to try to collect his thoughts. "Do you remember what it was like growing up?"

Talen shrugged, stuffed his hands in his pockets. "Sure."

Malek nodded. "Yeah."

"We lived with this shadow looming over our heads all the time, but we didn't know what it was, didn't know why we were afraid or why we were different. We didn't go to school, didn't play sports or join clubs or go on dates like our sisters did."

"They had to protect us," Malek pointed out.

"Sure." Drako sighed. All three of them had shared the same upbringing. They'd been isolated from their peers, left with only each other for companionship, support.

But then again, they didn't know anything else. Their childhood was what it was, and so maybe they didn't realize they'd missed out on some things. Wonderful things. Hell, Drako knew he didn't fully comprehend what a childhood was supposed to be like. All he had for a frame of reference was his own and what he saw on television and in movies. That wasn't the problem though.

He was now facing the reality of bringing his own children into the world, and bearing the responsibility of protecting them and preparing them to take his place someday.

He didn't want his wife to live in fear—not that she was now. To protect her from the stress of living under a constant threat, he hadn't told her anything about the Black Gryffons, The Secret, or the Chimera.

More important, he didn't want his children to grow up like he had. Like his brothers had. He wanted to be able to take them to the park, the zoo. He wanted to cheer for them as they hit a home run, sank a basket, or scored a touchdown. He wanted them to laugh with friends. And go to parties.

He wanted them to be normal children.

No matter what he did, as long as The Secret remained theirs to protect, and the Chimera continued to try to steal it from them, his children would be imprisoned. In a cell of duty, responsibility, and fear.

Could his brothers understand where he was coming from? Or would it take the pending birth of their first children before they'd see what he meant?

Then again, had those worries been the true cause of his father's almost-fatal mistake?

Talen stepped closer. "We'll keep going as long as you ask us to. We're not going to stop."

Malek relayed his assent with a nod.

Drako looked at both of them, seeing both the men they were now—loyal, trustworthy, brave—and the frustrated and lonely boys they'd been. There was no easy answer here. No cut-and-dried right or wrong. Good or bad. His reasons for taking action were as valid as his brothers' reasons for not.

What's my duty? What's most important? he asked himself.

The answer: to protect The Secret first and to prepare the future Black Gryffon members for their duty later.

Protect and prepare.

His son, he vowed, would be prepared for all possibilities. To lead an attack as well as defend against one.

"Let's go home." He pushed away from the van, heading toward his car, parked outside.

Malek and Talen both gave him a gape-mouthed stare.

"Are you sure?" Talen asked.

"We trust you," Malek said.

Stopping beside his car, he gripped the door handle in his hand. "We're not ready for this. Don't know what the hell we're doing. No, we'll keep going as we have, defending The Secret, just like our father and his brothers."

"It takes one hell of a lot of balls to admit something like that," Talen said, following him outside. "It's stuff like this that makes me respect and trust you more."

"I agree." Behind Talen, Malek smiled. "Makes me proud to call you my brother."

Each brother gave him a clap on the back as they headed to their cars.

"Don't go getting all sentimental and girly on me." Drako scowled.

Malek was half in and half out of his car when he said, "Hey, Drako, do you still want us to move back home?"

"Yeah. Why don't you come home tonight, and I'll introduce you." Drako watched them drive away before he closed the storage unit's rolling door and locked it.

So that was it. They were back to the same-old, same-old. Watching. Waiting. Hiding.

14

Rin stood in the kitchen, hoping, praying, the man standing next to Drako, the one with the spiked platinum hair and the razor-sharp gaze, wouldn't say anything about last night. Not only was she sure he was the dom from the dungeon, but she was 100 percent certain he recognized her.

"This is my wife, Rin." Drako, standing between his brothers, motioned for her to move closer. "Rin, these are my brothers." He pointed to the one on his right. "This is Malek."

Malek offered Rin a hand and a smile.

"Sure, I remember Malek. I never would've thought we'd meet again under these circumstances." She shook his hand and stepped back. "Good to see you again."

"And this is Talen." Drako introduced his other brother, the one Rin recognized from the dungeon. Had Andi known the dom was Drako's brother? If so, why hadn't Andi warned her?

"Good to meet you." She avoided meeting his gaze as she shook his hand. A very awkward silence fell over them. She decided to break it by saying, "I should go find my sister, so I can introduce her."

"Sister?" Malek echoed.

Drako cleared his throat, and Rin watched as the two men exchanged pointed looks. She guessed, by the stern expression on her husband's face, Malek was a player. Good to know. "Yes, why don't you go find Lei?"

"I'll be right back." She headed up to the bedrooms to hunt down Lei, still unsure whether Talen had recognized her or not. She knocked on her sister's door and, at Lei's invitation, ducked into the room and shut the door behind her. "Drako's brothers are here."

Lei didn't respond, which was so unlike the little sister she'd known her whole life. A year ago, Lei would've been dressed in her best, makeup perfect, satiny hair brushed to a glossy sheen. Even a few days ago. Not today. Although Rin had noticed when they'd gone on their shopping spree, Lei had mostly chosen oversized sweatshirts and loose sloppy pants. Not one garment was form fitting or stylish. As each day passed, Lei seemed to be withdrawing more. And today, she looked probably worse than Rin had ever seen her, the poster child for *What Not To Wear.* Her hair was scraped back from her face, hanging in a low ponytail. She had not an ounce of makeup on, not even lip gloss, and she wore the biggest, ugliest sweatshirt she'd bought. It practically hung to her knees. She'd claimed it was cold in the house.

"Lei, they're waiting to meet you."

"Why?" Lei snapped. Rin's heart lurched. She hadn't seen her sister act like this before. Her face was pale, her mouth drawn into a tight line. "Why do they want to meet me?"

"I'm sure they are just being nice." When Lei turned away, to grab a book and flop onto her bed, Rin sat beside her. "Is something wrong?"

"No, not at all." Lei gave Rin what she probably intended to be a smile. It was far from it. "I'm just busy. Reading. I have a test coming up."

"You told me your first test was next week."

"There's a lot to memorize, and I want to do well."

"And I appreciate that." Rin set her hand on Lei's knee. Was it trembling a little? She could swear it was. "Lei, you're acting a little strange. Are you sure you're okay?"

"I'm fine." Lei set aside her book. This time her smile was a tad more convincing. "Rin, this is an opportunity I never imagined I would have. I'm going to college, and not having to work my ass off to pay for it, like you had to. I don't want to waste the opportunity you and Drako have given me. I don't want you to have any reason to suspect I don't appreciate it."

"I know you appreciate it." Unable to shake the feeling that her sister's pronounced obsession with devouring *Psychology: An Introduction (11th Edition)* had nothing to do with her ambitions for school and everything to do with something else, something deeper. "I'll give them your regrets."

"Thanks." Without looking up from the book, Lei reached for a nearby notebook and flipped open the cover.

The first page was blank.

Rin closed her sister's door behind her and headed back down to the den. She was relieved to find all three brothers were gone. No need to try to cover for her sister yet.

Worried about Lei, Rin headed for the library, hoping she'd find a phone book there. It was time she faced the truth—Lei wasn't herself. She'd isolated herself a lot lately. Slept day and night, when she wasn't at class. And it seemed the arrival of Drako's brothers was making her withdraw even more.

She needed help.

Rin hesitated when she saw the library door was closed. Male voices rumbled inside, but they were too muffled for her to make out any of the conversation. She told herself they could be talking about anything, not necessarily her visit to the bondage club. It was easy to imagine they were though. And that inspired her to make a quick change of plans. She'd go to the public library, use the computer to look up local psychiatrists. While she was there, she'd pick up some books to read.

Thinking Lei might want to go with her, she headed back up and knocked.

Lei didn't respond. Instead, she inched open the door and peered through the crack. Once she saw it was Rin, she opened it wider. "I told you, I'm too busy—"

"No, I'm not here for that. They're doing something else now. I'm going up to the library. Want to come?"

"Yeah." Lei hurried inside, slipped on some tennis shoes, and, after peering down the hall, headed toward the back of the house.

Rin motioned to her room. "I have to get my shoes on. And I need my purse."

"I'll wait for you outside."

"Okay." Rin went to her room and exchanged the comfortable but frumpy sweatpants and T-shirt she had been wearing for a pair of cropped jeans, a knit top, and sandals. And once she gathered her purse and keys, she headed out to the car.

It was glorious outside. Not too hot; not too cold. The perfect early summer day. The air smelled wonderful. She wished Drako would open up the house, let some of this fresh, clean air blow through. She would be comfortable without air conditioning.

Rin found Lei sitting in the car, staring straight ahead. She started the car, backed up, and turned the car, driving down the long, meandering driveway toward the road.

Lei had very little to say as they drove the short distance to the library. And once they were parked, Lei hurried into the building, heading in one direction while Rin went in another. Rin researched psychiatrists, writing down some names and phone numbers, and then wandered through the fiction section, selecting a couple of mysteries, a romance novel, and a thriller to take home. After she applied for a new card and checked out her books, she went in search of Lei, finding her sitting in a quiet corner, curled up in a cozy chair, reading.

"Are you ready?" Rin asked.

"Sure." Lei set the book aside, cover facing down, and started toward the door.

"Don't you want to check out the book you were reading?"

Still walking, Lei waved an arm. "No, that's okay."

Rin flipped the book over. *The Post-Traumatic Stress Disorder Sourcebook: A Guide to Healing, Recovery, and Growth* by Glenn R. Schiraldi. It almost made Rin feel better, reading that title. At least, even if Lei wasn't willing to admit it to her, Lei recognized something was wrong.

When Rin got in the car, she started the vehicle and, without saying a word, handed her sister the piece of paper with the names and phone numbers on it.

Lei said a soft, "Thanks."

The rest of the drive was in silence, but Rin was feeling better about Lei as they headed back into the house. In fact, she was feeling better about a lot of things, until Drako stepped out of his office, his expression very cool. "Rin, may I please speak with you?"

So formal. Talen must have told him.

"Sure." She headed into his office, took a seat in one of the steel and leather chairs in front of his desk, and clasped her hands together. Her palms were sweating.

Drako sat in the chair next to her, instead of going around to the opposite side of the desk. He looked at her for a moment. Unsure whether jumping in and trying to defend herself would make things worse or not, she just waited for him to speak. "My brother Talen told me he saw you at a play party last night."

"Yes, I was. I went with a friend. I only wanted to watch." This might not have been the way she'd wanted this subject to come up, but at least it was out, and now was her chance to tell him how she felt.

"He told me what you asked him."

"I want to understand, Drako."

"Understand what?" He leaned forward, arms on his knees. At least he wasn't backing away. That was a good sign.

"Domination and submission."

"Why?"

"Does it matter why?"

He thought about her question for a moment, then shrugged. "Why didn't you come to me?"

"I wanted to, but I wasn't sure how to bring it up. With our situation being what it is, I was worried you'd take it the wrong way, like I was trying to invade your privacy or something."

Again, he took a moment to consider what she said before responding. "I might have."

"You see, then?"

He clenched his hands together. "So, what are you thinking? Would you like to explore D/s? Go to a dungeon?"

That wasn't exactly what she'd had in mind, but she wondered if a little experimenting might help her understand her husband better than talking about it. "Yes, I would. But only with you. I... I want to feel what it's like to be tied up."

His lips thinned. He shoved his fingers through his hair and stared down at the floor.

"Would you rather I find another dom—"

"No." He looked up. "For every one that knows what he's doing, there's one that doesn't."

Trying to pretend it wasn't a big deal, she shrugged. "You could recommend someone." She really, really didn't want him to do that, but she had a good feeling he didn't want to either.

Perhaps her husband had a bit of a jealous streak. That wasn't necessarily a bad thing, although it grated slightly, since he was expecting her to be fine with him playing spank-me games with other women. What was good for the goose should be good for the gander, as the old cliché went.

"No. I'll do it."

"Okay." She resisted the urge to beam a great big smile at him. "When? Where? I'd rather have privacy. I don't think I'm an exhibitionist."

"That's fine. We have a few things down in the basement, something of a private dungeon." He checked the clock sitting on the credenza behind his desk. "Meet me downstairs at nine. Wear something that's easy to get in and out of. When I get there, I expect to find you waiting and ready, on your knees."

"I will be, you can count on it." She set her hand on his knee. "Thank you."

He leaned back. "I've got some work to do, so..."

"I'm heading out to get ready." She hurried for the door, more than pleased with how that had gone. She couldn't have asked for any better.

Eight fifty-five.

Rin made one last attempt at adjusting the hem of her skirt. It didn't budge, one way or the other. She supposed that should make her feel better, but it didn't. Ironically, she knew it didn't matter how short the skirt was, or whether her ass was hanging out the back. Nobody was going to see her. Nobody but Drako.

But that was the point.

This was the first time. Their first time. And she wanted it to be better than any experience he'd ever had before.

Perfect.

No pressure there.

She shook out her hands, trying to release some of the tension. She was absolutely freaking out. For more than one reason. Yes, she'd been waiting for this chance for some time. She'd anticipated, hoped for, and fought for this. Now that the time had come and she was about to step foot into a strange new world of domination and submission, she wasn't sure if she was ready.

You can't back out. Not now. There's too much at stake.

That was the truth.

Remembering Drako's directions, she walked to the center of the basement dungeon, her fingertips dragging across a couple of pieces of wood and vinyl furniture as she passed them.

She lowered herself to her knees, back to the wall. Closed her eyes, and focused on breathing. In. Out. Innnn. Outttt. In the distance, she heard footsteps coming down the steps—thump, thump, thump, thump. She lowered her head just as he entered the room.

This was it. If he let Rin into this place, exposed this part of himself, there'd be no turning back. Would her submission bring him to his knees? Knock down the defenses he was struggling to hold up? God, he hoped not. Loving her could be the end of him, and his brothers.

Somehow, he would have to hold back the most vulnerable piece of his soul. If he focused on serving her, he might be able to do that. It was his only hope.

She looked so beautiful and delicate kneeling there, hands resting upon her thighs, fingers woven, palms clasped. Her hair was a silken tumble of waves that obscured part of her face. She was wearing clothes that were too sexy, the short, tight skirt not what he would have liked to see her in. But he couldn't fault her. She'd made an effort. That, he respected. He'd have to teach her what kind of clothing he preferred.

"Take off those clothes." He stopped directly in front of her, watched as her eyes snapped to his face, lingered there for a moment then dropped back to the floor.

"O-okay. Did I do something wrong?" She sounded so unsure. That wasn't what he wanted, but he understood her nervousness. This was all very new to her, uncomfortable. Someday, he would see her become the confident submissive he knew she could be. He would help her get to that point.

"No. I just would rather see you wearing something else."

"Tell me then."

"I'll show you. Later. For now, I'd rather see you unclothed. You're beautiful, and I want to look at you."

Her lips curled into a semismile as she wiggled out of the snug garments. She folded them and set them on the floor beside her. "Better?"

His gaze wandered over her form, slender legs, rounded hips, soft but flat stomach, round breasts. She truly was lovely, every inch of her. "Much."

Still standing, she clasped her hands in front of herself, straight arms hiding much of her torso, including her mound. "I-I don't know anything about this."

"I'll teach you."

"Will we pretend?"

"No. There's no pretending between us. Only reality." He went to her but didn't let himself touch her. Somehow, he had to maintain a little distance between them, while still gaining her trust. That was going to be one helluva trick.

Breaking a new submissive wasn't easy. Breaking a new submissive while holding back a piece of himself was even harder. For that reason alone, he couldn't take it that far with Rin. He'd have to keep it light, playful. Ironically, he'd just promised her the exact opposite. He looked at her hands. They were shaking. "Are you cold?" He checked her skin for goose bumps.

"Scared."

"You've learned to trust me. We've come this far."

"Yes, but this is different. I don't know what to expect."

He lifted her chin, waited until her eyes had found his. "I won't ask more from you than you're ready to give me."

From the look in her eye, the way her chest rose and fell with a long sigh, he guessed his reassurance had eased her fear slightly. It bothered him, though, that he'd had to actually tell her that. He thought he'd already proven, by deed, his trustworthiness. Hadn't he been a giving lover? A patient, gentle husband?

"Look around you." He gave her some time, watched as she glanced at one piece of furniture after another. When he was satisfied she'd seen them all, he said, "You told me you wanted to see what it felt like to be bound. I'm going to show you now. But you are going to choose. How will you be bound? Where?"

She gave him a puzzled look, then stood, circled in place, considering each piece.

Which one should she pick? There wasn't one piece of furniture that didn't intimidate her. They all looked like something a girl might see when touring a medieval castle's torture chamber. It didn't help the way they were constructed—sturdy. Wood and leather, big bolts holding the pieces together at the joints. Not to mention, there wasn't a single one that would allow her some small amount of control or freedom, at least not that she could see. Whether she was standing, sitting, kneeling, or lying down, she would be strapped in and utterly powerless.

Her pussy tingled.

It came down to a matter of deciding which position she could handle the best. Standing? No, sitting. She weighed her options. There was a swing, but that tangled mess of straps and buckles was more than she was ready for. But over by the wall, there was a benchlike thing with a little seat, a slanted back support. That one was more her speed.

"Over there." She headed toward the bench, thankful he'd let her make the choice instead of choosing for her. Knees quaking, she stopped next to it, turned to face Drako. Trust, it was all about trust. More than ever, she could appreciate that now. "Drako, can I ask you some questions first? Before you... before we do this?"

"Okay."

"What drives you to do this? Have you thought about it? Can you tell me?" She pressed her sweaty palms together, wove her fingers between each other.

"I have thought about it, sure. But I can't say exactly why I am a dom. It would be easy to say it's just a part of me, that I was born this way, but I doubt there's any proof of a genetic link to D/s. My brothers are both in the scene, and my father was too."

"I think that was the wrong question anyway. What I need to understand is what you feel as you play out a scene. What need does it fill?"

He didn't answer right away. Just like he had whenever they'd talked about important issues, he took his time; he thought through his answer. Did he ever just blurt something out?

He cleared his throat. "I feel respect for any partner who bestows their trust in me. Outwardly, you might not see any sign of respect if you were to watch me in a dungeon, particularly if the submissive has asked to be broken and the tool that they've asked me to use is humiliation. But it's always there, respect."

"It would seem like a contradiction." Rin struggled to understand. What he said seemed to contradict common sense; it was hard to fully grasp what he was saying.

"Much of D/s is, if taken at face value. You have to look

deeper, beneath the surface." Drako went to a rack bolted to the wall, pulled a little whip with slender ribbon tails from it. "For instance, if you were to watch a dom during a whipping scene, you might conclude he's punishing the submissive, right?"

"Sure."

"But the whipping might be a reward to some submissives."

"Really?" Rin thought back to the scene she'd watched, the one with Talen. His submissive had seemed to be enjoying what he was doing. Could it be the whip didn't hurt as much as she thought?

"Yes, really." Drako walked around her. When she started to turn, to face him, he stopped her with a hand on her arm. He stopped somewhere behind her. Her back prickled, the little hairs on her arms and nape stood on end. "A dom isn't focused on his needs as he scenes, he's completely tuned into his submissive's." Rin felt him move closer, felt the heat of his body warm her chilled skin. The ribbons tapped her shoulder, and she shivered. "He uses all of his senses to gauge his submissive's response. He reads her body language, listens carefully to her breathing, watches for signs of trauma to the body." He struck her again with the little ribbon tail, and she shivered. Her nipples hardened, the tips tingling ever so slightly. "I may give a submissive a safe word to use before we begin," he said, moving around her side as he spoke, "but I don't rely upon her to use it when she needs to. Sometimes a submissive can get too wrapped up in the experience, go too deep into her headspace, to communicate."

"I understand." She was beginning to see now, and it wasn't quite as scary anymore, knowing she would soon be completely at the mercy of a man who knew exactly what to look for.

He stopped directly in front of her, crossed his arms over his chest. "Today is going to be all about pleasure. Your pleasure. I'm going to make you come harder than you ever have. And then I'm going to make you come even harder than that."

That was one promise she was ready for.

"Ready?" he asked her.

She nodded. "Two questions before we begin. First, do I call you Master? And do you want me to use a safe word?"

Once again, he hesitated before answering. "Call me Drako. And use the word Red if you need me to stop. Yellow if you want me to slow down or ease up. You won't need it."

"Got it. Green if I want more?"

"Sure, you can use Green if you want more, but I may or may not give you what you want." The evil glint in his eye sent a little quiver of anticipation shimmying under her skin. What had she been so scared about? "Hmmm. I think a little bit of danger excites you."

She wondered if he wasn't onto something there.

He pointed at the bench. "Sit there."

After a moment's hesitation, she asked, "Should there be some paper or something on the seat? I'm naked."

"It's okay. The seats are sanitized after every use."

"Ah, okay." She sat, knees rammed together as tightly as she could hold them, arms crossed over her chest. Even she could read the get-the-hell-away-from-me message in her body language.

Unfazed by her nonverbal cue, he headed toward the armoire in one corner of the room, scooped up some things she couldn't name, and hauled them over to where she sat. She noticed, as he set them on the bench next to her, that several of the items were wrapped in plastic.

He stood in front of her, studying her for a few awkward moments, during which time she started getting jittery and nervous again. She had a feeling that was exactly what he was hoping for. Finally, he picked something up, something that wasn't tiny but was still easily hidden from her. He walked around the bench, stopped directly behind her, and when she started twisting to see what he was doing back there, he told her, "Stay still." She snapped back around and stared straight ahead.

The blindfold went on without any warning. One minute, she was looking at a table with straps connected to the thick legs and the next, everything was black.

Her husband explained, "I want you to focus on your other senses today. What you see will only distract you."

She heard him walk around her left side. Heard the crinkle of plastic, the clank of metal.

"Slide your hips forward, so your bottom is resting on the edge of the seat," he said.

She scooted a little. He helped her find the right spot, where she had enough support to keep her from falling off but was also completely accessible. Next, he eased her upper body back until she was resting against the slanted back support. He took one hand and lifted it up over her head. Some kind of cuff closed around it. The inside was padded and soft. Her heartbeat inched up a notch toward racing when he buckled the cuff and followed up with the other wrist, doing the same thing to it.

"How's that?" He checked the tightness of the cuffs.

"Okay."

"Now for the fun part."

She wondered what that meant.

He eased her knees apart. Wide, wider, wider still. She couldn't see, but she could swear they were almost straight out to the sides. The muscles stretched along her inner thighs burned a tiny bit, but it wasn't enough to diminish the pleasant warmth rippling through the rest of her body. He fastened a padded cuff around each ankle.

Now, she was sitting, semireclined, legs spread, completely nude, arms tied up over her head. And she was blindfolded.

She was already squirming and he had barely touched her yet.

Some music started playing very softly. Sultry jazz. And the scent of jasmine drifted to her nose on an almost imperceptible breeze when Drako moved toward her again. A candle? Incense? Whatever it was, he'd set the mood perfectly. Between the music, the fragrance, and the position in which he'd bound her, she was both relaxed and on edge. She hadn't realized she could feel those two things simultaneously.

Something very soft—a stream of air?—traveled down the center of her body and she shivered, goose bumps making her skin prickly. Before she'd stopped shaking, something bristly traveled down the exact same route, and her skin burned. Heat and chill buzzed through her, two extremes coexisting in a strange and unexpected way.

The sensations were kind of interesting, but not erotic. They weren't going to make her come harder than she ever had, like he'd promised. She didn't understand what he was trying to do.

What would do that was something hot and hard between her legs. Already, a steady throbbing heat had gathered there, and she knew it wasn't going to ease up until she came.

Gosh, what if this torment lasted for hours? She seriously doubted she'd have the patience to endure it.

"One moment at a time, Rin," he whispered, as if he could read her mind. She turned her head toward his voice, looking for a kiss. What she got was the faintest touch to her mouth. A teasing taste of ambrosia. She licked her lips, drawing the flavor into her mouth.

"I don't understand this," she murmured.

"You will. In time."

He poured some warm liquid onto her chest, once again between her breasts. It streamed down her body in little rivulets. The scent of jasmine grew stronger. She inhaled deeply, drawing it in as some of the scented liquid pooled in her belly button and more dribbled around her shaven mound and into the crease where her thigh met her pelvis.

A heartbeat later, shockingly cold liquid took the same journey, making her shiver and flush, hot and cold, all over again. Her pussy throbbed hotter. Her breasts ached. Her nipples were so hard she gritted her teeth.

How much longer would he make her wait? Was it too bold to ask for one touch? Only one? She arched her back, pushing her breasts out, hoping he'd take the hint.

He did. He laved one turgid tip with his tongue before doing the same thing with the other. She just about wept with gratitude.

Yes, more. That's it. Please, more.

He pinched a nipple and she yelped and jerked back, more surprised by the sensation than hurt. "You have perfect tits." His voice was rough and deep. The pain was instantly forgotten when he went back to licking her nipples. This time, it seemed the nerves were more sensitive, picking up the nuances of each flick of his tongue. A change in pressure, speed; she could sense it all. Each touch sent a ripple of pleasure through her whole body.

Now, she could appreciate what he was doing to her. Using opposite extremes, soft and hard, hot and cold, smooth and bristly, he was making her nerves so sensitive, she could feel every nuance of each touch, brush, and nip. And ohmygod, she didn't know if she wanted him to stop or keep tormenting her. Her pussy was pounding, blood rushing there in hard bursts, and she was aching to be filled.

No man had ever taken such care in lovemaking with her. Quite the opposite, she'd always been the one to lavish the attention on her partner, serving his needs. Sucking a cock, fondling testicles, teasing an anus with a fingertip, bending and contorting her body into any position her partner wanted.

But not this time, not with Drako.

If this was what bondage was all about, it was no wonder so many men and women enjoyed it, sought it out, and risked ridicule and shame.

She tried to pull her legs wider apart, needing him to touch her pussy so badly she could almost cry.

"Patience, Rin." His grazed her shoulder with his teeth and she jerked her head to the side.

"Kiss me, Drako. Please."

"I am." He nipped the back of her arm, not far from her armpit. "Here." He flicked his tongue against the tickly spot on the inside of her elbow. "And here."

Her pussy clenched. "No, kiss my mouth. Kiss me, please."

"You want me to."

"Yes."

"Not yet." He nibbled her neck.

She shivered. "Bastard."

"Remember my promise?" He suckled her earlobe, and all the air in her lungs escaped in one long sigh.

She gulped air into her imploded lungs. "The one where you vowed to make me come hard, that one?"

"Yes." He pinched her nipple again, harder, and her hips lifted off the seat. A fraction of a second later, a wave of heat blazed through her veins, so intense that she broke out in a sweat. He followed the pinch with a gentle suckle, and her whole body relaxed. Her butt eased back onto the seat, and a slow exhalation emptied her lungs again.

"This is torture," she half spoke, half moaned.

"Good torture."

"I'm not sure about that yet."

"You will be."

She heard him unwrap something. A few racing heartbeats later, the sound of electrical buzzing hinted at the nature of the unwrapped toy. That big vibrator had been one of the first things she'd noticed when he'd laid out his instruments of torture earlier. Her sex tightened and a gush of warm liquid seeped out, coating her nether lips. She couldn't remember the last time she'd been so wet.

He audibly inhaled. "You smell so damn good." Before she could respond, he touched the tip of her nipple with the vibrator, and once again, her hips thrust upward, her butt lifting higher off the seat. "If you keep doing that, I'm going to tie your waist."

A full-body tremble jerked the muscles of her legs, shoulders, stomach. She tried to lower her bottom back down but she couldn't, not until he took the vibrator away. Then, she didn't just sit, she melted, bonelessly.

She was gasping for breath, dizzy with need, on the verge of laughing and crying, in a state she didn't understand and wasn't sure she liked. She whimpered, unsure what else to do.

"It's the endorphins. Enjoy the rush, baby."

She closed her eyes behind the mask and concentrated on breathing. Innnn. Outttt. Slowly. Her heart was still pounding, her head still spinning, but she was beginning to feel a little giddy and high, like she'd guzzled a few glasses of wine. She felt herself smiling, even with her hands clasped into tight fists.

"Yes, that's it." He moved the toy, dragging the tip over the swell of one breast, down the crevice between them and then up again to the other one. When it found her nipple this time, she was able, barely, to keep from jumping up. It got a little easier the longer he left the vibe in place. "You see, the nerves lose sensitivity if I continuously stimulate them."

"I see." Trembling from head to toe, it was hard to embrace the notion that any of her nerves had lost sensitivity.

The vibrator went on the move again, this time heading toward the side of her body, skimming around the outside of her breast, tickling her under her arm, then meandering over the curves of her ribs. Lower it traveled, and she fought to spread her legs wider, hoping it was headed to the heated juncture, to the flesh that burned with the need for a touch, a caress, any contact.

How much longer would he torment her?

If Drako had known how painful it would be playing with Rin, he might have fought harder to avoid it. She was so fucking beautiful. But it was more than physical beauty that his wife possessed, and it was more than her very real reactions to his touches that made his cock hard and balls heavy.

Vulnerability. That was what it was. No, strength. Or maybe strength paired with vulnerability.

Oh, hell. He didn't know what he was thinking, but he knew what he was feeling, and that was what worried him most. He ached to break her, to strip away all the walls she'd built around her heart and set her free. But if he dared even try, he knew what price he would pay for the privilege. It was too dear.

Just keep it fun, he told himself. *She won't know any better.* He could focus on the sensation play, arouse her body and protect both their hearts.

Could, but he didn't want to.

Before he lost the strength, he dropped the vibe, shoved his pants down, and knelt. He hesitated one second, two, his gaze locked on his wife's flushed face. Her lips were parted, breasts rising and falling swiftly, the little hard peaks pebbled temptation. His gaze traveled lower, over a flat stomach, scented oil shimmering in the soft light. Down farther it wandered, to her shaven mound, the petals of her labia, the pink pearl erect, waiting for his tongue.

He'd made a promise; he would keep it.

Focus on building sensation. Forget everything else.

He grabbed a bottle of lube, dampened his fingers, and spread the slick jelly across her clit. He checked her pussy. The glitter of her juices told him she was wet and ready for him. She needed no lube.

He breached her in one swift thrust, his hand guiding his cock into her slit, then moving up to thumb her clit. Her tight pussy clenched him hard, and he had to remind himself with every thrust that he'd promised her the best orgasm of her life.

With lubricated fingers, he played with her clit, matching the tempo of the strokes with the timing of his thrusts. As he worked, he struggled to hold onto his willpower, fought to stay out of his head and watch Rin for every sign of climax.

There, he felt her pussy ripple around him, opening then clamping tighter. He jerked out of her and yanked his hand away, gritting his teeth at the agony of tearing himself from the pleasure her body had been giving him.

She cried out, arms and legs visibly tight. Panting, she demanded, "Why?"

Fighting to catch his breath, he cupped her cheek. "Trust me."

"I do." She sucked in an audible breath. He stared at her lips, tempted to taste them. They were the color of ripe berries, and he knew they were just as sweet.

His cock twitched and he felt a droplet of precum seep from the tip. He palmed the head, spreading the slick liquid over the ruddy skin, wishing he could finish fucking her and run away. Far away.

She had no idea what she did to him.

When he opened his eyes, he saw she was breathing easier. Now, he could take her to the brink of ecstasy again. This time, he'd let her orgasm, and she'd come harder than she ever had.

A fresh sweat broke out over his face, chest, and back.

He entered her again, this time slowly, allowing himself to relish the sensation of her body accepting his. Her slick walls tightened around him, enfolding him in warm, wet heat. That heat slowly moved up his body in slow, swelling waves, rising and falling. It was damn good.

He made himself go slowly so he'd build her pleasure at the optimum pace. He teased her nipples with one hand, using the other to grip the bar under the bench's seat. Her position allowed him to drive deep inside her. The tip of his cock pressed gently against her cervix at the end of each inward thrust.

She was getting closer. Her stomach muscles tensing again, making them visible beneath the smooth skin of her abdomen. Her tits were rising and falling swiftly as her breathing grew quick and shallow. And his body was right there with hers, coiling into a tight knot of need. A few more strokes...

He moved his hand back to her clit, knowing what it would do. He traced small circles over the swollen knot of nerves and shuddered as the first rush of orgasm slammed through his body.

Rin's pussy spasmed around him and his cum burned down his penis, escaping his body in hard spurts. They'd come together, their bodies working as one, their cries mingling, the scent of their need filling the air.

It was like nothing he'd ever experienced.

And he was terrified.

He wanted more. He wanted this again tomorrow, and the next night, but even better, even deeper.

He was like an addict on his first high. Already he wanted more. Still feeling a little less than solid after that orgasm, he carried her upstairs, to her room, set her on the bed, and held her.

"Will you read to me? We haven't read in a few nights."

"I'd be happy to." Rin got the book and settled next to him

again. " 'Every body in and about Highbury, who had ever visited Mr. Elton, was disposed to pay him attention on his marriage. . . .' "

Rin's soft voice soothed his nerves, calmed him. He closed his eyes and let Emma's story carry him away to another time and place, where he had no duties and he was free to just live and love and be.

15

The past eight hours had been the longest in Rin's life, thanks to the package that had arrived this morning. Or more specifically, the note she'd found inside it. As she'd gone about her day, she'd anticipated tonight with many of the same emotions as she had last night. But unlike last night, the overall feeling was positive. She was excited, eagerly anticipating her second session in Drako's dungeon.

Before marrying Drako, she'd never imagined she'd respond to domination and submission this strongly. She had an inkling Drako had taken it easy on her, was gradually introducing her to the practices he thought she might enjoy most. She couldn't have a more patient and more understanding man to teach her.

She also knew, without any doubt, she couldn't have a more generous one.

She checked her reflection in the mirror one last time.

The dress he'd bought for her was the most beautiful garment she'd ever seen. Hands down. Spectacular. And the fit, unbelievably perfect. It was as if the gown had been custom sewn to her measurements, which was impossible. Drako hadn't taken any measurements. There'd been no time to order a custom gown. And yet, she'd seen signs of alterations on the inside, as she'd gathered the silk charmeuse and translucent georgette overlay, preparing to slip it over her head.

How he'd known where to take the dress in was beyond her.

And the color, what she'd describe as a soft champagne, was unexpectedly flattering to her skin and hair color. Not only did Drako have an excellent eye for fit but also for color and style.

She felt, as she stepped out of her bedroom, as regal and elegant as a queen. Needing no fanfare, she paraded down to the private dungeon, where she took her position in the room's center, kneeling, head bowed, hands resting on her knees.

Her heart lurched when she heard him enter the room. Through her mascara-enhanced lashes, she watched him stroll across the room. She dropped her gaze to the floor just as he stopped, a few feet away.

"Stand up. Let me see you."

She carefully climbed to her feet, taking care not to catch the delicate material under the heel of her shoe. The material cascaded softly down her legs, the sensation just as sensual as a caress. Without being told to, she looked him in the eye and beamed. "It's so beautiful. Thank you."

His smile was genuine, and as striking as she'd ever seen it. "You're welcome. I'm glad to see it fits well."

"How did you know it needed to be altered?"

"Just a guess."

"A very lucky one."

"I see that." He circled her, and she stood still, loving the way it felt to be the center of his attention. "I think you look too good to keep to myself. I'd like to show you off a little. What do you think about that?"

"Show me off? Where?"

"There's a private club not far from here. I'd like to take you to it."

"A bondage club?"

"Yes."

"Will you do the same things to me there as you did here?"

"Only if you want me to. If you want to just watch, that's fine too."

One part of her was so happy to have the chance to go to a dungeon with Drako, to maybe learn even more about him, she wanted to jump at the chance.

But the other part wanted to tell him thanks, but no thanks.

She was in many ways a typical woman. She had issues with her body. Yet, at the same time, that little visit she'd paid to the bondage club had shown her that people of all shapes and sizes participated in D/s. Most of them didn't have the full, round butt she wished she had, or the perky boobs either. Nor did most of them have the slender, shapely legs or washboard stomach she possessed, thanks to a set of favorable genes. She had no more reason to be self-conscious or ashamed of her body than they did. "Okay."

"I promise, no matter what happens, my focus will be one hundred percent on you."

He led her out of the house with a hand pressed to the small of her back. He refreshed her memory about proper dungeon etiquette as they drove the half hour or so to the dungeon, which, like the one she'd visited with Andi, was set up in a beautiful old home, in a quiet suburban neighborhood where the manicured lawns, stately homes, and well-dressed residents screamed old money.

They parked in a hidden lot located around one side of the huge house and walked up to the door. He rang a bell. A man in a suit answered and, without exchanging a word with Drako, let them in.

Inside, what had once been a foyer was now a check-in desk, manned by one young male who could only be described as classically beautiful. Once Drako checked them in, he led her beyond the desk, down a stone-tiled hallway, to a large open dungeon area.

Like the other dungeon, this one was an open space set up with several stations dotting the landscape. Rin still didn't know the proper names of most bondage things, but, thanks to the laptop she'd picked up earlier today and a quick perusal of some sites that manufactured and sold bondage equipment, she could now name a few. Saint Andrew's Cross. Kneeler. Bondage table. Sex Swing.

Unlike the other place, this one had an added, interesting element. The longest wall of the dungeon was made of glass, allowing people in the main dungeon to see—but not hear—the scenes playing out in the three smaller rooms on the other side.

While Rin couldn't imagine doing anything in the main dungeon, she could easily see herself in one of those rooms, her legs spread wide and Drako tormenting her with the dildo he'd packed in the black bag he carried.

Her pussy clenched. Her face warmed. Oh, yes, that would be fun.

Fingering her burning cheeks, she crossed her legs and squeezed them together to ease the simmering. A man walked by, a big man who moved with the grace and ease of Drako and shared that strange air of authority that seemed to seep out of his pores and permeate the air around him. The man gave Rin a long, up-and-down assessing look.

Drako gave her the slightest nudge forward, toward the man, his response a huge surprise. What was he trying to say? Was he expecting her to go with that strange man? Just last night, he'd told her he didn't want her looking for another dom. Had he changed his mind for some reason? After what they'd shared last night, that just didn't make any sense. He whispered in her ear, "He likes what he sees."

"Who is 'he'?" she whispered back.

"A dom I've known for years. There's no reason to be afraid. His name is Nick Sandler." To the man, Drako said, "Nick, meet my wife, Rin."

Nick, who possessed the most interesting silver-gray-colored eyes and a set of charming dimples on either side of his full lips, extended a hand. "It's good to meet you, Rin." When she placed her hand in his, he lifted it to his mouth and ever so softly brushed his lips across her knuckles.

She couldn't help feeling both horribly guilty and turned on. She was married, and in the world-according-to-Rin, marriage meant commitment. Monogamy. In this strange world, it clearly didn't.

That said, she still wasn't ready to embrace a swinging lifestyle. After all, she was exploring D/s to hopefully encourage her husband to do the opposite—to give up the partner swapping and stick with just her. Was her plan backfiring? Was he reconsidering the possibility of her playing with another dom?

Oh, shit, say I didn't make the biggest mistake of our marriage.

She had no idea what protocol dictated in this situation. In general, she knew, as a submissive she had limited—if any—say in what she did or didn't do in a dungeon. But Drako had assured her she wouldn't be forced to do anything she didn't want to. She needed to make it perfectly clear to Drako she didn't want to play with another partner.

Mustering all the grace she could, she gave a little nod and a shy smile. "It's very nice meeting you, too, Nick." Then she eased her hand out of his grasp and pointed at the rooms beyond the glass wall. "Drako, those rooms fascinate me. Do you have to reserve one ahead of time? I'm sorry if that's a silly question. This is all very new to me."

Nick lifted his brows.

Drako said, “Excuse us,” and propelled her forward, past Nick, who in her opinion had made his interest crystal clear, and around one end of the dungeon. In one corner was a door. Rin soon learned where it led.

She also learned her husband leased one of the rooms with the glass walls. She tried not to think about the other women he might have taken in there as he ushered her inside and shut the door.

He leaned back a little, letting the door support his weight and silently studied her. She could swear he was breathing a little faster than normal. His lips looked a little thin. Was he mad? Upset? She couldn’t imagine why he’d be angry.

“Did I say something rude or inappropriate?”

“No, not at all.”

“I’m relieved to hear that.” She went to a small love seat against one wall and sat, crossing her legs. “I wasn’t sure what was going on. I kind of got the feeling you were trying to offer me to him . . . or something. Silly, huh?”

“No, it isn’t. I thought about it.”

“I don’t want that, Drako. I didn’t come here to do anything with other men. Only with you.”

He jammed his fingers into his hair and dragged them toward the back of his skull. “I know.”

“You look upset.”

“I’m not.” He couldn’t honestly expect her to believe that. Every one of his features was pulled tight, eyes squinty and sharp, jaw clenched, neck and shoulders taut. He was like a rubber band being stretched to its breaking point.

“Are you sure?”

“Yes.” He pushed away from the wall, and gaining some of the control she was so used to seeing, he walked over to a storage cabinet and opened the door.

That was quite a collection he had in there. Was all that stuff his?

A little uneasy at seeing all those intimidating gadgets and gizmos, she strolled around the room, checking out each piece of furniture. "So, does all this stuff belong to you? Or does the club provide it?"

"It's mine. All of it. And everything is sanitized after every use."

Fingertips exploring the rounded edge of the wood bondage table's top, she nodded. Her eyes jerked toward the wall of glass, and she realized a few people were standing on the other side of the window, in a group, watching her. "I feel a little like a carnival sideshow."

"You're new." He went to her, eased her around so she was facing her onlookers fully. "See the anticipation in their faces?"

She couldn't miss that if she were blind, which at the moment she wouldn't mind being. A little breathless, she nodded.

Drako's hand slid around her side to warm her lower stomach. His fingers were splayed, his hand big enough to cover most of her abdomen. She couldn't ever remember feeling more vulnerable. Or more aroused. Her lips parted a little, and she realized, as she watched a young woman on the other side of the glass moisten hers with her tongue, her lips were dry. She mirrored the woman. Drako's hand moved higher, and Rin's breathing sped up even more. She tried to close her eyes and shut out the woman's face on the other side, but for some reason, she couldn't. Her eyelids kept fluttering up.

Drako's friend Nick stepped up behind the woman. He placed a possessing hand on the woman's waist and looked straight into Rin's eyes, making her feel almost as if he was taking possession of her too somehow.

"That sweet little submissive is getting hot watching you, Rin, feeling what you feel now and remembering her first time here. That's why they love it when a new submissive comes to play." He unfastened the halter neck of her gown and let the material skim over her breasts as it fell.

Her nipples tightened instantly.

She sucked in a little gulp of air.

She was standing in front of a window and letting dozens of people see her tits. And ohmygod, she was almost hot enough to melt. There was no embarrassment, no shame. Not at all.

She shuddered, not because she was cold or scared but so overcome with carnal need her whole body was pulling into a hard, tight knot.

Drako clamped his hands around her wrists and lifted them up high and apart, so they formed a wide vee. He pressed her flattened hands against the cool glass and then, his fingers between hers, smooshed himself against her back, the hot, hard length of his body a stark contrast to the cool glass now chilling her chest and stomach. Her nipples were hard little points, poking at the glass. Little tremors of pleasure spread up and down her limbs, and a churning warmth circled round and round deep inside. The world's longest second passed. Maybe two. She was about to beg him to do something, to wedge a knee between her legs so she could grind away the building ache, or pinch a nipple, or kiss her to oblivion, when he stepped back and murmured, "Don't move."

Her wobbly knees just about buckled, but by some miracle, she managed to stay standing. "O-okay." Listening to the clank of metal and crinkle of wrapping, she stared straight ahead and concentrated on taking slow, even breaths. It was a lot harder than she would have thought.

He gathered her hair to one side and sweetly placed it over her shoulder, leaving her back exposed to the base of her spine. Something sharp, prickly dragged down her spine, and she gasped and shuddered. Her knees wobbled but didn't give out, as much as she wanted them to.

How long would he torment her like this?

Pulling herself out of her head, she focused on the faces before her, on the other side of the glass she was now using as support. So many eyes, pupils dilated with carnal need. So many mouths, lips parted, some quirked into naughty half smiles that sent blood racing through her veins in sharp bursts.

Her skin both burned and prickled with a chill, the bizarre pair of sensations making her quiver. The sharp thing disappeared, and in its place something whisper-soft stroked her shoulders, nape, spine. When it moved around one side to tickle the sensitive skin stretched over her rib cage, she wriggled and swallowed a giggle.

"Don't move." His voice was soft but, impossibly, sharp as well. It was a command she wouldn't have ignored.

And since he was performing magic on her body, she was going to do her damnedest to do exactly what he said.

"They can't see all of you yet," he said, leaning in close enough for the heat from his body to drift over her skin in a gentle caress. "Your pussy, ass. They want to."

She could swear her heart skipped a beat or two.

Drako pulled the zipper at her waist, dragging it down the center of her bottom, and her dress slowly slid over her butt and down her legs. And then she was standing in front of even more people, wearing nothing but a blush, her shoes, and a tiny G-string.

He knelt to gather the beautiful garment off the floor, and trembling now all over, Rin waited for him to put it somewhere safe and return to her. She ached to have him near right now, so much that her chest literally hurt. This kind of vulnerability was so new to her, she felt hot tears gathering in her eyes. And yet, being practically nude in front of a horde of strangers did something else too. It made her sex clench, and gushes of hot juices trickle down the inside of her thighs. She wondered if she might come before Drako had even touched her pussy.

"I'm going to let you take off that G-string." He was close

again, and she was so grateful, she would do just about anything to keep him there, close enough to touch, for the rest of the day, month, year. Forever.

Hands barely able to function, and sense of balance way out of whack, she somehow managed to get the little bit of lace and elastic off without making a total fool of herself. When she handed it to Drako, she tried to turn around and meet his gaze, but he caught her hair in his hand and tugged, forcing her to look straight ahead.

The submissive on the other side of the glass visibly gasped. And Rin, caught in a moment she didn't understand, mirrored her, gulping in a sharp mouthful of air.

"I see the goose bumps, Rin. Your nipples are hard and tight. I see the slick honey coating the inside of your thighs. I know your body craves my touch. But are you ready to surrender to me, mind, body, and soul? Are you ready to accept me as your master?"

"I... think so, yes."

"Why? What are you looking for?"

"I want to be close to you, Drako. I want to understand you, to share the most vulnerable moments of your life with you."

"No. You should never make yourself this vulnerable for another person, not even me." He eased her back around with gentle hands and cupped her face, his thumbs wiping away tears she hadn't realized were there. "Rin, you are the most precious person in the world to me. That's why I can't let you do this."

"I don't understand." She closed her eyes, squeezing her eyelids to try to stop any more tears from escaping. "What's wrong with my wanting to be closer to you? Why can't you share this world with me? Why must it stay separate?"

"I have never asked anyone to submit to me for my pleasure alone."

"But I was enjoying it. The proof is all over my thighs."

Drako slid a hand between her legs and spread the warm liquid up to her pussy. Rin shuddered and fell forward, bracing her hands against his chest for support. "Sure, you like the physical aspect. That couldn't be clearer. A little sensation play would probably keep you contented. But it wouldn't be enough for me, and I would be doing you a huge disservice if I let you go on thinking this is all D/s is supposed to be."

"I don't understand. Tell me, explain it to me."

Drako got her dress, handed it to her. As she stepped into it, he explained, "D/s is different things to different people, Rin. It's a casual pastime for some, a way to blow off steam or express repressed emotion, but for others, like me, it goes much deeper." He placed his hands on her shoulders and stared into her eyes.

"I understand that, and that's why I'm here."

"No, you don't understand." Gently, he forced her to turn around, then, as she looked out and watched the crowd that had gathered in front of their window disburse, he zipped her dress.

She whirled around, grabbed his wrists. "Then help me." When he shook his head, she swallowed hard. Her heart hurt, like it had been squeezed in a vise. "I—I'm falling in love with you."

She knew she'd made a mistake saying those words the minute they'd slipped past her lips.

Drako changed. His face, his body, his energy. The man she knew, the sweet, gentle, caring one she'd married, was suddenly hard and cold. "This is why we can't do this again. Not ever. Rin, we agreed, you agreed, there'd be no expectations, no love."

"I know, we agreed, but dammit, I can't help what I feel. I'm sorry." She could hear the sarcastic bite in her voice, knew it wouldn't help anything, but she was frustrated and hurt and so angry she could spit. "If I can live with a one-sided love, why can't you accept it?"

"I..." He jerked away from her, stomped across the room, and yanked open the door. "I won't talk about this."

"Fuck you," she growled as she rushed past him. Knowing he was behind her, she forced herself to walk slowly, exaggerating the swinging of her hips. In the main room, just before she reached the exit, Nick stepped directly in her path, and an absolutely insane impulse charged through her like an electric jolt. Before she knew it, she had a hand pressed against the man's thick chest and was asking, "Are you, perhaps, in the market for a new submissive?"

Behind her, a low growl signaled her husband's wrath. He looped a thick arm around her waist and hauled her back against him. She tried to twist around to tell him what she thought of his possessive streak, but one of his hands clapped over the side of her face, forcing the opposite side against him. "You're playing with fire, Rin. You don't want to do that."

"If you won't be my master, what's to stop me from finding someone who will? After all, you have your submissives. Shouldn't I be allowed to have what I need too?"

"It's different."

"Why? Because I'm a woman and you're a man?"

"No, because I come here for me, because I need it. You don't. You came here because of me."

He was right, and for a split second, she had a tenuous grasp on what he'd been trying to say. Unfortunately, all the other emotions swirling inside her didn't let her hold onto it for long.

A surge of fresh fury blazed through her, and she unleashed it on Drako's shins. Her heels her weapons, she kicked until he released her, then gathering what little dignity she had left, hiked up her chin, grinned at Nick, and said, "On second thought, I think I'll pass. Thanks, anyway," and headed out to the car.

Stupid two-seater. She would have sat in the backseat, if there'd been one, just to put more distance between herself and her insufferable husband.

She was mad at him, but she was madder at herself. She knew, from the start, he wasn't going to fall in love with her. And she'd been 100 percent onboard. Why did she have to let herself fall in love with him? Why?

16

Weeks passed in a blur of empty, meaningless activity. On her daily walks, Rin watched the leaves on the trees turn from vivid green to rich gold and vibrant red. Gradually, the limbs released the foliage, letting the leaves fall to the ground where they grew crisp and brown, a crunchy bedding under her feet.

It didn't happen overnight, but as the world around her changed, the hurt from the night in the dungeon slowly faded. It helped that Drako didn't come to her at night for sex, or so she told herself. She'd never imagined it could be so fucking hard to love someone. When she saw, heard, or smelled anything that reminded her of him, her insides twisted into an agonizing knot and she gritted her teeth against the urge to unleash a fresh river of tears.

He'd warned her about the risk of loving him, but it hadn't mattered. She'd gone ahead and fallen in love with him anyway. Damn her heart. Why did it have to go and do something so stupid?

She could say one thing about all of this. It had made her take a good long look at herself. All her life, she'd done what everyone else had expected. She was a people-pleaser to the core. She took care of her sister. She took care of her mother. Any disappointment on their parts, any criticism, was more agonizing than a physical blow.

That was, no doubt, why she'd thought she would be okay in a loveless marriage. Normally, she was too focused on the other person to care what she was gaining in return. She'd thought she would be content, knowing she was pleasing Drako.

Ironically, she felt selfish, wishing he could love her back.

Standing at the river's bank, her boots sinking into the mud, she tossed a rock into the water. As it plunked through the surface, she said, "I need a shrink." Then again, she suspected a counselor would wonder how she'd become so fucked up to get herself into this predicament in the first place. No, she didn't need anyone to tell her where her mistakes had been.

"Rin."

Drako. Her spine stiffened. Her heart lurched, thumping painfully against her breastbone. "Yes?" she asked, forcing herself not to turn around yet, knowing all the pain she felt would show in her eyes and scare him away. Better to seem cold and aloof.

It had been so long since he'd touched her, or since she'd touched him. Her palms burned, her fingers curled, as the urge to spin around, wrap her arms around his neck, and lose herself in his embrace charged through her body.

"Do you know where Lei is?" he asked.

She shook her head. "Sleeping, I'm guessing. It's early."

"When was the last time you saw her?"

"Last night." Why was he asking about Lei? "We watched some television."

"Did she tell you she was leaving?"

"No." She couldn't put it off any longer. Her curiosity and a little pang of worry made her turn around. "Why?"

"We received a delivery this morning." He extended his arm,

displaying a piece of clothing that looked familiar. Rin's gaze jerked up to his face, and right away she saw the hints of rage simmering in his eyes. "Is this Lei's?"

"I don't know." She reached for the garment, but stopped herself when she saw the deep brownish-red stain. "Is that . . . ?" She couldn't say it.

Drako did. "Blood."

Campioni. Had he stolen back *his property*?

The shirt. It looked familiar. Very. Her stomach imploded, sending her breakfast up her throat. She spun around and wretched, but nothing came up. Strong hands settled on her shoulders as a second wave of nausea gripped her.

"I checked her room. It looks like her bed hasn't been slept in."

"Ohgod, ohgod, ohgod. Lei." Rin wrapped her arms around her waist. "We don't know yet, if that's her shirt or her blood. It could be someone else's." She needed to cling to hope right now.

"I know someone who can get it tested. We'll need a sample to compare it to."

"A sample of blood?"

"Yes."

"Mine?"

"That'll work."

Rin started hiking back toward the house, determined to locate her sister. "It's not her blood. You'll see. It can't be. She's in the house somewhere. Maybe she was in the shower when you checked her room? Or—"

Drako grabbed her wrist, halting her progress. "Rin." When she didn't look at him, he caught her face between his flattened hands and forced her to meet his gaze. "I need you to think. Has Lei talked about anyone new recently? Met anyone?"

"Anyone, like a man? No . . . I don't know." God, why was it just occurring to her now that she'd barely spoken two words to her sister the past couple of months? "She's been different since your brothers moved in. Quiet. Barely comes out of her room. But she's been going to school. At least, I think she has." Rin curled her fingers around Drako's wrists and blinked back the tears gathering in her eyes. "Maybe she just... met a guy and spent the night with him." She knew that suggestion was way off base as soon as she'd said it. She'd noticed how Lei was around men now. The last thing her sister would do was hook up with some stranger. No, if Lei was truly missing, it couldn't be by her choice. Not after everything they'd both been through. Lei's experience with the sex slave traders. Rin's arranged marriage to buy her freedom. "Do you think the bastard slave trader kidnapped her? Is that what you believe?"

"If he did, why would he send her shirt to us?"

"So you'll pay him more money. It makes sense, Drako. I can't think of anyone else who would do something like this. Assuming, of course, she isn't out... somewhere...." Her whole body was shaking so badly, she had to squeeze her arms very tightly to contain the tremors at least a little. "What do we do now? I can't think. I can't breathe." She sank to the ground and sat back, letting a nearby tree trunk support her upper body. As Drako stood before her looking like he wanted to tear somebody from limb to limb, she closed her eyes and tried to focus on inhaling and exhaling. Ages ago, she'd learned when things were bad she had to live one second at a time. Then she could expand it to a minute. Ten. A half hour.

"Let's get you inside." Thankfully, Drako was sweet now, when she needed him most. He wrapped a protective arm around her shoulder, and Rin slid one of hers around his waist, using his body to steady herself, just as she had the day of their wedding. He might not have the capability of loving her, but he was incredibly stable and didn't mind it when she leaned upon him during times like these. Drako's two brothers met them at the door. "Would you like to go lie down for a while?"

"No. I don't want to be alone."

There was a moment of heavy silence. Drako cleared his throat. "I need to talk to my brothers, figure out what we're going to do next."

"Why can't I be a part of the conversation? She's my sister." She heard the fury building in her voice, felt the anger spreading through her body like a cancer. And she knew from experience how foolish it was to do anything when she was in such a state. She'd not only be useless to them in this condition but would probably make things more difficult. Still, she couldn't stomach the fact that she was being put to bed like a toddler while her husband and his brothers solved her problems for her.

"Rin." Drako walked around her, putting his body in the center of her vision so she'd have no choice but to look at him. "You can join us when you feel you're ready. We need to work fast. The longer I stand here, talking to you, the less likely we'll find your sister..."

Alive. She knew that's what he meant.

It just about killed her, but she somehow managed to walk herself into her room and close the door. Drako had proven himself trustworthy, since the very first day of their marriage. There was no reason to doubt him now. And like he said, once she was calmed down, she could join them.

She hoped it wouldn't take too long to get her body to cooperate. God only knew, her heart took a hell of a long time listening to reason.

Drako took his brothers into his office and shut the door, so Rin wouldn't overhear their conversation. "Let's keep it low." The two brothers agreed with a nod. "So, what do we know? Anything?"

Talen pulled a chair up to Drako's desk and sat. Malek remained standing.

"It's not the Chimera, at least, I don't think it is. There's no mention of The Secret." Malek pushed an envelope into Drako's hand.

No address. No return address. No postage or postmark. "Are you sure? When did this come?" Drako walked around his desk, sat, and turned on the lamp. He checked the exterior of the envelope carefully, looking for suspicious marks, substances, anything. Once he was fairly certain there was no poison or bug, he flipped the envelope over. "You opened it already?" Malek nodded. Drako flipped up the back flap.

Malek rested a hip against Drako's desk. "It arrived maybe ten minutes ago, just after you went out to find Rin. Delivered by courier. I asked the delivery guy to describe the person who'd hired him. The description doesn't fit Oram or any of the other Chimera operatives we know of."

Drako pulled the piece of paper out and unfolded it. The paper was blank, giving him reason to suspect what Malek said was true, that the letter wasn't from the Chimera. The demands listed gave him reason to know for a fact who it was.

Campioni was looking for a buyer. For two sex slaves.

"Dammit." Drako surged to his feet. How the hell had that bastard found Lei?

"What's this all about?" Talen asked.

Drako read the letter a second time. "Rin's sister was a sex slave. Rin married me for the money to buy her sister from him."

What would he tell Rin? She deserved to know what happened to her sister, but it was going to kill her. And it was going to kill him to tell her.

"Shit! Why didn't you tell us about this?" Talen shot to his feet. "Since when are we keeping secrets from each other, Drako? Aren't you the one always talking about telling each other what's going on?"

"I handled it. It was done. I didn't expect... Let me think about this." Drako looked each of his brothers in the eye. "I'm sorry. I'm telling you now, asking for your help."

Both his brothers nodded.

"You got it," Malek said.

"We have to move fast, but we also have to move carefully," Drako said, curling his fingers into a tight fist. The paper in his hand crumpled into a hard, compact ball. "I want this bastard stopped. For good."

"Okay." Talen settled back in the chair. "So what's the plan?"

"Whatever we do, we'll do it together." Drako threw the paper ball across the room as hard as he could. It bounced off the opposite wall and landed on the floor. "No more secrets. I promise."

17

Rin hit the button on her cell, cutting off the call. Oh, God, what a relief! Lei was safe. The bloody shirt had been hers, but she hadn't been kidnapped. She'd had an accident while jogging this morning, had sent a note with a teenage boy who'd witnessed it. Lei didn't know how he'd ended up with the sweatshirt or what had happened to the note.

Didn't matter. Lei was safe. Her injuries were minor. She'd just been released from a local emergency room and needed Rin to pick her up. She was waiting at a nearby coffee shop.

Rin galloped downstairs, headed straight for Drako's home office. She knocked. No answer. She checked the kitchen, the den. Gone.

She tried calling him on his cell. No answer. She left a message, telling him she'd heard from Lei, grabbed her purse and keys, and jogged out to her car. The drive to the coffee shop was short, thankfully. She didn't see Lei outside, so she cut off the engine and headed inside. Still no Lei? She pulled out her cell phone and hit the speed dial, calling her sister. No signal. Damn.

She went up to the counter and described her sister to the teenager taking orders.

He nodded. "Yeah, she was here a minute ago." He pointed at a table up in front, adjacent to the wall of windows facing the parking lot. A few balled-up napkins were scattered over the table. "She was sitting there."

Rin took another glance around. Where would Lei be? "Do you have a restroom?"

"Sure. It's back there." The teen pointed to a narrow corridor Rin hadn't seen when she first came in.

That had to be it.

Rin rushed into the bathroom. It was a small space, dimly lit. Two stalls. One was occupied. Rin spotted a familiar pair of tennis shoes under the door.

She didn't knock, respecting her sister's privacy. Instead, catching her very scary reflection in the mirror, she went about trying to tame her messy hair. She was almost finished twisting the elastic ponytail holder she'd dug out of her purse when the stall door swung open. She turned to say something to Lei, but before she'd even seen her sister, something sharp jabbed her in the leg. Next thing she knew, her limbs felt too heavy to move and her head was spinning. What the hell?

"Lei . . . ?" Her knees buckled and the floor flew up, smacking her in the face. Stars glittered everywhere, obliterating her vision.

Tired. Woozy. Something was wrong.

Just before the darkness completely closed in around her, she heard the man say, "Let's get her in the van."

Oh, God, she'd drank too much last night. Sharp needles of light were pricking her eyes, and her eyelids weren't even open yet. And her head . . . holy shit, what had she done to herself this time?

Wait. She hadn't been drinking. What happened?

Oh...

Like a heavy fog lifting, the haze clogging her brain cleared and she remembered. She'd been at the coffee shop, in the bathroom. A strange man had said something about a van.

Had she been kidnapped?

With great effort, she somehow managed to lift her eyelids enough to snatch a quick peek at what was in front of her. But the pain allowed her to get only the tiniest glance. It was enough to let her know she was in a bed, in a house. That was it. The light blazing through the window blinds was enough to fry her retinas and scorch her brain to a crisp. There was absolutely no way she could bear it for any longer than a fraction of a second.

A wave of nausea rolled through her stomach, and she wrapped her arms around her waist and rolled to her other side, where the light wasn't so bright.

"Tsk, tsk. I can't let you sleep the whole day away."

Rin hadn't realized she had company. The hairs on her nape stiffened, and a chill buzzed up and down her spine. The voice, a man's, had come from general direction of the foot of the bed.

More afraid than she'd ever been, because she felt so weak and powerless, she struggled to sit up. Her head spun, almost forcing her back into a horizontal position, but she clamped her eyelids closed and willed the spinning to stop. It did, by some miracle.

"That's better," her visitor—captor?—said.

"That depends upon what side of my skull you're on. From this point of view, nothing's looking 'better.' " Grimacing, she tried opening her eyes again. She needed to see who was speaking. As of this moment, all she knew was it was a male.

She blinked a few times and concentrated on focusing.

He was a pretty good sized man, tall and solid, late fifties to early sixties. Something about his features seemed familiar. Had she met him somewhere before? "Not doing well?"

She gritted her teeth and pressed the heel of her hands into her eye sockets. "I feel like I've just come down from a month-long bender. Who are you? Where am I?"

"I can get you something for the pain."

"That would be nice. Where am I?" she repeated.

"Someplace safe."

"Safe?" Did Drako have something to do with this? Where was Lei? "What's going on?"

"I'll explain later, after you've had some time to recover. I would've preferred to avoid the drugs, but there wasn't another way to get you out of that shop without raising suspicion."

"Whose?"

"Later."

"What's your name?"

"I'll answer all your questions. But not now." He headed for the door. "I'll send up some breakfast. Something light."

"Th-thanks." Completely confused, Rin watched the man leave. Once the bedroom door was closed, she hefted herself out of bed and half walked, half stumbled across the room to the window. Between the slats of the blinds, she saw a row of pretty Cape Cod homes with well-tended lawns and bare-limbed oak and maple trees marching down the street like huge skeletons.

With the pack of children skateboarding up and down the street, the young couple walking a little white fluff ball of a dog, and a pair of women racewalking, ponytails swishing back and forth, this hardly looked like the kind of neighborhood a kidnapper would hold a victim against her will. It would be so easy to open the window and scream for help.

Rin tried it. The pane slid up with no effort, and a gust of cool air chilled her face. She looked down. Couldn't be more than a ten- or fifteen-foot drop. Nowhere close to fatal. Clearly her host wasn't expecting her to try to escape or call for help.

He'd told her she was safe. He had to be working with Drako.

Feeling a little less freaked out about the situation, even though she was far from over her drug-induced hangover, she headed back to the bed, sat, and buried her face in her hands. If only the excruciating pounding in her head would ease up.

Someone knocked.

"Yes?" she croaked.

"I have some breakfast for you." Another male voice, this one different.

"Okay." When the door didn't open, she sighed, forced herself to her feet, and made the long journey to the door. This one was younger, barely out of high school, if she had to take a guess. He held a tray with some foam cartons, a rolled-up paper napkin, a carryout paper cup with a plastic lid, and a bottle of water. "Where am I?"

He gave her a guilty shrug as he handed her the tray. Without a single word, he turned around and headed back down the hallway, toward the stairs at the end. Rin shut the door with her foot, then carried her breakfast—which smelled delicious—to the bed. She flipped open the cartons, finding scrambled eggs and buttered toast. Not exactly what she'd call a light breakfast, but it would do. The cup had orange juice in it. Her stomach wasn't ready for that. She cracked open the water first, took a few long chugs—she hadn't realized how thirsty she was—and, finding a small bottle of over-the-counter painkiller, dosed out the maximum number of tablets. They went down with another mouthful of water.

She ate a little bit of the eggs. A slice of toast. By the time she'd swallowed the last bite of the toast, her head wasn't thudding quite so painfully. Her stomach wasn't feeling so bad either. Looked like she was going to survive.

After her meal, she was almost feeling human again. She located a full bathroom behind one of the two doors that didn't lead out to the hall. There were fresh towels hanging on the rods and hotel-sized, packaged soaps and shampoos in the shower. She decided those were meant for her use and got herself cleaned up, but only after locking herself into the bathroom. When she came back out, she discovered a set of new clothes, in her size, lying on top of the freshly made bed.

Breakfast in bed. New clothes. Such service.

Not at all sad to give up the clothes she'd slept in, she took the new ones into the bathroom, locked the door, and changed. This time, when she came out, the man from earlier was waiting for her. Standing, arms crossed over his chest, shoulder leaning against the door frame.

"Okay, I've eaten, showered, and am feeling much better. Now, will you please explain to me what's going on? Did my husband arrange this?"

"Not exactly." The man with no name motioned for her to follow him. "This way."

Together, they walked downstairs and into the living room. The space was furnished with a comfortable-looking couch and love seat, a couple of chairs, and a wall of bookshelves. It looked lived-in, the books on the wall of shelves opposite the couch well loved. Between the two bookcases hung a small widescreen plasma television. Under it were shorter bookshelves, stacked with volumes, paperback novels—mostly thrillers, from the look of it. A coffee table sat in front of the couch, the top completely empty except for a small remote control.

Her host waved her toward the couch. "Make yourself comfortable."

After a moment's hesitation, Rin sat. There were a lot of questions bouncing around in her head, the most pressing being, *Why am I here?* and *Where is Lei?* Even though the man said Drako hadn't arranged it, exactly, she still had to believe he had something to do with it.

It was tough, but she could wait a minute or two for some answers—no longer than that though. Definitely no longer.

The man, still standing, asked, "Can I get you something to drink? Water? Coffee?"

"No, thanks. I'd rather you sit down and tell me what's going on."

He nodded. Took a seat on the love seat, positioned next to the couch. "My name is Bob. I'm your husband's uncle. His father was my brother. And I'm guessing there are a lot of things you don't know about your husband." He sat forward, resting his elbows on his knees and steepling his fingers under a chin that looked enough like Drako's for Rin to believe there was a genetic connection between them. "Drako and his brothers Talen and Malek are in trouble."

Bullshit. "What kind of trouble?"

"They stole something. From the U.S. government. Something extremely dangerous. It isn't safe for you to be anywhere near any of them right now."

Right... "Stole something?" That sounded nothing like her husband, but she wasn't going to let this man know she didn't believe him. "What kind of something?"

"You're skeptical. I don't blame you."

"Do you have proof?" She studied his features carefully. His mouth sure looked like Drako's. And his eyes were the same shade. His hair, much of it gray now, was thick and wavy. It was easy enough to believe Bob was a relative of Drako's. A close one.

Regardless, none of this made sense.

"I have some surveillance footage," Bob said.

Some grainy video wasn't going to convince her of anything. But she shrugged her shoulders. "Let's see it."

Bob scooped up the remote, hit the power button with his thumb. A little red indicator light on the TV started blinking. Rin studied him even closer as she waited for the television to power up. Deep groves cut into his forehead, and his once-firm jaw had softened. His mouth was a thinner, older version of Drako's too. Yes, she'd say he was old enough to be Drako's uncle.

The screen glowed blue. Bob hit another button, and a second later Rin was watching a black-and-white recording, filmed in some kind of building with white walls, white ceiling, and tiled floor. The date, displayed in red digital numbers in the upper left hand corner, suggested the video was more than ten years old. Drako, carrying some small tube-shaped canister in his hands, looked straight at the camera, then reached up. The picture went black, but the sound didn't cut off right away. Rin heard one, two, three hollow pops; men's voices; a name she couldn't quite make out being shouted. Shuffling followed, the slam of a door. Then silence.

That didn't tell her much, although the video didn't exactly jive with Drako's claim to be a jeweler. Of course, who was to say Drako hadn't decided on a career change? A lot of people did that these days. Maybe once upon a time, Drako had been a security guard? Or... or... ?

"That tape was filmed in a highly secure government facility not far from here," Bob explained.

"What's in the canister?" Rin didn't expect an honest answer.

"Something the government will do anything to get back."

"Are you trying to tell me my husband's a spy?" Rin stood up, crossed her arms over her chest, and wandered toward the front window. It was hard to believe that Drako would be involved in some kind of secret spy work, but if she were honest with herself, she'd admit she knew very little about him.

Could this be why he'd decided to marry her in the first place? Why he kept insisting she not fall in love with him? Was he still involved in some kind of spy work? Or undercover work?

No. That's so silly.

Shit, maybe.

He'd done everything he could to avoid any deep intimacy with her. He didn't talk about his work. He spent a lot of time away from home, and there was no way for Rin to know where he was going or what he was doing. But, and this was a big but, he didn't live like a man on the run, living a lie, or hiding something the government would "do anything" to get back.

She moved to the front door, curled her fingers around the knob, and tested it. Unlocked. "Am I free to leave? Or am I a hostage?"

"You can walk out whenever you want. But I hope you'll stay, listen, try to set aside what you think you know about your husband, and take a long, hard look at what you really know about him."

"Like what?"

"For instance, Drako Alexandre isn't his real name." Her host went to the bookshelf and pulled out a large atlas. When he set it on the table and opened it, Rin realized it wasn't what it looked like, a book. It was a hollow box with some kind of complicated locking mechanism. Inside was a file. He handed it to her.

Still confused and unsure what to believe, Rin flipped the file open. On top, she found a picture ID. A military ID. With a photograph of Drako. Beneath the picture was the name Kane Zacharias.

Zacharias? That was the same name Rin had heard shouted on the videotape.

Her insides twisted. If Drako was keeping such a huge secret, how could he talk to her about trust? How could he say things like "it's real between us"? He couldn't. He wasn't the kind of man who would talk out of both sides of his mouth.

Her host pulled a leather wallet-like thing from his pocket and flipped it open, revealing a federal ID that wasn't much different from the one in the file. The name, Robert Zacharias. "I'm a federal agent, but that's not why I brought you here. Kane—Drako—is my older brother's boy. I've loved him since he was a kid, and I don't want this to go down the way it's heading. I want your help. I need your help."

She flipped through the documents in the file, all military reports. They looked real enough, but she still couldn't believe what she was hearing, seeing, reading. Drako's name wasn't Drako? Everything she'd known about him was a lie? He'd stolen some kind of top-secret weapon or something from the government. She felt sick, like her insides had been yanked out of her, wrung like a wet shirt and stuffed back in. "What do you expect me to do? If what you're telling me is true, then I don't know *anything* about Drako. Not a goddamn thing. I certainly haven't seen a metal tube lying around the house." She shook her head and tried to hold back the anger slicing through her. "And say he did steal whatever that thing is. I saw the date on the recording. It was made ten years ago. Why would he keep anything that dangerous for so long?"

"Because he doesn't want anyone to have it. Not our government. Not anyone."

"Why?"

"Because he believes it's too dangerous to be used by anyone." Bob picked up his identification and tucked it back into his pocket. "He believes he's doing the right thing by protecting it." Now, *that* Rin could believe. If there was one thing Drako had shown her, it was how strongly he felt about duty, protecting people, including her and her sister. "We think you can get him to tell you where it's hidden."

"How? He hasn't even told me his real name. How am I ever going to convince him to tell me where he's hidden something for ten years?"

Bob leaned closer, lowered his voice. "He has one weakness that we know of. But it won't be easy."

"What's that?"

"When he's in a dungeon, he's most vulnerable. Especially if he's the one submitting."

"Oh, I don't know about this." Even as Rin's heartbeat kicked into double speed, she shook her head. "I don't know anything about that stuff and you're asking me to dominate him. What if I do something wrong?" Considering how she felt right now, she couldn't trust herself not to beat his ass bloody.

"What if we had someone train you? Someone you know and trust?"

"Who?"

Bob indicated with an index finger that he wanted her to wait. He produced a cell phone from his pants pocket, dialed, said the word "Now," and ended the call.

Less than a minute later, Rin was standing face-to-face with her sister.

Rin was too overwhelmed with relief, seeing that her sister was safe and unharmed, to worry about why she was with these men, or ask how she'd come to be a part of this whole mess. The first thing she did was throw her arms around her baby sister and hug her, asking, "Are you okay?"

"I'm fine. Perfectly fine." She didn't sound fine, not even to her own ears.

"I'll let the two of you get caught up." Bob headed toward the kitchen.

Rin waited until she was sure he couldn't overhear her before asking, "Lei, what's going on?"

"It's kinda crazy, isn't it?" Lei sat, coaxing Rin to sit beside her. "I believe them. What about you?"

"I don't know. The documents and tape all look real, but I can't picture Drako as some kind of secret agent-slash-spy. Or maybe I don't want to believe because that would mean everything he's told me has been a lie."

"Oh, Rin. I feel for you. But I think you've long suspected

there was something about him that didn't fit, that there's more going on than making jewelry."

"Maybe, but I thought the other stuff had to do with his hobby rather than his work." Rin dropped her face into her hands. "It's so hard to accept that all that talk about trust and being honest and real was a bunch of shit." Lei rubbed her back. Right now, she couldn't be more grateful to have her sister there with her. "Speaking of trust, Drako's uncle wants me to go to a dungeon with Drako and make *him* submit to *me.* That's crazy. And even more insane, he more or less suggested you could show me how to . . . how to make him submit."

"I can." Lei nodded. "One of my owners trained me to be his domme."

Another shock. "How did Bob know that about you? I didn't even know." Rin threw her hands in the air. "Do I know anything about anyone? My God, I'm being hit by surprises from all sides."

"I'm sorry, Rin." Lei grimmaced. "I met Drako's uncle at a dungeon. He was going by another name—"

Dungeon? Lei had been going to a dungeon. She was a domme. Truly and honestly. Not because she was being forced to be one, or paid to be one, but because she chose to. Rin wondered what other secrets her sister had kept since coming home. "Why didn't you tell me?"

"About the D/s?"

"Yes."

Lei smiled. It wasn't an ear-to-ear grin, it was more of a wry semismile. "Why didn't you tell me you were going to a dungeon? You went with that flake, Andi."

"You know about that?" Despite knowing Lei was a domme and wouldn't be shocked, Rin felt her face burn with embarrassment and shame anyway. And here she'd been judging Drako and her sister for keeping secrets.

"I was there."

"You were? I didn't see you."

"You didn't see me because you weren't looking for me. But that's beside the point." Lei shifted to face Rin fully. "The point is, we've both been keeping secrets, right, Rin? And so has Drako. He has his reasons. I'm sure he'll tell you. Some things are hard to talk about, even with people we trust and love."

"Yeah." Rin's gaze dropped to her hand again, to the blue stone shimmering on her ring finger. If Lei, the sister who'd loved and trusted her for years, was keeping secrets, why wouldn't Drako? And if she hadn't told Lei about the dungeon because, in a way, she was trying to protect her, how could she judge Drako too harshly? Perhaps he was ashamed. Or maybe he felt he was protecting her by not telling her about this spy thing? Yes, that made a lot of sense.

"You met Bob at a dungeon and then what happened?" When Lei didn't answer right away, Rin asked, "Did he drug you like he did me? Kidnap you?"

"I was never locked up. I could leave whenever I wanted." Lei added, "I was never afraid."

"Did you know what he was going to do?" Rin pressed, wondering how much of a role her sister played in Agent Bob Zacharias's scheme. Not because she was angry with her sister, but because she wondered if she'd ever been in danger.

"He explained it all to me, just like he did to you."

"Why didn't you just tell me the truth, Lei?"

"Would you have believed me?" Lei gave her a pointed glare.

"No," Rin admitted. "I wouldn't have. But dammit, I wish there'd been another way to handle this whole thing. I was terrified that bastard, Campioni, had taken you away again."

Lei placed her hand over Rin's. "I'm so sorry you were worried. The truth is, I wanted to call you and tell you I was okay, but they told me I shouldn't, that they'd bring you here, to me, when it was safe. I didn't want you to get hurt. I was petrified something would happen to you." Lei curled her fingers around Rin's hand and squeezed. "Rin, if I were to lose you, I think I'd go crazy. Or die."

Rin stood, wrapped her arms around herself, and walked over to the window. The western sky was streaked with salmon and deep purple, the heavy sun barely hanging above the horizon. The weakening light left much of the surrounding neighborhood cloaked in shadow. Still, there was nothing sinister or threatening about the homes. They were, just like the one she now stood inside, charming cottages. Rin didn't need to hear another word to know that Lei was genuinely convinced Drako was up to something dangerous. But why would Lei be willing, then, to let the sister she loved risk her life by going back to him? "Why aren't you trying to talk me into leaving him, Lei?"

Lei stepped up behind Rin and placed her chin on Rin's shoulder. "Because I also believe you love him. You can't leave him. Am I wrong?"

She wasn't. No matter if Drako was Drako Alexandre or Kane Zacharias, or John Smith, jeweler or spy or auto mechanic, she loved him. With everything she had and was. She'd married him, promising for better or worse, and she had been looking forward to living up to that promise. She wanted to have his children, watch them grow up, and eventually begin lives of their own.

He had to have a damn good reason for lying to her. She knew it in her gut.

Still standing behind Rin, Lei wrapped her arms around Rin's shoulders. "If we can get that thing, whatever it is, away from your husband safely, with Agent Zacharias's help, then you can go back and live like nothing has changed."

"You think?" Rin watched a little boy toddle down the street, pulling a wagon. His dark, wavy hair poked out from beneath a baseball cap. Rin could easily imagine that was their child, hers and Drako's. Could they truly find some kind of normal life after this?

"Honestly, I think the only chance you have of living the rest of your life with that man is if you help them. If you don't, the government is going to arrest him. He'll spend the rest of his life in federal prison."

Lei's words struck her with more force than a blow to the stomach. Rin went back to the coffee table, picked up the military ID, and ran her thumb over the photograph, staring at the face that was so familiar, paired with the name of a stranger.

She battled with doubts and fears as she read through every piece of paper in the file again and again. Lei didn't try to convince her to believe or do anything. She sat by her side, one arm resting on Rin's shoulder.

Finally, after one last, long breath in and out, Rin nodded. "Okay. I'll do it. Because I love him. I just hope I won't be sorry."

Lei gave her hand a hard squeeze. "Rin, you've always done what's right. When we were growing up. Then, after I was sent away. Now, you're doing the right thing for your husband and the family you'll have with him someday. I know you don't regret what you did for me. You won't regret helping him either."

Her eyes were burning. Her heart felt heavy, and her insides felt raw, as if they'd been run across a cheese grater. She dragged her thumb under one eye, then the other, and tried not to cry. "You can teach me? I don't know how to . . . what to do."

"I'll teach you everything I know." Lei looked as if she might cry too as she wiped away the tear that seeped from Rin's eye. "You'll get my crash course in being a domme, starting right now. You don't need to know everything, just the basics. Safety first."

Rin pulled Lei into an embrace and whispered as she buried her nose in Lei's satin-smooth hair, "Thank you."

"It's the least I can do, after all you've done for me."

18

Convincing Drako that she and Lei had escaped from Campioni without any help had been a lot easier than convincing him to take her back to a dungeon. In fact, after trying every night for more than two weeks, Rin was ready to give up. Until Lei brought her a letter one day, addressed to her. It was from Agent Zacharias, letting her know the FBI was planning a raid in exactly forty-eight hours.

Rin folded the note and handed it back to her sister. "I've done everything you told me to. Suggested, seduced, practically pleaded. He won't take me back there." Feeling utterly defeated, almost overwhelmed with hopelessness, Rin sat on her sister's bed, shoulders slumped, chin resting on her knees. "Time's running out. What do you think will happen to him?"

Lei, looking at her with worry-filled eyes, shrugged her shoulders as she sat beside her. "I don't know. I suppose the best we can hope for is they'll arrest him, put him in prison."

The air in Rin's lungs rushed out in a heavy sigh. Even the thought of Drako being taken from her left her feeling empty.

She couldn't give up, not until she'd run out of time. "How can I convince him to do what I want?"

Lei jumped up, grabbed a textbook off her nightstand, and plopped back down beside Rin. She ran her fingertip down the book's spine. "We're studying behavioral psychology, you know, motivation, reinforcement, salivating dogs, that kind of thing. If you want to make someone do anything, you've got to know what motivates them."

"I don't know what makes Drako go to the dungeon. I've tried to figure it out."

"Maybe not, but you do know what makes him do other things, like, for instance, marry a woman he doesn't know."

Wondering where Lei was going with this, Rin nodded. "Sure, duty."

"Exactly."

"So how do I convince him that it's *his duty* to take me to the dungeon?" Rin asked.

"Hmmm." Lei thumbed through the pages of her psychology book. "If you could convince Drako that you *need* to go to the dungeon, and that he's the only one you trust, then he'd have to take you. Right?"

"Sure, I guess." Rin sighed. "The problem is, what do I say to convince him of that? He took me to the dungeon once, and he knows I went there for him, not for me."

"Don't say anything."

"Huh?"

Hugging her book to her chest, Lei surged to her feet and began pacing back and forth. "I don't think he'll believe you if you tell him you need to go to the dungeon. He'll only believe you if you *show* him. Let him see you heading out the door, a bag of bondage gear slung over your shoulder, and let him make up his own mind."

"Bondage gear? I don't own any."

"No problem there." Lei sent Rin out of the room with a

shooing motion. "Go, get dressed. I'll take you shopping. When he sees you tonight, he won't doubt for a minute you're serious."

Rin dashed back to her sister, gave her a quick hug, then raced to her room to change into some jeans, a T-shirt, and some tennis shoes. She brushed on a little blush, ran a comb through her hair, and applied a little lip gloss before heading out to find her sister. Lei was waiting for her in the kitchen, her purse on the counter, a glass of diet cola in her hand.

"Ready?" Lei took a swallow of her soda.

"Let me grab a quick something." Rin went for the protein bars in the cupboard and a bottled water from the refrigerator. Fast and simple. And, most important, portable.

"I'll drive." Lei pulled her car keys out of her purse, slipped on some fierce D&G sunglasses—the only true luxury her sister had indulged in—and hurried out the door.

The day was glorious. The air was heavy with the perfume of earth and leaves, an undercurrent of cool freshness playing beneath the surface. The sun, still hanging far to the east, was brilliant. Only a few little white puffy clouds broke up the expanse of true, clear sky blue stretching from one horizon to the other.

Rin inhaled deeply before sinking into the passenger seat of her sister's little car. As Lei navigated the vehicle out of the parking spot next to Rin's car, Rin munched on the chocolate protein bar, washing it down with the water.

The store wasn't far, to Rin's surprise—she hadn't expected to find a sex toy shop out in the burbs. When Rin entered the store and saw all the gear, she was extremely grateful to have her sister there with her. She had no clue what half of it was used for.

They shared laughs and a few awkward moments, when one or both of them found themselves facing a topic they weren't comfortable talking about. Even though Lei had spent hours helping Rin learn how to safely bind a submissive; how to use paddles, whips, and other toys safely; and how to help a submissive find her headspace by volunteering to be Rin's guinea pig, Lei still didn't talk about some things. And neither did Rin. They both respected each other's limits.

Once Rin had made her selections, the sisters headed out with hands full of bags. They put everything in the trunk, drove to a favorite restaurant for some lunch, and discussed a strategy for that evening.

If Rin couldn't convince Drako this time, she never would.

That evening, she dressed carefully in something a little sexier, a little more dangerous than he cared to see her in. She called him about a half hour before he normally got home, asking him if he was going to be home at the normal time and asking if he'd stop for some milk.

At time minus ten, or roughly ten to six, she had a small panic attack as she gave herself one last up-and-down look in the full-length mirror. If she failed...

Don't think about it, or it'll become a self-fulfilling prophesy.

"It's going to work," she told her reflection.

Her cell phone rang, just once, then cut off. That was the signal. She dragged the heavy bag off the bed, sliding the strap over her shoulder. Metal clanking sounds accompanied her every step as she headed toward the door, where she'd "accidentally" run into Drako.

"Rin." Drako was half in and half out of the door when he saw her. His eyebrows shot to the top of his forehead; his eyes widening for an instant before narrowing. "Hi."

"Hello." She raised up on tiptoes to give him a kiss. It was as brief as she could bring herself to offer. A metallic clank sounded from the bag the instant her heels came back into contact with the ground.

Drako grabbed the bag's strap in a fist, raising it, the motion causing a few more clacks and clatters. "What's this?"

She lifted her chin. "Well, you know I've been asking you to take me to the dungeon?"

"Yeah."

"You keep telling me 'no.' So, I have no choice. I'm going without you."

He pulled the bag's strap off her shoulder. "No, you're not. It isn't safe, not after—"

"I'll be careful." Pretending she wasn't nervous as hell, she patted his shoulder and tugged on her bag's strap. He had no idea how vital it was for him to take her to the dungeon. And that was only the beginning. Next, she had to get him to trust her—she had no idea how she was going to do that—and then, she had to somehow get him to tell her where the stolen thingy was. She wasn't facing any uphill climb; she was about to scale Mount Everest. And the scariest part—she had no safety net to catch her if she fell. And not only was she facing a horrible fall, but she would pull Drako down with her.

No pressure there. None at all.

Wishing she could turn the whip over to Lei, who seemed so much more capable of pulling this off, she gave Drako a little smile and wave. "I'll be home in about an hour and a half. Unless I'm having too much fun and decide to stay longer." She gave Drako a step-outta-my-way look. When he didn't move from the doorway, she turned sideways, facing him, and sidestepped through the narrow opening.

Unfortunately, she didn't make it all the way through. He stopped her by clamping his hand around her wrist, as tight and unyielding as any metal cuff could be.

"I said, you're not going."

She narrowed her eyes, meeting his gaze. "One question. Have you stopped going to the dungeon since Lei and I were kidnapped?"

His gaze jerked from hers. A tense silence, frosty and hard, fell between them.

"Are you going to suggest your need for D/s is more urgent than mine?" she asked.

"Since when did you *need* D/s?" he bit, his teeth clenched so tightly that Rin could make out the muscles of his face. A large blood vessel on his neck protruded. That couldn't be good.

"Does it matter when?"

As impossible as it might have seemed, his jaw clenched even tighter. He wasn't annoyed; he was furious. Every bone in Rin's body was screaming for her to stop this ruse and back step out of what could potentially be an ugly fight. But the fear of the unknown, of what might happen, was enough to push her to keep going.

She glared at the side of his face. He wouldn't look at her. "Drako, I've been through a lot lately, a terrifying experience. I haven't slept in over a week. I'm terrified of every stranger I see. I went out today with Lei and had a panic attack in a store. If I don't get out of this house, and face my fears, I'm going to become a prisoner of them. Now, does this make sense?" By the end of her speech, her voice was shaky and her eyes were burning and blurry.

Drako didn't speak for a few seconds. The tense space between them—no more than a couple of inches—was filled with nothing but the sound of her shallow, panting breaths. His gaze found its way back to her face, where it lingered on her eyes. Gradually, his face relaxed. "Okay. I'll take you."

She dragged her hand across her eyes. "Thank you." It was a good thing she was wearing waterproof mascara or she'd be washing off the raccoon eyes before going anywhere.

He let her go outside first, then followed her. During the drive, she watched the familiar landscape whiz by in a blur, her mind racing as she tried to anticipate the next battle she was about to face. Convincing him to take her was only a small victory.

By the time Drako had parked the car, she had recited in her head at least a dozen different speeches, each one saying, essentially, the same thing.

She was ready. Until they were in that room again.

All the words flew from her head, like pigeons from a kicked cage. Drako gave her a funny look, probably wondering why she was standing there, just inside the door, her hands curled around the strap of her bag so tightly her knuckles were white.

"Are you okay?" His voice was heavy with concern, and she realized he was reading her body language and interpreting it as terror. That wasn't far from the truth.

"I'm okay." She took a few slow breaths.

"Come, sit down." He motioned toward the love seat.

"No."

His jaw practically dropped to the floor. If he thought that little bit of rebellion was a surprise, he had no idea what was about to hit him. If things hadn't been so life-or-death, Rin might have actually enjoyed this more, watching his reaction as she exorcised an independent streak he didn't realize she had.

Clearly insisting on making her sit, he walked to her, placed one hand at the small of her back, and tried to give her a little nudge.

"Drako, I'm not here to be your submissive."

"You're not? Then who were you planning on scening with?"

"You."

He looked like she'd just spoken to him in Swahili. "Huh?"

She strolled across the room, set her bag down on the table, unzipped it, pulled out the single tail whip, and flicking her wrist, sent the tail sailing through the air. It snapped a couple of feet from him, at about chest level.

She was relieved to see those many hours of practice had paid off.

Drako's face went white.

Remember, show no weakness, no doubt, no fear. If he's going to trust you, you have to show him you're trustworthy. His life depends upon it.

Was this his wife, wielding that whip like a professional domme? Couldn't be. No fucking way.

He was so stunned, speechless, he didn't know how to react, what to do next. For one thing, his heart was telling him that the stranger standing in the room with him was Rin, the woman he'd come to know and care for. But his eyes... what he saw just wasn't jibing with what he felt.

For another, he was as far from a submissive man as a guy could be. He was the oldest of three, comfortable taking responsibility, acting in the name of duty, and taking control of a situation. He not only didn't want to put himself in the role of submissive but was almost afraid to.

He knew how vulnerable a submissive was to his or her dom. There was no way he could take that risk. But what would happen if he downright refused? Would she go find a willing submissive?

Maybe that would be best.

"Haven't you ever switched roles, Drako?" Rin looked extremely confident as she sauntered closer. Sexier than hell. The fact that his cock was hard enough to bust through concrete surprised him. Normally an aggressive woman made his libido take a nose dive. She trailed a manicured fingernail over his shoulder as she stepped around his side. "Are you afraid to let any woman take control or only me?"

"I'm not a sub."

"That doesn't mean you haven't stepped into the role. Don't a lot of doms try it? To learn to appreciate a submissive's perspective, needs, feelings?" She stopped directly in front of him. She was tiny, delicate. Maybe that was why he'd always found himself wanting to protect her, take care of her. But at this point, her size didn't seem to matter so much. She possessed a tangible strength, an energy he couldn't ignore. This new confidence and power made his feelings for her change, but not in the way he would have expected.

He wrapped his fingers around her slender wrist, felt the quick pace of her pulse beating beneath her skin. She was either excited or nervous, or both. Was it all an act? "Do you really think you know how to use this?" He twisted his hand, forcing hers to turn over, palm up. He laid his other hand over her fingers, curled around the handle of the whip, expecting them to open, releasing the toy to his care.

Instead, she jerked her hand away. She pointed at a painting hanging on the far wall. "See the pearl earring on the woman in the portrait?" Before he responded, she sent the tail whirring through the air. It struck the painting exactly where she'd indicated. "I haven't been at this long, but I had a good teacher and I'm a quick study."

He couldn't deny that. Nor could he deny the waves of heat blazing through his body. "Impressive. But I'm not your boy. I'm not going to get on my knees. Not for you. Not for anyone."

"Let me make something clear." She focused those almond-shaped eyes on his. "I don't want a *boy*. I want a man. I want you." She hooked her arm around his neck and pressed her body to his. And his cock grew impossibly harder.

She tipped her chin up, offering her plump lips, and there was no way he would refuse them. But just as his mouth met hers, she shoved him back.

Holy shit, did he want her badly. Who was this woman? She was playing him and he was fucking loving it.

Her smile was pure seduction. "You're going to earn a kiss from me."

Maybe he could play along a little, make her think she was getting what she wanted. Sure, that could work. He drew his hands behind his back and wove his fingers together, damp palms pressed tightly. "Okay. How can I earn a kiss?"

Her lips, the ones he'd been about to taste, and would taste again soon, curled into an enchanting smile. "Good choice." She circled him, her skirt ruffling away from her legs as she walked. Her shoes did everything for her legs that they should do. As soon as he had control over this situation, those long, shapely legs would be wrapped around his waist, his cock driving into her tight little pussy.

"Undress. Take off everything," she commanded.

That was a good start. He let her suffer a little as he stripped off his clothes, making sure to move in ways that showcased his body to its fullest. Arms, chest, shoulders. Those were her favorite parts of his body, he'd figured that out long ago. So those were the parts he made her wait to see. And when he did finally reveal them, he pumped his muscles so they were tight, defined. He was rewarded with plenty of heated looks, but she said nothing. Her nostrils flared slightly as she moved closer. And he could see her pupils were dilated, the irises almost completely overtaken by them. A sheen of sweat coated her chest, and the air was sweet with the scent of her arousal.

She might be the one holding the whip, but he was the one in control.

He decided to test her by sliding a hand over her hip and stepping closer. She didn't stop him. Not when his hand glided around to the small of her back, or when he dragged her against him. But when he bent his head to take the kiss he believed he had earned, she gave his ass a sharp smack and twisted out of his hold.

"I didn't tell you to kiss me yet." Her chest was rising and falling quickly, her breathing visibly fast. She wanted him. Yet she was still insisting on playing this game, denying herself, denying him. She pointed at the kneeler. "There."

He could be patient a little longer. He nodded. "Sure."

Without being told, he knelt down and bent over the upper support. His ass was still tingling a little where she'd smacked him. It wouldn't bother him if she did it again.

She buckled leather cuffs around his wrists, securing them down by the floor. He couldn't stand up now. Couldn't use his hands. Not a big deal, but it wasn't the most comfortable situation he'd ever been in either. "How's that?" She stooped down to look at his face.

"Fine."

"Green light?" she asked, her eyes searching his.

"Green light." He tested the restraints with a little tug.

"Not used to being powerless, are you, Drako?"

"Nope."

"Are you uncomfortable?" Her tongue swept cross her plump lower lip.

He shook his head. "Not at all."

She checked the snugness of each cuff. "Do you trust me?"

"You seem to be able to handle that whip okay."

"Thank you." She dragged the whip's tail across his back. "My sister's an excellent teacher." She cupped his chin, brushed her lips across his, and with her mouth barely touching his, murmured, "Don't worry. I know my own limitations. Now, tell me yours."

"I can handle pain."

She nipped his lower lip. "I have a feeling that would be the easiest part of submitting for you." She had him pegged. "Losing control. That's where you struggle, isn't it?"

"Maybe." He didn't like where this was going.

She trailed little soft kisses along his jaw. Each one seemed to light a little spark in his blood. "I bet you're so good at controlling people, situations, you've never lost a power struggle. I bet you've been tied up, bound, gagged, and still been able to somehow dictate what happened."

Damn, she knew him too well.

She stood, circled him, the whip's leather tail skimming across his lower back as she walked. "The few times you've 'submitted' to someone, it's been an illusion, hasn't it? You've always had the power because you've always picked partners who were willing to hand it to you. I'm not going to." She kicked his knees apart.

He felt a cuff wrapping around one ankle, then the other. Now, he couldn't stand either. He wasn't completely immobilized, but damn well close enough.

With eyes and ears, he tracked her movement as she went to her bag to gather some toys. After setting an array of toys on a table, within his sight—including a prostate massager—she dragged up a chair and sat facing him. "Have you ever had a woman tell you when to come?"

"No." A drip of sweat fell from his forehead, striking the floor beneath him with a soft pat.

"I didn't think so." She bent down and lifted her skirt, dragging it up her thigh, over her hip. She shifted her weight forward and pulled the material out from under her buttocks and parted her legs.

Her pussy was wet, pink temptation. He inhaled deeply, pulling in her scent, deep down into his lungs. His tongue swept over his lips, and he wished he could have one taste, just one.

She fingered herself, parting the damp folds to push one digit into her tight canal. He could almost feel those silken walls gripping his cock. "Do you want to taste me?"

"Shit, yes." He licked his lips again.

"Do you want to make love to me?"

"Yes."

"Then you're going to do what I want. You're not going to pretend. If you try to control me, I'll make myself come and you'll watch, but you won't touch me. Understand?"

"Yeah." He felt his fingers curling into fists, his jaw clenching.

She stood and the material cascaded down over her hips. "Is it really so bad, letting me lavish you with some attention for once?"

Yes. "No."

"Good. Enjoy." She poured some oil onto her hands and massaged his shoulders, back. The air filled with the soft scents of lavender and vanilla. "Your tattoo is so hot. This is the first time I've gotten a good look at it." His skin tingled as her oil-slicked fingertips walked up and down either side of his spine. When she started kneading a knot down in his lower back, he actually moaned. "Yes, that's nice, isn't it?"

"Yeahhhh."

She worked lower, strong fingers pressing into muscles wound tight.

Damn, that felt good. He'd forgotten about her stint at the massage parlor. Clearly she'd learned a thing or two there. Perhaps this was the Rin she was in that setting. Maybe she'd had to be more aggressive there?

Her hands slid down over the curve of his ass, and he tensed up again, remembering she had a prostate massager. He'd never taken anything in his anus, though he'd taught plenty of subs to take toys in their asses. He knew, having scened with men before, what a prostate massager could do to a guy. Make him come in a heartbeat, hard, fast, and against his will. The thought of losing control to that degree...

Her fingers slid between his ass cheeks, explored deeper until a fingertip was stroking his anus. Just like a new sub, he tightened up.

"Have you ever used an anal toy?"

"No."

"Okay." Her voice quavered ever so slightly, enough to let

him know she wasn't as confident with exploring anal play as she was targeting that single-tailed whip.

"If you're unsure—"

"Don't," she interrupted. "I told you, don't try to control me. You won't like the consequences." She returned to her seat, pulled her skirt up, and slid her bottom to the edge of the chair. Next, she grabbed a vibrator off the table, squirted some lube into her palm, and smoothed it on the toy. Her gaze locked to his. "Look at me." He watched, mouth dry, heartbeat pounding in his ears, as she parted her pussy lips and pushed the toy inside.

That shouldn't be a piece of plastic, gliding in and out of that tight sheath. It should be his cock. It was his right, as her husband, a fact that made this situation all the more frustrating. He bit back a rant of frustration, knowing she was more than cruel enough to mete out some serious punishment if she wanted.

Was it one minute, two, or a lifetime, she tormented him by fucking herself with that damn vibrator? He completely lost track of time. It was meaningless to him. She plunged it in and out, in and out, over and over, filling the room with the sweet sounds of her breaths and tiny moans. To torment him more, she dragged her chair closer and fucked her pussy harder, faster, until her face was flushed, her lips parted slightly, a sheen of sweat glistening over her forehead, cheeks, and chest.

Just when he was sure she was about to come, she stopped; set the vibrator, still wet with her juices, on the table, and smiled at him.

"Next time, I won't stop," she vowed.

He had no reason to doubt her.

19

She had him where she wanted. She could sense his change. It felt like a shifting energy field, an almost-imperceptible sensation. He would submit now. He'd surrendered. She'd gained his respect. And his trust. The hardest part was over.

Now, the fun began.

Feeling more confident, not having to play a role anymore, she walked around him, admiring his beautiful body. So much power lay in those thick arms and legs, strength in the muscle and sinew and bone that formed his body. And it was all under her control now.

She squirted some lube onto her fingertips and caressed his balls, firm and snugged up tightly to his body. She let herself indulge in a couple of strokes up and down his cock, enjoying the way he shuddered at her touch. And finally, sensing he was ready, she touched his anus again. Unlike the first time, her fingertip slipped past the ring of muscle easily. To reward him, she gave his cock a couple more strokes with her other hand, moving the two together, finger in his ass, hand tightly gripping his penis.

He probably had some idea of what she was planning for him. If he did, he wasn't anxious. His breathing was fast and shallow, his body tight, skin warm, but that wasn't from fear. She could tell by the way he groaned and whispered her name.

The air smelled so good, of man and sex, that she wanted to gulp in great big lungfuls and hold it in until her head started spinning.

Convinced he was ready for the toy, she lubed it up like Lei had shown her and, after helping prepare his anus with a couple of fingers, eased it into place. She was so happy and relieved when it went in easily and he seemed to enjoy it.

"How's that?"

"Good."

Holding the end of the toy, she played with his cock and balls with her free hand, appreciating every shiver, every sigh, every moan. This experience was so unlike any she'd shared with him, or any man for that matter. She was clear-headed, concentrated fully on his pleasure, not her own. It made it so much easier to read the nuances of his reaction as she touched him all over, whispered dirty words into his ear, and licked and nibbled her way up and down his body. Goose bumps coated his arms. His skin grew warm under her touches. A deep ruby flush stained his chest, neck, and cheeks.

It was time.

"Come, Drako. Come now."

"No," he whispered. "Not until you have your pleasure first."

She turned the toy on, setting the vibrate on low, and watched in fevered awe as Drako's muscles pulled into taut, thick ropes. "I said, come," she whispered. He trembled, fought the restraints binding his arms and legs, jerking against them and cussing. But he didn't say "Red." His cock jerked. He howled, tossing his head back, and, still struggling against the bindings, came.

She'd never seen anything so chilling and yet so beautiful.

"Dammit!" he shouted.

"What's wrong? Didn't you like it?" She shut off the vibrator and walked around him, squatting so she could see his face.

"No."

"No?" She took his still-semierect penis in her hand and gave it a slow swipe. It jerked in her palm. A droplet of cum seeped from the tip.

"I mean, yes, and no. I'm not used to this, to an orgasm hitting me from nowhere."

"You mean you're not used to having someone or something else make you come." She ran her flattened hands up his arms and over his shoulders. His muscles rippled beneath the golden skin. She traced the outline of his tattoo, the griffon that stretched from one side of his upper back to the other. "You're such a beautiful man. I like this, taking my time with you, dictating what you feel and when."

"But wouldn't you rather have me touching, kissing, stroking every inch of your body?"

"No. Not yet."

"Sure you would." He twisted an arm, trying to free it from the cuff. "Let me loose, and I'll show you how good I can make you feel."

"No, thanks."

He gave a little dissatisfied grunt.

"This is just the beginning," she promised, knowing he'd need to come at least a couple more times before he'd be tamed. But he'd need some time to recover. At least a couple of minutes.

She'd give him a little encouragement to keep playing.

Straightening up, she removed her dress, which left her nude except her shoes. She returned to the chair, positioned directly in front of him, parted her legs, and found a vibrator that looked like fun. This one had a second little part that would stimulate her anus, as well as a collar of rotating beads.

She placed the tip on her clit and turned it on. After about two seconds, she decided that wasn't such a good thing. The stimulation was too direct, sending her hurtling toward orgasm too quickly. She inserted the toy and shuddered as a wave of sensual heat rippled through her body.

Now, this was better.

She glanced at Drako. Were those flames flickering in his eyes? Deep blue ones, like the uber hot flames on a gas stove. The toy's vibrations hummed along her nerves, making her heartbeat race, pound in her ears. It would be so easy to surrender to the pleasure, let it carry her away, but she couldn't. She had to focus on Drako, on breaking down the walls he'd erected around his heart.

She pulled the toy out just before orgasm had her in its tight grip. Gasping for breath, she set it aside.

"This isn't what you want, Rin. Why are you doing this?"

"Because it's what we both need." She took his face in her hands, ran her thumb along his bottom lip. This was the face she loved, the man she loved. She had to do everything she could to help him, to save him.

"No. I don't believe that."

"It's too soon for you to agree with me." She kissed him, softly, patiently, exploring his warm, delicious mouth and letting him do the same. It was the kind of kiss she'd remember a long time, full of raw emotion. Sweet and tender. Provocative and sensual.

"Release me and let me show you true pleasure," he murmured into her mouth.

"Are you uncomfortable?"

"No."

"In pain?"

"No."

"Can you say the safe word if you needed to?"

"Yes, the word is 'Red,' but I'm not going to use it."

"Very well." She released his face, strolled around him, this time stopping at his side. She played with his cock and balls, using her hands to bring him to the verge of orgasm and then she commanded, "Come, Drako."

He clamped his jaw. "No."

She turned on the anal stimulator again.

He fought even harder against the second orgasm. He cussed, he begged, he pleaded, he yanked his arms and jerked his body from side to side. But nothing worked. He lost the battle within minutes.

"Say it," Rin demanded, her heart in her throat. "Say 'Red.' "

"No, dammit."

He was a lot more determined than she'd expected.

"Then you'll come for me again." Instead of turning off the vibrator, she turned it up a notch, increasing the level of stimulation to his prostate. He shook and growled, like a caged beast, the sensation sending him racing toward yet another orgasm.

"Say the word, Drako. Say 'Red' and I'll stop."

"No! That damn thing isn't going to control me. You're not. Nobody, nothing is. It can't. I can't..."

"Can't what?"

Drako shook his head, and a droplet of sweat fell from his forehead. He jerked as a second orgasm raged through his body. Rin stood by his side, waiting for him to say the word she knew he had the strength to say but not the will. She didn't shut off the toy. She didn't give him a moment's relief because she knew it would set him back. He didn't fight the third orgasm much at all. When the fourth had him in its grip, he mumbled, "Red."

With tears in her eyes, Rin removed the toy and unfastened the cuffs at Drako's wrists and ankles.

He sank to the floor, and she sat next to him, pulled him to her. It wasn't an erotic embrace. It was more the meeting of bodies and souls. Skin to skin, yes, but so much more. Heart to heart, spirit to spirit. "I had no idea," he said softly, his voice breathy as he struggled to catch his breath. "No clue how to let go. I was afraid." Looking up, into her eyes, he smiled. "You did it. You broke me. You took it all away."

"And now I can give it all back, and it'll mean something to you." Rin didn't know how long they sat on the floor and held each other. She was far too content to stay that way. The world could go on without them and she wouldn't care.

"Yes, you're right. It will."

This was what she'd been waiting for, longing for. She lifted her head and realized she'd been crying. Her face was damp with hot, salty tears.

"I can trust you. No, I . . . need you." Drako placed his hands on either side of her face and kissed each eyelid, each cheek, her forehead, the tip of her nose, and finally her mouth. As their lips brushed against each other's, he whispered, "Thank you for helping me accept the truth."

A little sob slipped between her lips. "Will you make love to me now?"

His response didn't take the form of words, but a kiss. A soul-shattering kiss, at that. He caressed her neck, shoulders, upper arms before dragging his hands to her breasts. She responded with a full body shudder and a tiny whimper. She'd never wanted a man this badly before, never needed one this badly either. Did it matter anymore that today had started out as an exercise to manipulate Drako? No, not at all. Because somehow it had turned into something far more essential. She was sure her husband's heart was finally hers.

He gently coaxed her onto her back and she drew her legs apart, allowing him to settle his hips between them. He entered her slowly, the ecstasy so delicious she arched her back and moaned into their joined mouths. He lowered his upper body onto hers, and she slid her hands around his sides to his back. His weight felt so good, so right, resting on top of her. This was heaven.

Their bodies worked in harmony, moving to the same rhythm, coming together and then shifting apart. Rin kissed every inch of Drako she could reach, touched every bit of skin she could too, knowing he was hers, all hers and only hers at last. Never would she share this man with anyone again.

And he did the same. Sprinkled kisses over her face, neck, shoulders. He kissed her fingertips, her eyelashes, her hair. He touched her with such gentleness while looking down upon her with wonder, reverence.

But even though his lovemaking wasn't what she'd expected—it wasn't the hard, feral possession she thought it would be—that didn't make this moment any less perfect.

So he wasn't fucking her with the harsh abandon he might once have Andi and his other submissives. So what? It might have been her wish once, to be what they were to him, the receptacle for all the pent-up energy he kept so carefully contained. She was more to him now than they had ever been, the sanctuary of his soul.

And he was her hero, and the man who had earned the title Master of My Heart.

They brought each other to the crest of passion. With kisses and touches and whispered promises. Their lives and hearts were forever bound, the threads of their souls woven into one.

When the first wave of tingling heat crashed over her, Rin dug her fingertips into Drako's shoulders. She felt him come with her, his cock thickening at the same moment, his cum filling her as her pussy spasmed, pulling it deeper. She laughed and cried, clinging to Drako's slick, hard body, wrapped her legs around his hips, pulling his cock deeper inside. He laughed too, trailed fingertips down the side of her face, kissed the corners of her mouth.

"Rin, you are my world," he said, rolling onto his side and taking her with him. And she believed him. "You don't know how fucking scared I was when I found out you'd been kidnapped, when I thought I'd lost you. I was a wreck. Couldn't think. Couldn't do a goddamn thing. My brothers . . . I don't know what I would've done without them. But I'm so glad you're back and safe. And I don't want to let you out of my sight again, but I don't want to cage you either." As she settled her head in the crook of his arm, she smiled into his eyes. They were open now, the shield that had once been there completely obliterated. "Thank you for waiting, for being so fucking patient with me. I was such an idiot."

"No, you were never an idiot. You were doing what you thought was best for both of us. Not only do I respect you for that, but I love you for it. You're always thinking about what's best for people."

She waited, hoping he'd say the words she longed to hear. He didn't. He kissed her. But in that kiss was all the unfettered emotion he couldn't communicate in words.

He loved her.

She loved him.

Their story was almost complete. There was only one small hurdle to their happy ending. But how could she bring it up now, when they'd just shared such a magical, intimate moment? She didn't want to ruin this or to destroy the trust she'd worked so hard to gain.

She was terrified that if he learned why she'd brought him there tonight, he'd think it was all an act.

God help her. God help him! She couldn't do it. Not now, now while the memory of that beautiful moment, when Drako had finally surrendered, was still so fresh in their minds. And with the imprint of that change so new on their hearts.

"Are you hungry?" He brushed her hair from her face, uncovering her eyes. "What's wrong?"

"Absolutely nothing's wrong." She gave him a reassuring smile. "I'm not exactly overwhelmed, because this is what I've wanted for a long time. I'm just really, really happy."

"Good." He brushed a thumb over her lower lip, kissed it, then sat up. "I need to eat something."

As if on cue, her stomach rumbled. "Me too."

Drako helped her up and then they helped each other into their clothes, sneaking in a touch here, a kiss there. It was a way to hold onto that intimacy a little longer, the magic. Once they had all their clothes on, they joined hands and headed out of the dungeon into what had become a cool, damp night.

"What do you want to eat?" Drako asked after he'd escorted Rin to the car, opened her door, strolled around to the driver's side, and folded his bulky form behind the steering wheel.

"I don't know. But what I would love is to take it home where we can relax and enjoy it, maybe watch a movie."

"Sounds perfect. How does Italian sound? There's a great place a few miles from here."

Visions of rich cream sauces played through her mind. "Yes."

After a few minutes, at a red light, Drako glanced at her. "You said your sister taught you?"

"Hmmm?" Having been lost in her thoughts for a few minutes, she wasn't sure what Drako was talking about.

"You handled that whip like a pro. How long have you been practicing?"

She fingered her cheek, which was burning. "Well, not very long, just since we, er, escaped. But we made good use of the time. I couldn't tell you how many hours we spent working together. I learned that one of my sister's owners taught her to be a domme. He had a lot of play parties, and evidently she was very popular with his friends. She didn't mind it so much because she was in control. Imagine that. Some guy bought a sex slave to be his domme." Rin stared at his profile as she talked.

"She's still dealing with some of the stuff that happened when she was being sold to one owner after another. But I can tell D/s is going to be a big part of her future. It's the only way she feels safe in interacting with men anymore."

"Time will help."

She looked down at her hand, played with her ring. "I know. But I won't stop worrying until I see her happy. I mean, genuinely over-the-moon happy. Like I am."

He touched her cheek, coaxing her gaze back up to his face. "I've never met anyone like you, Rin. You give so much."

She laid a hand over his, sandwiching it between her face and palm. "I've never met anyone like you either. You'll do anything in the name of duty. You're dedicated, loyal."

"And stubborn, an ass," he added, laughter making his eyes glitter brightly. He returned his hand to the steering wheel, using the other one to hit the turn signal.

"Hey, I'm not perfect either. We're both flawed. But maybe that's why we fit so well together."

"Maybe." After he navigated a right turn, he glanced at her. "Rin, I want our marriage to be different. I want to be open, honest, about everything. I want to make a new start, hold nothing back. Our marriage won't be just one of name only. Not anymore." She was so happy, she didn't know what to say. "Most important, I want you to feel you can tell me anything, ask me anything."

It had worked. Just like Lei had said. That unbelievable experience in the dungeon had changed their relationship, and Rin was beyond happy. She hated the idea of risking that happiness already, when it was still so fresh, so new. She'd waited a long time to hear these words. What if he pulled back again? Built up those walls around his heart, this time out of even stronger stuff. Would anything knock them down?

When Drako pulled the car up to a red light, Rin shifted nervously in her seat.

Drako, being the perceptive man he was, looked at her. "What's wrong?"

This was it, her chance to try to get to the truth. It was her only hope to save him from being arrested, imprisoned. "I don't know how to bring this up."

"What?" A horn sounded from the car behind them, and Drako reacted, punching the accelerator. The car lurched forward. But instead of moving along with traffic, Drako turned into a gas station driveway and parked next to the air pump. Once he had the car shifted out of gear, he twisted to look her way. "Is it about what happened in the dungeon?"

"No."

His eyes narrowed. "What is it?"

Rin dragged the back of her hand across her face, smearing tears over her cheeks. "I wish this wasn't necessary."

Drako's eyes narrowed even more.

"I wasn't exactly honest with you." Rin took a few deep breaths, let them out. "Lei and are weren't kidnapped by Campioni. Another man did. He told me things about you."

"What things?"

"He said your name isn't really Drako, and you aren't a jeweler. He said you'd stolen something very dangerous, and you're in danger now because of it."

Something flared in Drako's eyes. Rin waited for him to deny what the man had said. She prayed it had been a lie and Drako would tell her everything was going to be okay, that she had nothing to worry about.

"What else did he say?"

"He said there's going to be a raid, that the thing you'd stolen belonged to the United States government and they were coming to get it back, before it landed in the wrong hands."

"The government?"

She nodded. "The FBI." Drako hadn't denied anything yet.

Why hadn't he? "He said he was telling me because he's worried about your safety."

A deep crease appeared between Drako's brows. "Did this man tell you his name?"

"He said he's your uncle."

The crease became even deeper. "My uncle?"

"He looked a lot like you. His name was Bob Zacharias."

Drako's lips thinned. His fingers curled tighter around the steering wheel. "That's impossible. My uncles are both dead. He lied."

She wanted to believe that. But after what she'd learned about her sister, and knowing she tended to believe what she wanted, rather than the truth, she asked, "Why?"

Staring straight ahead, Drako shrugged. His indifference, however, wasn't convincing. "To manipulate you into helping him. What did he want you to do?"

"Convince you to tell me where the thing you'd stolen is being hidden."

Chewing on his lower lip, Drako shook his head. "If he was really my uncle, he'd know I wouldn't tell you that. I can't tell anyone."

"Then it's true? You're not Drako Alexandre? You're Kane Zacharias? And you did steal something, whatever it is?" Rin's heart was thumping so hard in her chest, she felt her breastbone being bruised from the inside. "Are you in danger?"

"That depends."

"On what?"

Drako's gaze snapped to hers. His stare was hard, sharp, almost intrusive. "On a lot of things. How much of what you told me earlier is true?"

"Most of it. I got a call from Lei and went to the coffee shop to pick her up. I was drugged, taken to a house. Lei was there, and she knew all about you. Agent Zacharias showed me some things, a video from ten years ago, your military records. He asked us to help him find out where you're hiding the weapon or whatever it is. I didn't tell him I would. And then we escaped."

Drako's eyes widened. "Oh, shit. He didn't want you to find out where we're hiding anything."

"What?"

"Oram knows we won't tell anyone, not even our wives. He just wanted you to get me away from my brothers long enough..." He jerked the car's shifter into gear and slammed his foot on the gas pedal. "We need to get home now."

"Why? He said the raid was going to happen tomorrow. He's waiting for me to tell him where the—"

"No, he's not." Driving like he was trying to win the Indy 500, he crammed his hand into his pants pocket and pulled out his phone. He handed it to Rin. "I need to keep my eyes on the road. Call Malek and Talen and warn them Oram's on his way."

"Okay." With one hand, she scrolled through Drako's saved phone numbers while she held on for life with the other. She found one of the brothers, hit the button to put the call through, and waited, hoping Malek would answer. "Drako, is everything going to be all right?"

"I wish I could say yes, but I don't know." Drako zigged and zagged through traffic.

One ring, two, three, four. The call went through to voice mail. Rin hung up and tried Talen's number. "Would it have been better if I'd told you about Agent Zacharias sooner?" she asked.

"It's not your fault. If I'd opened up to you earlier, you wouldn't have been afraid to tell me what happened. It doesn't matter whose fault it is, anyway. We've just got to deal with what comes, as it comes."

20

Rin rode the entire way home with her eyes squeezed shut. She hadn't prayed in eons, but that didn't stop her now. She prayed up a blue streak, making all sorts of promises to the Almighty if he'd give what was beginning to look like a desperate situation a good ending. At the very least, she prayed the people she loved—her sister, Drako and his brothers—would be kept safe.

Supposedly, the big raid was going to happen tomorrow, so even though Drako thought they might be raiding today, she held out hope that he was wrong. That hope was shattered when the car turned onto their street and Rin saw all the black SWAT trucks. The road was completely blocked off by police cars, angled across the width to keep any vehicles from coming in or leaving.

"Ohmygod," she whispered, slapping her hands over her mouth. "What're we going to do?"

Drako jerked the car over and slammed the gear shift into park. "I have to help my brothers." Leaving the car running, he pushed open his door.

"No!" Rin threw herself toward him, catching his sleeve in her fist. Before he could pull himself free from her grasp, she looped an arm around his neck. "You can't rush into that mess. They'll arrest you. Or... or shoot—"

"I have to." He'd never looked so torn, so desperate. "Rin, the man isn't my uncle. He's dead. And that's not the SWAT. It's a secret group that's been trying to get their hands on something for a very long time. They've killed before. They'll kill again."

"More reason to stay out of the way." She squeezed her hand, tightening her hold on his shirt.

"No, if my brothers die, I won't be able to protect The Secret. I can't do it alone."

She yanked, desperate to keep him from leaving her. "So, let them have it. Who cares about some stupid secret weapon or whatever?"

"I wish it were that simple. But it isn't. If The Secret falls into their hands, there isn't a man, woman, or child alive who won't suffer. This is what I was born to do, to set my life aside to protect The Secret. I can't just walk away." He fought out of her clutch, bending to look into the car. "I'm sorry, Rin. Very sorry."

"I love you, Drako Alexandre."

"No matter what happens, don't come after me. Stay here. Stay safe. Just in case... I don't want you to be hurt."

Sure her world was about to shatter around her, she watched her husband run toward a house full of men with guns. She didn't want to think of any "just in cases," but as she sat in that car and watched dozens of men swarm her home, she couldn't help imagining all kinds of horrible outcomes.

How ironic, she was once again waiting for Drako to pull off some miracle, just like she had the first day of their marriage. Then, it had been her sister's freedom, her future at stake.

Now there was so much more to lose, including her sister's life. She hadn't heard a word from Lei since she'd left with Drako.

Hands shaking so badly they were hardly useful, she dug through her purse, found her cell phone, called Lei.

No answer. It went straight to voice mail. Either the phone was shut off or Lei was talking to somebody else. Rin checked her call log to make sure Lei hadn't been trying to get in touch with her.

Nothing.

Rin literally clawed at the seat as she stared over the back. Her lungs were barely inflating. Her nerves were stretched to near snapping point. All kinds of horrific images were playing through her mind.

More men in black charged up to the house. Those guns were going to be pointed at Drako and his brothers, and maybe her sister too. Everyone she loved, everyone who mattered in her life, was inside that house.

She belonged there with them.

This time she couldn't stand by and wait, watch. No way in hell.

She didn't bother shutting the car door. She just ran, arms and legs pumping as fast as she could make them. Her lungs burned with the need for air and her stomach lurched into her throat, but she didn't stop. She kept her eyes focused on the open front door and kept going, following the zigzagging path Drako had taken up to the house, using trees and shrubs for cover.

She was hoping, with the melee, nobody would notice the petite woman racing toward the house. She was almost there. One second, the big, yawning, black gaping doorway was bouncing closer, the next the world was a blur, and then some green grass flew up and smacked her in the face.

So much for hope.

It took her less than a second to realize what had happened. Somebody had tackled her from behind. And her lungs had completely collapsed. Lying flat on her stomach, she fought to inflate them.

"Where do you think you're going?" asked whoever had knocked her off her feet as he yanked both of her wrists behind her back and bound them.

"My husband. My sister," she said between frantic gasps, spitting dirt and grass out of her mouth. Her nose hurt like a sonofabitch, and she was still seeing stars as she was hauled to her feet and shoved forward, her captor's hand holding onto the plastic bands circling her wrists. "I'm not a criminal."

"That may be, but you're running into the middle of a police raid, Miss. We can't have you doing that." He steered her toward a black camperlike vehicle, shoved her inside. "Look who I found skittering around outside like a little mouse?"

She found herself standing in some kind of mobile police station, face-to-face with the man who had claimed to be Drako's uncle. "You!" she shouted, teeth gritted. She fought against the man still holding her. "You lied to me!"

The man smiled.

How she wished she could kick him in the balls. She threw herself forward, hoping she'd catch her captor off-guard and get a shot at the bastard grinning like he'd just been told he'd won the lottery. No such luck. All she managed to do was hurt herself, the tension yanking on her shoulders so hard she staggered backward, falling against the man behind her.

He wrapped an arm around her neck and squeezed, threatening to cut off her air supply.

She froze in place, her sense of reason finally kicking in. She'd let her emotions get her into this situation, but she'd have to think her way out. "Okay, okay. I'm not going to fight anymore."

Agent Zacharias—or whatever his real name was—motioned to the man holding her. "Leave us."

The thick arm slid away from her neck, and Rin sucked in a few shallow gasps, staggering forward to lean against a bench seat bolted to the vehicle's floor. She glanced over her shoulder, toward the exit, down at the bottom of three steps.

"It's locked," he said.

"From the outside?"

He shrugged. "You're free to try it if you want."

She did. Locked. Bastard. "You used me." She stomped back up the steps.

"Yes, I did."

"Why?"

"Because most of what I told you was true. The Secret doesn't belong to Drako Alexandre, or any other man for that matter."

"This isn't a real SWAT truck. Drako told me." Another glance around almost convinced her otherwise. Sure looked real.

He didn't look worried that she knew it wasn't a real police vehicle. "If you try to convince any of those men out there that this is anything but what they believe, they'll laugh in your face and then haul you to the nearest hospital for a psych evaluation."

"And you're not Drako's uncle. He's dead."

The man shrugged. "Sometimes the ends justify the means. Even men you respect believe that. Ever been to a doctor? They cause pain sometimes, don't they? But they do it to heal you, to save your life. This is no different."

"Drako said The Secret needs to be protected, that it's dangerous."

"Sure, that's because that's what he's been told." The man stood, strolled toward the back. He pulled open a panel, stuck his arm into the space behind it, and produced a cola. It seemed the camperlike vehicle had some of the luxuries of a regular camper, like a refrigerator. "Nobody actually knows if that's true." He returned to his seat. "Who's to say all those ancient cultures perished because of The Secret? Nobody's alive to say one way or another. Written testimony didn't exist. There are no records, only conjecture." He opened the can, took a couple of gulps. "In the meantime, mankind is denied a power source that could put an end to gas shortages, global warming, and break the grip the Middle East has on the U.S.'s economy. Imagine a world where there is enough energy to fuel every need, and it's free. There would never be the need to drill into wetlands or haul millions of gallons of oil back and forth across oceans."

Rin could hardly imagine all of that. Was it possible? She had a hard time believing it.

He took another drink, then set his cola on the small counter behind him. "Guess who your husband is related to?"

"Who?"

He sat back, crossed one leg over the other. "The men who have the power now, the richest, most influential men of our world. The wealthiest families of Russia, Saudi Arabia, and the western U.S. Do you think they have an interest in keeping secret a power source that would make oil, natural gas, and all other fossil fuels obsolete?"

"Maybe. But that isn't why Drako is protecting The Secret or whatever it's called. He's doing it because he believes it's best for everyone. Maybe if you talked to him—"

The man interrupted her with a raised hand. "Kane's been brainwashed since he was old enough to understand spoken words. No amount of talking will do anything."

A tense silence fell between them, as thoughts churned through her mind like a wildly thrashing river. If the words she'd just heard had been spoken by any other human being, she might believe him. If she could set aside her fury and fear, she could almost believe this man, one she'd come to distrust. Only one thing stood in her way.

He'd lied to her once already. Could she accept anything he said as truth?

"Who are you, really?" she asked.

"I am who I said I was, your husband's uncle. Full name's Robert Henry Zacharias."

"Drako said his uncles are dead."

"He believes his uncles are dead. He's about to learn one isn't."

The door opened, and Rin, believing Drako was about to join them, twisted to look over her shoulder. She was disappointed to see it wasn't him, and even more upset to see the man who'd entered slide into the driver's seat, start the vehicle, and pull it away from the curb.

Rin stumbled, a bump sending her flopping into the seat she'd been clinging to for balance. "Where are we going?"

Drako's uncle answered, "Somewhere private, where the three of us can have a chat. Can I get you a cola? Water?"

Drako swallowed a scream of rage and curled his fingers into a fist. "He has Rin. Dammit!"

Talen, surveying the situation, waved him away. "Go on. We've got things under control here. Dobbs and Wilkerson are out back, taking care of the last of them. Get her back." Drako hesitated, and Talen gave him a shove. "I said, go. Now. Before it's too late. They've retreated. Battle's over."

Drako wanted to believe that was true, but he couldn't quite convince himself of it.

"Where's Rin?" Malek asked, strolling toward them. He was red-faced but otherwise looking no worse for wear. The attack had been swift and unexpected, but it hadn't been well organized. A few bodies were scattered over the house's first floor, the enemy's loss, but that was the extent of the death toll. They'd come in, guns blazing, and beat a hasty retreat minutes later when Drako's brothers and their two hired guns had returned fire.

"Rin's been taken hostage again," Drako said.

"What're you doing here, then?" Malek shoved a 9mm into his hands.

Holding the gun, Drako shook his head. "I can't leave you two here."

"We're fine. They're gone." Like Talen, Malek gave Drako a shove toward the door. "I think we've proven today that we're more than capable of keeping Lei and The Secret safe until you return."

"Dammit." Drako hesitated for one more second before dashing toward the door. He hoped Rin had left the keys in the car's ignition. Even more important, he hoped Rin had taken her cell phone with her. As he ran, he hit the speed dial for her number. It started ringing before he'd reached his car, sitting exactly where he'd left it, keys still hanging in the ignition.

Rin's phone rang once, twice, three times. Just before it cut to voice mail, she answered, her voice barely audible. "Drako?"

"I'm here, baby. I'm on my way." When she didn't respond right away, his insides twisted. He said, shifting the car into gear and punching the gas, "Are you there?"

"I'm here. I'm scared."

So was he. More scared than he'd ever been. This whole thing wasn't sitting right with him. Oram was up to something. "Everything'll be okay. Where are you?" He turned onto the main road, opting to head toward the closest freeway, hoping that was the right direction.

"In a big black SWAT truck."

"I know. Can you tell which way it's traveling?"

"I'll try to look. Gotta put the phone down. Don't hang up. Please, don't leave me."

"I'll stay right here and wait." The traffic light ahead turned yellow and he slowed, gritting his teeth against searing frustration. If he didn't believe he'd get pulled over for running it, he would've shot right through. He wasn't willing to test his luck.

"We're on M-14, heading east. There's an exit up ahead. Ford Road."

"I'm right behind you." The light changed and he slammed his foot on the accelerator, sending the car rocketing forward. The freeway entry ramp was just ahead. The truck had a several mile lead on him, but the vehicle was big and slow. His Corvette was small, fast, and had a 430-horsepower V8 under its hood. He could close the distance without risking his life.

He was grateful for the fact that this leg of the freeway was lightly traveled and rarely ever patrolled by police. He watched the speedometer's needle climb to eighty, ninety, ninety-five. His eyes occasionally strayed from the road ahead to the mirrors. He didn't need to be pulled over for speeding any more than he needed to be pulled over for running a red light.

"We're exiting," Rin said.

"Where?" He tucked his cell phone between his shoulder and ear.

"Sheldon Road? Heading north."

That was another few miles up ahead. He'd closed the distance slightly, but not enough. And once he was in traffic, it would be harder. He pushed the accelerator to the floor. His speed climbed. One hundred. One hundred five. One hundred ten.

The sign for the Sheldon Road exit passed him in a blur of green. He slowed, taking the cloverleaf exit at a speed that had him holding white-knuckled to the steering wheel. The phone dropped into his lap as he roared around the sharp curve. As he slowed to a stop, he picked it back up. "Are you still with me, baby?"

"I'm here. Trying not to talk too much. Don't want them to find out I have the phone."

"That's okay."

"We're turning."

"Where?"

"Six Mile Road. Going west."

He checked the sign up ahead. "I'm less than a mile behind you."

"Okay."

The road up ahead was congested, but he timed the lights perfectly, hitting the intersection in less than three minutes. "I'm on Six Mile."

"Still going west."

The road quickly turned into a rural two-lane highway, and with each mile that passed with hardly a car in sight, Drako pushed the accelerator harder. Trees rushed by him in a blur, the road ahead a gray expanse, empty and lonely.

"We turned. Metal gates. Unpaved driveway heading northeast. No road sign. No landmark."

He looked for an opening along the right side as he raced down the road. "What was the last intersection you passed?"

"Ridge Road. A school. Some subdivisions."

"I see it." He eased up on the gas.

A muffled sob echoed in his ear. "Be careful, Drako. I love you."

"I see the truck." Heart thumping, hands quaking, as adrenaline charged through his system, Drako raced down the bumpy dirt road, his car's undercarriage slamming to the ground more than once. He thought he might have to ram the car into the truck to stop it, but after the truck hit a deep rut, it lurched to the right and slammed into a tree.

Drako barely had his car out of gear before he jumped from it. He led with the gun, his finger next to the trigger, not on it, for fear he'd accidentally shoot Rin.

Just as he reached the vehicle's door, it swung open and Rin came stumbling out, held against her captor's body with an arm around her neck and a Glock pointed at her temple. Her face was the shade of paper, with the exception of her eyes, bloodshot and tear filled.

His gaze slid up to the man holding her, and the air in his lungs left his body in a rush.

She hadn't been misled. That was his uncle, one of three brothers who had once served as the guardians of The Secret.

"What the hell?" Reeling from what felt like a sucker punch to his gut, Drako just about dropped his gun. Never had he suspected he'd be in this situation, his wife being held hostage by a man he'd known for decades, loved, respected, and had mourned.

"Expecting someone else?" his uncle asked.

"Yeah. Oram."

His uncle shook his head. "They couldn't bury the coffin empty, could they?"

What the hell?

"How did you find us?" Drako moved his index finger, setting it on the trigger.

"You walked right into my trap. At least you got smart, though it took you a while. You should stick with what you do best. I told you that. So did your father. Why didn't you listen?" His uncle sneered. "You don't know what I'm talking about, do you? How's that beanhead you sent into the old Chimera hangout feeling? What was his name, Wilkerson? You pump a few drugs in that boy's veins and he don't stop talking."

Holy shit! Drako wished he could turn back time and do things differently. Malek had been right. They shouldn't have sent those two men in there. If they hadn't, Rin wouldn't have been kidnapped and he wouldn't be having this conversation with his enemy now. "Why are you doing this? Why now, when you had access to The Secret when you were one of us?"

"Because I learned some things after I retired."

"What things?" Drako asked, trying to sight a clean shot. His uncle was smart; he wasn't giving him a shot. Drako had no choice but to be patient, wait.

"I learned the world isn't black and white. It's all shades of gray. Right. Wrong. Good. Bad. Nothing is all one and none of the other, not mankind, and not anything man has created."

Drako inched his gun to the right. Still no good. "So we're here to talk philosophy?"

"Not exactly." His uncle pushed the Glock harder against Rin's temple, and Rin visibly tensed. A fat tear dripped from her lashes.

"You want The Secret. You know I can't give it to you."

His uncle tightened his arm around Rin's neck. "We don't have the right to keep it hidden away. We're playing God."

"No, we're protecting millions of innocent people."

"I'm not in the mood for a debate." His uncle lowered the gun, and before Drako could react, before Drako had even realized what he was about to do, he shot Rin in the leg.

Her scream tore through Drako's body, the shock of what he'd just witnessed freezing his muscles.

"You fell in love with her, didn't you, boy? That was your first mistake. You know a man can't think straight with all those sissy emotions turning his brain to mud. Look what it did to your father." Drako's uncle jerked Rin, now sobbing and shaking, tighter against him. "Clock's ticking, Drako. It's not a mortal wound yet, but if she bleeds for too long it will be."

"Drako." Rin's bottom lip quivered. Her eyes bored into his. She mouthed the word, *no*.

"Call your brothers," his uncle demanded. "Have them bring it to us."

Drako tightened his fingers around the gun, wishing he could get a decent shot. But he couldn't. Rin's head was too close to his uncle's, and her body blocked most of his chest, stomach, and groin. At best, Drako might be able to shoot him in the hand, but he was too afraid Rin would get shot again to try it.

"Call them," his uncle repeated, calmly. "Now, or I'll have to speed up the clock. And tell them to come alone. This party's already too crowded."

Rin whimpered and mouthed, *nonono*.

"Okay." Drako jerked his phone out of his pocket and dialed.

"They have exactly fifteen minutes to get it here, or she's dead."

Talen's phone rang once, twice. He answered on the third ring. "Did you get to her in time?"

"Yes and no. Talen, Uncle Bob isn't dead. He's the one holding Rin hostage, and he wants The Secret brought to this spot. Or he'll shoot her. He already has once." He couldn't help staring at the growing stain on her leg. "Sheldon Road north to six mile west. Down a few miles, past Ridge. You'll see a pair of metal gates."

"Holy hell. Got it."

"You've got fifteen minutes," Drako told his brother.

"What're you going to do?" Talen asked.

"I wish I knew."

"Hold him off. We're coming." Talen ended the call.

Drako shoved his phone back in his pocket. "They're coming."

"That's good." His uncle shot Rin again, in her other leg. "Now, to make sure they bring it."

Drako's heart stopped for a split second and then started racing as white hot rage ripped through his body. He shot, intentionally aiming high, hoping his uncle would move. He didn't bat an eyelash.

"Call them back and tell them to bring The Secret."

Drako yanked his phone out again and dialed. When Talen

answered, he said two words, "Bring it," and hung up. "There, I did it."

Rin was trembling, visibly weakening. Her eyelids were heavy, her lips milky white.

He couldn't stand there and watch her die. He couldn't lose her. She was his world, she was his reason for taking his next breath.

"Rin," he said, sure she was about to lose consciousness. Her eyes were rolling around in the sockets. Somehow she managed to focus on him. "I love you, baby. I love you."

The corners of her mouth lifted slightly. "I love you too."

He dragged his hands down the sides of his legs. His fingertips were burning, like he'd held them against a stove's burner. "I need you."

"Me too. I won't leave." Even as she said the words, Drako could see her slipping away.

"I hope Talen and Malek are fast drivers," his uncle said, so calmly and casually it made Drako want to shriek.

The rage inside him swirled hotter, faster. He could almost feel the heat racing along his nerves, down his spine, his arms, to his fingertips. He curled his hands into fists, but the pain grew unbearable.

The gun in his hand fired. He hadn't meant it to.

Time seemed to slow, each fraction of a second lasting an eternity.

Drako looked up and saw his uncle, surprised, clap a hand over his arm. The Glock fell to the ground. Rin slid from his grasp, falling like a lifeless rag doll. Drako lurched forward, swept her into his arms, and, praying his uncle wouldn't shoot him in the back, ran to his car.

A bullet whistled by his head.

There was no way he could go back for his phone or to try to warn his brothers. He raced to the nearest hospital, every mile stretching forever, every minute more excruciating than the last.

He screeched up a U-shaped driveway, rammed the car into park, and yelled at the security guard, "My wife's been shot!" Everything happened in a blur from that point on. Doctors and nurses came running; she was put on a gurney and wheeled out of his sight. He answered questions in between asking when he could see her, and once he was told she was being taken up to surgery, he found a phone and tried calling Talen.

There was no answer.

Torn, he told a nurse he'd be back as soon as he could and left, hoping his brothers had found nothing but a corpse and an empty truck. But he couldn't shake the feeling that he'd just sent them into a trap that might cost them their lives.

21

Drako's worst fears had come true.

No sooner had he turned the corner onto the dirt drive did he see them. His two brothers, standing with arms caught behind their backs, their posture telling Drako what their faces couldn't, because their backs were to him. Why were they just standing there? Why weren't they fighting?

He didn't bother cutting the car's engine, he just tumbled out of the driver's seat and raced toward them, the 9mm ready. With every footstep, he made a promise to make his uncle and the rest of the Chimera pay for what had happened.

But before he was close enough to get a decent shot, somebody hit him from behind, knocking the gun out of his hand. It sailed through the air, landing in some scraggy brush about ten feet away. Drako swung around to face his assailant, but the bastard slammed his head with something hard. Drako dropped to his knees, stars obliterating his vision. By the time it cleared, Drako's hands had been tied behind his back and he was standing next to Malek and Talen.

Where the hell had this asshole come from?

His uncle sneered, a large scarlet stain covering much of his shoulder and arm. "So glad you decided to come back, Kane. How I love family reunions. It's been what...ten years? How you've all grown." It was hard to believe that cold voice belonged to a man Drako had once trusted and respected. Who would have ever imagined they'd have to worry about an ex-guardian joining the enemy? "Unfortunately, this isn't going to be much of a party. Your brothers forgot to bring my present."

"They didn't *forget*."

"I kinda figured that out already." His uncle lifted the gun he'd recovered as Drako had raced off with Rin. He aimed it at Talen.

Drako's heart jerked up into his throat. He was about to watch his brothers being slaughtered. Then he guessed he would be tortured until he either died or gave up the information.

He would never do that.

Maybe this was all for the better. It would be over soon, the stress of keeping such a vital secret for so long, the heavy weight of duty, responsibility lifted from his shoulders. With the three brothers gone, The Secret's location would be lost, at least for a while. With any luck, the Chimera wouldn't find it until mankind was ready for it.

Drako glared at his uncle. "We won't tell you where The Secret is. No matter what you do to us."

"I got that too." Their uncle squeezed the trigger. A sharp pop echoed through the air. "Good-bye, Eagle." Talen jerked to one side. And a couple of heartbeats later, he silently sank to the ground.

Dammit! Drako started trembling. His blood burned. His fingers curled into fists. He clenched his jaw as the temptation to give up and give the bastard what he wanted charged through him.

Be strong. At least he wasn't tortured.

With absolutely no warning, his uncle fired again. "Farewell, Lion. Two down, one to go."

Drako spun around, met Malek's gaze. He watched at least a half dozen emotions play across Malek's face before his eyes became empty and cold. Slowly, Malek fell next to Talen.

Both brothers were down. Drako looked at the men and saw the boys they had once been. Full of life, full of hope. Was it all over for them? Had they failed?

Had he failed them?

On the tail of horrid, gripping despair came tooth-gritting fury.

No. It wasn't all over. Not until he'd taken his last breath.

He charged his uncle. As he ran, as hard as he could, his vision narrowed to a single point, the end of the Glock's barrel. The bullet would be coming soon. In the next blink. Or the next.

Something grabbed him from behind. The same bastard who'd caught him earlier. He fought. He kicked. He swung his body, using his rage to give him strength. Nothing worked, and he knew why. He'd been so fucking busy strategizing, and sitting in fucking vans, watching video feeds, he hadn't been keeping himself in top condition. Another fuckup.

Soon he was standing next to his brothers' still bodies, facing a man who, thanks to two mistakes on Drako's part—Drako wasn't convinced anymore that falling in love had been a mistake—was about to take everything that mattered from him, including the future he'd hoped to share with Rin.

"Why not just shoot me?" he spat.

"I'm going to, Dragon. But I wanted to let you know something first." His uncle's smile was pure evil. "That sweet little wife of yours is going to suffer every day until I get The fucking Secret in my hands. She's going to beg to die." His gaze sharpened. "She won't have a minute's relief, not a fucking second without pain, until I have what I want. And it'll be your fault."

Something inside Drako snapped. He and his brothers had lived with the knowledge this day might come. But Rin, sweet, innocent, loving Rin...

His skin felt hot, on his back, up over his shoulders, along his neck. Blistering.

His uncle laughed. It was a hollow, empty sound, nothing like a real laugh. "I knew you wouldn't be able to fight it. You fell in love with her." His uncle actually tsked him like he was still a little boy. "How many times had I warned you? Was it the way she kissed you? The way she touched you? Or was it something else? Something... deeper? Maybe I'll figure it out for myself." He winked.

All the anger and rage seemed to charge like an electric current through his body. The heat on his skin seemed to seep inside where it sizzled and whirled and churned deep in his gut. It grew stronger until Drako felt like he had been consumed by an inferno. It was out of control, and he was at its mercy. His wrists broke free and he pointed a finger at his enemy. "Go to hell, you bastard!" A scarlet flame arced across the space between them like the blaze of a flamethrower.

What the hell? He looked at his hand. Not a burn in sight. His toe caught something as he took a step back. The plastic handcuffs. They looked like they'd been heated and stretched out of shape.

At the sound of a scream, Drako glanced up, finding the bush next to his uncle was nothing but a charred skeleton and his uncle's shirt was on fire. His hair. His uncle screamed again, the sound almost inhuman. While Drako watched, confused, his uncle wheeled around in circles, arms flailing. The man who'd tied Drako's wrists came around the side of the black truck, raced toward the screeching man, now fully engulfed.

He knocked the burning man to the ground, trying to smother the fire.

Snapping out of his stupor, Drako lunged for his brothers. He hefted Talen onto his shoulder and half carried, half dragged Malek. He stuffed them into the car, dashed around to the driver's side, and climbed in. A curl of smoke wafted from his fingertip as he curled his fist around the gear shift.

Not knowing if it was too late to save his brothers, he drove straight to the hospital.

22

She'd waited so long for this day. Waited, hoped, despite everything that had happened, even though more than once she'd feared this day would never come.

She was ready to finally face all the pain, to cleanse her soul, and break down the walls she'd built around it. She had realistic expectations; she knew D/s wasn't a replacement for therapy. Yet she'd read the stories online, in which people described very powerful, tangible benefits from exploring BDSM. Were there other ways she might get the results she was looking for? Perhaps.

Perhaps not.

She wasn't afraid as she dressed, as she rode to the dungeon with her husband, or as they walked side by side to the room. She wasn't excited either. She was at peace.

After they entered the room, Drako told her to take off her gown. She removed everything, draped her dress over the back of a chair, and set her G-string on a table next to it.

"Remember, Yellow means slow down, Red means stop."

Drako guided her to a kneeler and positioned her on it. "I'm here to help you, to guide you. Use me."

"Okay."

He blindfolded her. And in that dark space, she found herself focusing on her other senses, monitoring Drako's movement around the room by the sound of his footsteps, the occasional draft of air caressing her bare skin, the scent of his skin growing stronger as he neared. As she waited for him to move her into position and secure her arms and legs, she started wondering what would happen. Would she recognize that moment, when she slipped into "headspace"? Would it be as life-changing as she'd read, or a complete disappointment?

"Are you ready?"

"Ready." She liked being bound, being completely under Drako's control. There was no doubt she trusted him. Perhaps that was why she wasn't worried she couldn't move, couldn't signal to him, couldn't see what he was about to do to her. Rather, the bindings felt like extensions of him, his fingers curled around her wrists and ankles, holding them in place. His body supporting her stomach as she rested against him. She felt safe, cherished.

No, she felt free. Free from responsibility, from obligation and duty. She couldn't step into his place and take over for him, like she had with her mother, over and over again. That alone was enough to make her want to weep with joy.

The first sensation was soft and tickly, something soft cascading over her shoulders, pattering across her back. There was no pain, but the sensations still made her warm and relaxed. She breathed in slowly and evenly, enjoying every minute, knowing it was only the beginning.

A part of her wanted to move on to the next thing already, the next pleasure, but she trusted Drako to know when the time was right. She knelt bent over a padded support and fought to concentrate on what she felt right now, this second, rather than wondering what was coming next.

The next tool he used was the bristle brush, and ohmygod, it felt good. The bristles scraped across the skin of her shoulders, easing the tickling. He followed the line of her spine with the brush, scrubbed over her bottom, leaving her skin burning and tingling. It was easier to focus now, the sensation was a little stronger, and she noticed when he stopped for a few moments, she was breathing a little faster and shallower than normal.

She hadn't reached that magical plane yet, at least she didn't think she had. "Drako, is it working?"

"Patience, love. Concentrate on the sensation. What do you feel?"

"My skin is burning a little. It's a good burn."

"Are you ready for more?"

"Yes, please, yes."

She heard a sharp smacking sound before the pain registered. When it did, it sent the air rushing from her lungs, and she had to gulp in a mouthful to reinflate them. Where he'd struck her, the skin burned hotter, a slightly more intense tingling heat than what had followed after the brush.

The second strike, on her other buttock, didn't surprise her as much. Still, she spent a second or two in a breathless state in which time seemed to crawl at an impossibly slow pace, where fractions of a second lasted an eternity. After the third and fourth time, she felt like she was sliding deeper into herself. All thought swept from her mind and she just was, existed, the pain more a part of her than her own mind.

Behind her closed eyelids, colors swirled and took form. She saw her grandmother, her mother, and Lei, but they were younger. Lei was barely out of diapers. Their voices echoed in her ears. Laughter.

When had there been laughter in their family?

She looked into her mother's eyes and saw something she

couldn't ever remember seeing—the glimmer of happiness in their dark depth. She didn't remember her mother this way at all. She'd been hard, cruel, detached.

Rin wanted to ask her what had changed, why she'd turned her back on her children, but something stopped her. There was a touch, gentle but firm, on her back. The whisper of words she couldn't quite understand in her ears. A voice calling.

When she blinked against the light burning through her eyelids, Drako was holding her cradled in his arms and was kissing her cheeks, eyelids, nose. The blindfold was gone. She wasn't bound anymore either. "What happened? Did I pass out?"

"No, you were awake. You responded when I asked you questions. You don't remember?" Gently, he stroked her hair back from her face.

"No." Feeling a little odd, like she'd just woken up from anesthesia, she glanced around the room. They were still in Drako's suite. Drako was sitting on the love seat, holding her.

"How do you feel now?"

"I feel . . . like I want to laugh and cry at the same time." She dragged her hand across her face. Her hand was damp.

"That's exactly what you were doing."

She wiped her face again and sat up. "Oh, God, how embarrassing."

He ran a knuckle up the side of her cheek. "No, Rin. I've never seen anything more beautiful, and I'm grateful to have witnessed it." He brushed his mouth across hers, and it felt like an electric jolt jumped between their bodies. He looked deeply into her eyes now, and for the first time, she felt as if his defenses had crumbled. He was as vulnerable as she. "Please let me make love to you."

"Yes." She started to climb onto him, but he stopped her with a soft touch on her shoulder.

"No, not here. Home. In my bed."

His bed.

Still a little unsteady after her first real experience in the dungeon, as well as emotionally all over the place, she swallowed a little sob and nodded. "I'd like that very much." Her bottom burned as she put her gown back on, the smooth material chafing it just enough to make her breathe a little sharply and smile as the memory of those wonderfully intense moments played through her mind. Her head felt a little foggy still, but it was a pleasant feeling. Overall, she felt a lot like she did after a really long, hard cry—but without the inevitable migraine afterward. It was as if she'd emotionally purged her soul.

That had to be what made people come back, over and over. That sense of being at peace. Her mind seemed to be working slower. The tension was gone. And she was content to simply be. To live. In this moment. With Drako holding her hand, sweetly.

Out they went, into the evening. Across the parking lot to the car. Drako asked her several times if she was feeling okay as he drove them home.

She was. Better than okay.

A mile or two from home, he stopped asking.

She heard voices as they entered the house. Male voices. And one female. Lei was talking to Drako's brothers, laughing. The sound made Rin's heart soar. They'd all endured months of pain after the attack. Rin, as well as both Talen and Malek, had gone through emergency surgery and rehab afterward. Drako's brothers were still recovering. Their injuries had been more serious than hers. And although Lei had been spared the trauma of a physical injury, she'd still suffered. She'd been in too delicate a condition to handle almost losing Rin. They'd all had to adjust to a new life, with new names and a new home. In one way, it was good leaving the past behind and moving on. In another, it was surprisingly difficult.

It was good to hear her laughing, to hear them all laughing.

Finally, it seemed things were getting back to normal, that the horror of that awful time was behind them.

She smiled at Drako, slipped her hand in his, and followed him down the hallway, past her room and Lei's. Past Talen's room. Malek's. They stopped at Drako's closed door. He swept her up into his arms, pushed open the door.

"I never carried you over the threshold. What kind of husband am I?" he joked as he set her gently on a bed big enough to fit a small village.

"You're the very best kind of husband." Her bottom burned as her weight settled on the mattress. Her gown gently chafed the warm flesh as she leaned back, letting the pillows and headboard support her upper body.

He stood there for a handful of heartbeats, just looking at her as if she was the most incredible, miraculous thing he'd ever laid eyes on. "No, I haven't been the best husband, but it wasn't because I didn't want to do better. I did." His sigh was heavy and full of regret. "No excuses. I don't deserve you." He lifted an index finger and a tiny yellow flame flickered on its tip. He used it to light the candle on his nightstand. "I don't know if I'll ever get used to this." He blew out his finger. "I wish I knew how it works. At least I'm getting a little better at controlling it."

"That's good to hear. Accidentally igniting the curtains once is more than enough." Laughing, she extended her arms to him, took his hands in hers, and pulled until he was sitting next to her. He was facing her, his ass next to her knees, a hand flattened on the mattress, on the opposite side of her legs, trapping them. "Now, to get back to what we were talking about. You most definitely deserve me." She hooked her hand around the back of his head and pulled him in for a little kiss. "You're my hero. You saved my life. My sister's. I understand what it means to be bound by duty. Of all people, you must know I get it."

"Thank you." He kissed her cheeks, her eyelids, her chin and nose. Finally, he kissed her mouth, and it was like no kiss she'd ever experienced before. It started a little shy and uncertain, which surprised her, but in the span of a few shaky breaths, it changed, turning desperate and full of raw need. His hands, trembling, started at her face but gradually moved down her neck, over her shoulders, and down her arms. His fingertips traced tingling lines as they traveled over her skin. When he broke the kiss, leaving her breathless, he looked like he was on the verge of tears. "I love you, Rin. More than life itself. And I promise I won't let a day go by without showing you how lucky I am to have you as my wife."

This moment was almost too sweet to feel real. She cupped his cheek and dragged her thumb across his cheekbone. She had no doubt she'd ever grow weary of gazing upon this face. Even when his strong jaw softened and his skin grew creased, the dark stubble and eyebrows turned from deep brown to gray and then white.

She helped Drako out of his clothes, each garment removed revealing more of his beautiful body. When he was nude, he lay back and let her explore, with hands, lips, tongue. She flicked her tongue over his hard little nipples, tickled the sensitive skin on the inside of his upper arms and along his rib cage with light touches, kissed a path from the center of his chest down to his hard cock, jutting out and tempting her with a droplet of precum on the tip.

Just as she was about to lower her mouth, to swipe that tempting pearl of moisture with her tongue, he shuddered and whispered, "Please, Rin. I can't wait another minute."

She could appreciate the hunger and desperation she heard in his voice. She'd been in those shoes once or twice. But where he'd been cruel—in a strictly good sense—she would be kind. She didn't have the patience, the stamina, or the discipline to make either of them wait.

"You, my dear, are lucky. I can't wait either." It didn't take much effort to get herself out of her dress, especially with Drako aiding her. Once she was nude, he forced her onto her back by crawling on top of her, raining dozens of kisses all over her stomach, chest, neck, face. His hands skimmed along her rib cage, the touch so soft it felt like a warm summer breeze.

Their mouths met again, tongues stroked and caressed, lips tormented, breath mingled. Drako was absolutely intoxicating, addicting. Rin just knew she would cry out when he took that sweet mouth from her. And his touch, which was growing bolder with every heavy beat of her heart. What were once soft, tickling brushes of his fingertips became firmer caresses and then hard possession. His fingers curled around her wrists, locking tightly. He lifted her hands up over her head, like he so loved to do, and murmured against her mouth, "Don't move."

She was quite happy to oblige him, even when he snatched those delicious lips away from hers. Down, they traveled, accompanied by tongue and teeth, along the side of her neck, over her collarbone, between her breasts. He pinched her nipples, both of them, applying just the right amount of pressure. Sharp little blades of pleasure-pain shot through her chest. As they zipped down her body, the pain lessened, the pleasure increased. And by the time the sensations reached her pussy, they were 100 percent glorious delight.

Beneath her husband's touch, she squirmed but she didn't move her arms. Not even when he pulled a nipple into his mouth, alternating hard suckling with tiny nips with his teeth.

The man knew exactly how to drive her crazy, and she was so thankful. But there was a problem, one that was growing more urgent with every lick and nip. Her pussy was clenching, achingly empty. Wet and hot, and when would he drive that cock into her and stroke away that throbbing need?

It seemed, as he moved to the left nipple to lavish it with the same attention he'd paid the right, that he'd turned the tables on her. Now she was hot and tight all over, trembling and gasping for breath.

"Drako," she whispered.

He answered with a kiss on her stomach and a rough "Mmmmmm" that sent a shudder quaking up and down her spine. "You're more delicious than any dessert." He moved lower still, kissing her belly button, the sensitive skin of her lower stomach, her freshly shaved mound. He audibly inhaled. "And smell better than the most exquisite flower." A fingertip slipped between her nether lips, more torment.

She arched her back, then rocked her hips forward, powerless to stop the movement, timed perfectly with the thumping of her heartbeat and the throbbing of her pussy. When he finally filled her, she was going to rocket to the stars.

"I bought something special for tonight," he said, sounding so casual, so in control, his finger gliding toward her anus and then up to circle her clit.

"What did you buy?" Her voice was breathy and soft. She was having a hard time filling her lungs. "I just want you to fuck me. Now."

"No, you don't." He sat up. "Don't move."

She started to clench her thighs, desperate to do something to relieve the aching between them.

"No." He pulled her knees apart and pushed them back, exposing her to his hungry gaze. The look in his eye only made her more desperate. "Don't move. Not even a toe." He shook his head, moistened his lips with his tongue. "You're so fucking beautiful and I love you so much." He went to the nightstand, opened a drawer, and pulled something out, wrapped in plastic. He held it to her so she could see. "Do you know what this is?"

She did. She nodded.

"Have you ever used a butt plug before?"

"No."

"I guessed as much." He pointed to the narrow, tapered end. "This is for a beginner, but it'll feel good. I promise."

She believed him.

He sat beside her, a tube of lubricant in one hand, the little pink rubber toy in the other. "Trust me."

How could she not, considering everything they'd been through? "Of course, I do."

He squeezed some of the lube onto a fingertip and teased her pussy first, tracing a circle around the opening. He bent down and flicked his tongue over her clit a few times until she was shaking. He slipped a finger inside her vagina and she practically came. "Mmmm," he said, smiling at her. "You're so hot and tight and wet. I can't wait to fuck you."

"I can't wait either."

"Soon, baby. You're not ready yet."

She didn't think she could get any more ready.

Evidently reading the signs her body was sending, her erect nipples, flushed skin, shallow breaths, and trembling muscles, he warned her, "Don't come yet. Wait. You'll be glad you did."

Did he know what he was asking? "Are you sure this isn't revenge for what I did to you?"

"Of course not. What you did was for me. My pleasure. My benefit. And what I'm about to do is for you."

"Okay, I'll try." She didn't sound committed. He gave her a hard look and immediately stopped what he was doing, letting her know, without any doubt, that *trying* wouldn't be good enough. Of course, he'd made her so hot, so desperate, she'd promise the moon if she thought it would make him happy, so she amended her response. "Okay. I won't come. But you'd better help me out a little. I'm weak."

"I'll help you." As if he wished to illustrate exactly what he meant by that promise, he pushed two fingers into her pussy.

She wanted to claw his shoulders, to dig her fingernails into his skin and make him pay for that. An eye for an eye, as they say. But she knew he was far more wicked than she, much more devious. And any punishment she doled out would come back to her, only ten times worse. So, instead, she bit back a curse, clamped her jaw tight, and tried to think about something that wasn't sexy. Naturally, the only thing that came to mind was that glorious face of his, the glitter of erotic hunger in his eyes, the way his lips curled into a naughty semismile when he looked at her.

Her brain was on his team.

Against her will, her pussy tightened around those fingers, increasing the sensation as he slowly fucked her with them.

Her pussy was on his team too.

A slick fingertip moved toward her anus, ringed around it a few times, coating her with warm lube. She squeezed her eyelids tightly, wove her fingers together, and prayed she wouldn't come. If she lost control, he would put her through hell—a carnal hell where she'd be denied satisfaction for God only knew how long.

God, she loved this man!

As he applied the slightest pressure, her anus puckered tightly, resisting the invasion.

"Relax, baby." He stopped tormenting her pussy and only touched her ass. That helped a little. Not much. She still couldn't seem to relax enough so he could slide his finger inside. "Take a few slow, deep breaths."

She did exactly as he suggested. Once, twice, a third time. Okay, now maybe she could relax. He pressed. She tightened up all over.

Maybe not.

She shook her head. "I can't."

"Yes, you can. You have to trust me. I'll go slowly, just like I did in the dungeon. You liked what happened there, didn't you?"

He didn't need to hear her answer; he knew exactly how much she'd liked it. But she answered anyway, "Yesyesyes."

"Focus."

She concentrated and planned for his touch, anticipating it like she did the blinding light of a camera's flash. She tightened her anus before he touched her and then, the second she felt his finger again, released the tension. The tip of his finger slipped past the ring of muscle just before it closed up again, this time around his finger.

The sensation was out of this world hot. And then he started pushing it deeper, and a blaze erupted in her pussy. She clawed at the headboard and fought to breathe through the ecstasy, fighting to cling to a thread of control so thin she didn't know if it would snap.

She was losing the battle. A rush of heat rippled out from her center and the tingling start of an orgasm gathered between her legs. Drako's finger slipped out at the exact moment when she was sure she was going to come.

She released the breath she hadn't realized she'd been holding. "Ohmygod."

"Good?"

"That's an understatement."

"You're going to enjoy what I have planned for you."

She had no doubt.

"First, I need to help you settle down a little."

"Thank you."

He kissed her forehead, which felt like it was blistering hot. "On your stomach. I'm going to rub your back, help you relax."

If she didn't know better, she'd swear Drako was a figment of her imagination. He was too wonderful to be real, and for the briefest moment—not long enough to ruin the mood—she wondered if some other horrific secret would come up and destroy everything they'd fought for since they were married. She shoved that toxic thought aside and relaxed her arms and shoulders as he swung a knee over her and began working on a couple of hard knots at the base of her neck.

"Drako, I thought the submissive was supposed to serve the dom."

"Actually, what I define as 'serve' may be different from other doms." He placed a kiss at her nape, and she shivered. Goose bumps prickled all over her back and shoulders. "You don't think you're serving me?"

"Sort of. But you're the one who's rubbing my shoulders, not the other way around."

"True. But I'm setting the pace. I'm controlling everything in this situation by manipulating your body. The massage is just another tool. It helps you relax your muscles, slows your heart rate and breathing. The tools of D/s don't have to be sex toys."

"I understand now."

Moving lower, he worked a couple more hard knots out of her muscles, on either side of her spine. After he was finished, he dragged his hands up and down her back. She felt like a queen. A very relaxed, satisfied queen. With a hot consort who knew her body better than she did.

"Now, you're ready."

"For what?" she asked, having more than a good idea what the answer would be.

"For me." He helped her up onto her hands and knees and settled behind her. He entered her slowly, filled her completely, and the muscles he'd worked so hard to soften tightened up again. But she could understand now why he'd taken the time. The change was exquisite, sending a wave of warmth rippling through her body.

He moved in and out, his intimate strokes hitting just the right spot. He kept the pace easy, building her need back to the level where it had been before gradually. She closed her eyes, tossed her head back and rocked back and forth, taking him deeply, fully appreciating every stroke as they sent bigger and bigger waves of carnal need surging through her.

This time, he'd let her come... she hoped. She was getting closer. Trembling, tight. She curled her fingers, clenching the sheets that smelled so sweet, like Drako, closed her eyes, and prayed he'd let her come.

He stopped. His cock slipped out of her pussy.

She whimpered.

"You're going to thank me for this. I promise, Rin. You've been so good, baby. You deserve this. You've deserved it since the first night we fucked." He parted her ass cheeks with his fingers, licked her anus, her pussy, her clit. "Relax, baby. I'm going to insert the plug."

She did what she'd done earlier, clenching her ass and releasing it the moment she felt the tip of the plug pushing its way in. It slipped in, glided into place. A giant tidal wave of need practically knocked her over.

Drako pressed on her shoulders, encouraging her to drop her chest down until it rested on the mattress. His cock slid home, and Rin saw stars.

A cock filling her pussy. The plug filling her ass. It wouldn't be long, a few strokes, maybe, and she'd lose all control.

She gasped. "Drako. Come. Please."

"I am. Right now." He dug his fingers into her hips. She felt his cock getting thicker as his cum surged down its length.

That tingling, buzzing sensation charged through her system. She couldn't fight it. "Drako!"

"Come with me. Come now."

Their voices blended as they cried out in ecstasy. Their bodies worked as one, their energies whipping between them, coursing through each other. Mind, body, and soul, they were joined, their love shattering the final barriers.

There'd never be any question, any doubt or fear. Rin belonged to Drako. Drako belonged to Rin. They would share everything for the rest of their days, pain and pleasure, hopes and fears. And above all else, love.

When the bliss of their lovemaking faded, they curled up under the covers, and Rin read the final pages of *Emma* to her husband, with her head resting on his shoulder, one of her legs draped over his.

Their own story might bear no resemblance to *Emma*, or any other classic work of fiction, but in its own way, it was timeless and beautiful and uniquely magical. And of course, despite the bumps they'd endured, Rin had known all along it would have a happy ending.

Turn the page
for a sneak preview
of Logan Belle's
BLUE ANGEL

Available May 2011!

1

During the entire cab ride he kept telling her, it's a surprise.

"I don't like surprises," Mallory said, following him into the dark, barely marked building off of Bowery.

"It's your birthday! What's a birthday without a surprise?" He winked at her, and she couldn't resist smiling back. That was the thing about Alec: no matter how much he aggravated her, she loved him too much to stay angry.

And why should she be in a bad mood? They'd finally moved in together after three years of dating long distance while she finished law school. She had a good job at a midsize firm. And yes, it was her birthday—the big twenty-five—and Alec was taking her out for a night on the town, in her new city, just the two of them.

Except...the dark location did not seem to be a romantic restaurant.

A woman with a clipboard greeted them inside the door. She had a butterfly tattoo on her neck and a perfect face. Behind her, a blue velvet curtain prevented Mallory from seeing into the room.

"Alec Martin and Mallory Dale. We're on the list," Alec said, taking Mallory's hand.

Once inside, Mallory saw that the venue was a bar of some sort, with a seating area and a stage and . . . dwarves. Two that she counted. And a topless woman wearing a garter belt, black-seamed stockings, and red patent leather stilettos. And a man dressed for a rodeo carrying a bullwhip.

"What the hell is this?" Mallory asked.

"It's the Blue Angel. A burlesque club," Alec said, smiling like he'd just presented her with a diamond.

Burlesque—the topic of the article Alec was writing for *Gruff*, the pop culture magazine he worked for. And his latest excuse for constantly ogling other women.

"We're spending my birthday doing research for your article?"

He steered her to the table closest to the stage. The room was packed, but the table had a reserved card on it. Now she *knew* the evening was a *Gruff* magazine gig. The owner of *Gruff* was a rich kid named Billy Barton. Alec had met Billy thanks to the long tentacles of the Penn alumni network. And unlike Alec and most of their friends, who had only been in New York a few years, Billy could open any door, pull any string, and reserve any table.

"No," Alec said. "We're doing something fun and interesting on your birthday that I happen to be writing about but that I know you will enjoy. Wait here—I'm going to get our drinks."

And he was off to the bar before she could protest.

She wished she had worn something different. Her long, houndstooth Ann Taylor skirt suddenly seemed overly prim. There was a lot of leg showing in the room—bare legs, garter-belted legs, legs in fishnets and heels. At least she was wearing a simple black turtleneck, so the overall effect wasn't too dressed.

In the corner at the far end of the room, two women were laughing and talking to the guy in the Western getup. The one in the faux leopard coat was the first person Mallory had noticed in the room. How could she not? Aside from being model gorgeous, she had an ultrastylized look, with dramatically pale skin, full red lips, and straight black hair cut in a fabulous, razor-sharp bob. As if sensing Mallory's stare, the woman turned and looked at her with sharp blue eyes. Startled, Mallory quickly looked away. But when she glanced back, the woman was still watching her, as if expecting that her gaze would return. Their eyes locked, and Mallory's stomach did the oddest little flip.

"Hey," Alec said, sitting next to her and sliding over a bottle of Stella Artois. "You're not mad, are you?"

Mallory accepted the beer, trying to resist the urge to look back at the beautiful dark-haired woman. "What? Oh, I don't know. A little. Come on, Alec. Admit it—you're just killing two birds with one stone: you want to do research, but it's my birthday and we're going out so this is what you chose to do. It has nothing to do with how I'd actually want to celebrate."

She hated the way she sounded, but she was worried. It wasn't just about her birthday—it was about *them*. She didn't want to admit it, but their relationship hadn't felt right since she'd moved to Manhattan six months ago. Alec was consumed with the cutthroat world of New York media. She was working crazy hours at the law firm and studying to retake the bar exam. And lately, he kept bringing up the idea of their hooking up with another girl—with having a three-way. At first when he brought it up, she had thought he was just being provocative. But she finally realized he was completely serious. She didn't quite know what to make of this, so she mentally filed it under Things I Can't Deal With Right Now.

And it wasn't that she was appalled at the thought of being

with a woman; she'd had minor girl crushes when she was younger. There was that one girl at overnight camp, Carly Klein. She wore tube socks pulled up to her knees even in ninety-degree heat, and she spiked a volleyball like she was going for the gold medal. She'd even had a sex dream about that girl and felt guilty about it for weeks. But this wasn't overnight camp, and she didn't have girl crushes anymore. She was an adult, and she was allegedly in an adult relationship.

Alec put his hand over hers, but before he could tell her how wrong she was or whatever he was going to say, Lady Gaga's "Beautiful, Dirty, Rich" pulsed through the room, the lights dimmed, and the thick, blue curtain on the stage slowly parted.

Rodeo guy stepped into the spotlight, and the crowd erupted in hoots and applause.

"Ladies . . . and those annoying creatures you felt compelled to bring with you tonight," said Rodeo Guy, "Welcome to the Blue Angel!"

He cracked his whip, and Mallory jumped in her seat.

More hollering. Despite herself, Mallory felt a slight rush. The energy in the room reminded her of being at a rock concert. She didn't want to give Alec the satisfaction of smiling—because no matter what he said, this night was just about his story—but for the first time since stepping inside the club, she was just a little excited to see what would happen. But her history with these types of places made her less than optimistic.

She had gone to a strip club in Philadelphia sophomore year of college and again, reluctantly, when she first moved to New York. She'd hated both experiences. The girls seemed miserable, and she felt like a perv for looking at them, even though there was little else to do. And giving them money had made *her* feel exposed. Both times, her friends had just had a laugh and told her to lighten up. But she'd minored in women's studies, for God's sake. She couldn't just walk in the club and check her mind at the door.

She dreaded that feeling of not knowing where to look or what to do with her hands, of feeling both sorry for the girl and embarrassed for just being in the room.

And so when the first girl came onstage, Mallory was nervous. But the crowd was raucous and exuberant, and she was aware of being the only one in the club not making some sort of noise. Alec, especially, was yelling, clapping. He looked over at her only briefly, and winked.

Mallory turned back to the stage. The song "Diamonds Are a Girl's Best Friend" played, and the stage lights bathed the dancer in fuschia. She was blond, and she wore a surprising amount of clothes: thigh-high, pink patent leather boots with a platform heel, a white corset, long white gloves, and in both hands gigantic fans made out of pink and white feathers. She waved the fans around so that sometimes they concealed her face and most of her body. Other times, she just covered her body and looked at the audience with a sly smile. When the hooting and hollering reached a peak, she tossed the fans aside, stood with her feet squarely apart, and slowly tugged off one glove. The crowd roared as if she'd just flashed her bare breasts. Did women get completely naked in these shows? Mallory didn't know what to expect.

Little by little, the blonde peeled away her costume—first the gloves, then the boots, and then she turned her back to the audience and eased down the zipper of her corset so slowly, Mallory was shocked to realize she could not wait for the woman to get it off. And when she finally shook herself free and turned to face the audience with her hands over her breasts, Mallory found she was holding her breath.

The blonde moved her hands away, striking a pose like Madonna in her "Vogue" video. Her breasts were small, pert, and perfectly shaped, the nipples covered in red sequined flowers. When she danced around in her pasties and red thong, Mallory was simultaneously relieved and disappointed—the performer was probably not going to get totally nude, after all.

The crowd was in a frenzy, and Mallory joined in, whistling and clapping. The woman responded to the crowd, seeming to feed off of the excitement, gyrating close to the edge of the stage, where she slowly bent over, flashing her ass to the crowd, playfully squeezing both cheeks.

Once again, the cheers escalated, though Mallory did not think a higher decibel level was humanly possible.

Rodeo Guy returned to the stage.

"One more round, everyone, for Poppy LaRue," he said, though he didn't have to ask. The room was still wild.

"What do you think?" Alec asked, squeezing her leg.

"It's . . . I like it," Mallory said.

"I knew you would." He leaned over and kissed her cheek.

As Rodeo Guy launched into a brief monologue, surprisingly clever, full of sly political commentary and pop culture references, Billy Barton slipped into the seat next to Alec. He wore a lavender shirt and purple suspenders. He was handsome and rich, so he could get away with dressing like Scott Disick on *Keeping Up with the Kardashians.*

"Did I miss anything?" he asked, a little too loudly.

"I don't know. What do you think, Mal? Did he miss anything?"

She rolled her eyes.

"Ladies and gentlemen, please give it up for the gorgeous, the glamorous, the *dangerous* . . . Bette Noir."

The regulars in the crowd chanted the dancer's first name. The curtain remained down, but Marilyn Manson's "I Put a Spell on You" began to play. As the low, pounding, eerie first beats filled the room, the curtain slid back to reveal two wooden chairs and a small table with a crystal ball. In one chair, a woman was crouched, a towering black witch hat obscuring her face.

She rose slowly, her figure shrouded in a long black dress. She swayed and looked directly at the audience, moody and defiant; Mallory saw that it was *her*—the stunning, leopard-coat woman.

Mallory knew the song well—had heard it long ago in a David Lynch film and loved it. It had been years since she'd heard it, but it had an unforgettable early crescendo, and when it reached that initial peak, the dancer pulled off her black dress to reveal her perfect body in only a bullet bra, black lace panties, black seamed stockings, garter belt, and six-inch, patent leather stilettos. In one hand, she held a shiny black wand. This time, when she looked at the audience, she focused on Mallory.

And then—and at first Mallory thought she was imagining this—she pointed her wand at Mallory and gestured for her to come onstage.

Mallory looked away, pretended not to see. But the crowd was cheering her on, and Mr. Rodeo appeared to assist her. Damn Billy Barton and his front row seats! She looked back at Alec, but he was laughing and waving her on.

The exact mechanics of how she got onstage were details she would never quite grasp. But somehow she found herself seated in one of the wooden chairs, in front of the crystal ball, with Bette Noir dancing around her. And then Bette sat in the chair opposite her, back to Mallory, and gestured for her to undo her bra.

Hands shaking, Mallory somehow managed the metal clasp. Her fingertips brushed the woman's pale skin, as remarkably soft as it was fair. And when Bette turned to face her, bare breasted, Mallory felt she was an audience of one. She did not hear the crowd or the music. She did not know if she even heard Bette speaking to her—but it felt like she was. And Bette was telling her to remove her sweater. The only reason she did it was because she couldn't be responsible for ruining this gorgeous spectacle. She hesitated for maybe twenty seconds, and then, with a rush of adrenaline, Mallory slowly pulled off her sweater.

Bette did not smile, did not even bat her fake eyelashes. She calmly took the turtleneck from Mallory, walked to the edge of the stage, and tossed it to the seat Mallory had vacated. The crowd was roaring—yes, she heard it now, like a television set that had become unmuted. Mallory, now wearing only her Ann Taylor skirt and white Victoria's Secret bra, felt her heart pounding. She wondered how much longer she would have to be onstage, but at the same time didn't want to leave. It was like she was hyperalive—everything felt louder, brighter, and bigger than life off the stage. It was dizzying, and to ground herself she looked out at the audience to find Alec. She could see that his gaze was riveted on her, only her. She took a deep breath and stood still as Bette worked the stage around her, wearing only a bejeweled thong and impossibly high heels and still holding the wand and dancing—all the while dancing, moving in the most deliberate and perfectly choreographed way.

And then the curtain came down.

Poppy LaRue peeked at the crowd from behind the curtain. She could not believe Bette had pulled that brunette onto the stage. Her nerves had barely settled after her own act—it was flat-out sadistic that Agnes had made her open the show on her second performance ever. She thought about telling Agnes just that, but Agnes was too busy reaming Bette for pulling one of the audience on stage.

"What are you thinking? This is not a circus!" Agnes fumed in her thick Polish accent. Agnieszka Wieczorek, former Warsaw ballerina turned proprietress of the Blue Angel, did not take kindly to broken rules.

"Of course it is," Bette said, calmly lighting a cigarette. "Why else do you think these people come here?" Bette walked past her without another word, into the dressing room. She closed the door with a sharp slam.

Who else but Bette Noir could get away with that?

"I need to get my shoes out of there," Poppy said. Agnes mumbled something in her native tongue and waved vaguely in the direction of the closed door with disgust.

Poppy waited until she was out of sight, then rapped lightly on the dressing room door.

"Fuck off," Bette said.

"It's Poppy." She took Bette's silence as an invitation to enter. When she'd started at the Blue Angel six months ago, she would never have followed Bette Noir into a room if she was in a snit. But she'd finally gotten close enough to feel comfortable; she only hoped she could get a lot closer. She'd never been with a woman before, but she knew Bette only liked girls, and, if that's what it took to get Bette to take her under her wing and show her the ropes, she had no problem with it.

"I don't think Agnes's really mad at you," Poppy said. She paused in front of the mirror and couldn't help admiring herself. She'd recently cut her white-blond hair into a chin-length bob, much like Bette's black one. They were both fair skinned and blue-eyed, although Poppy was a few inches taller. She'd always liked being five nine, but ever since meeting Bette she wished she were a bit shorter. Everything about Bette seemed more perfect, more right for burlesque, more special. Regardless of the height difference, with the black/blond bob thing going on Poppy liked to think they were like photo negatives of each other. More and more, she imagined what it would be like to be in bed with Bette, her lovelier twin.

"I don't really care," Bette said, looking up from her iPhone, fixing Poppy with her unnerving cat-eyed glare. "I'm not working here to make one hundred and fifty dollars a night for the rest of my life. Do you know who that was at that table?"

"The girl you pulled onstage? No—is she an actress?"

"Not her! The guy in the stupid suspenders."

Poppy was the one who felt stupid. Was he an actor? She'd barely even noticed him. She decided it was best to say nothing. She knew Bette was going to tell her, regardless.

"It was Billy Barton," Bette said. When Poppy still showed no sign of recognition, Bette sighed in exasperation. "The owner of *Gruff* magazine. You know *Gruff*, right? They have that annual "Hot" issue. I think it was Megan Fox on the cover last year."

"Oh, yeah—sure. I read it all the time," Poppy lied.

"Well, the publisher was here—tonight! That's a big deal, Poppy. If the magazine writes about the club, we could get some industry people in here. Not just these horny NYU kids."

"Cool. So... do you want to get a drink?"

Bette turned abruptly in her seat, looking at Poppy closely. She eyed her up and down, her gaze lingering at her chest. Poppy, wearing a pink satin robe over her pasties and G-string, felt more naked than she had onstage in front of fifty strangers. She forced herself to stand still.

Bette stood so they were almost face to face. She reached out and slipped her hand under the robe, cupping Poppy's breast. Poppy couldn't even breathe. After months of being ignored, then barely getting conversation out of Bette... this! Poppy had never been so invisible to another human being.

But not anymore.

"Take these off," Bette said, her thumb brushing over the red sequined flowers hiding Poppy's nipples. Bette sat back in her seat, content to be the audience, while Poppy slowly removed her pasties. In the background, Poppy could hear the chords of "Fever" by Peggy Lee; it was Cookies 'n Cream's number—the final act. Usually, Bette closed the show. But she and Cookie had made some crazy bet, and Cookie won. They wouldn't even tell Poppy what the bet had been about. She felt like such an outsider, and wondered when that would change. How long would she have to be at the Blue Angel before she understood the place? Before Agnes spoke to her? Before the customers shouted her name? A year? Two?

But none of that mattered right now. All that mattered was that her robe was on the floor, her pasties were in her hand, and Bette was staring at her bare breasts.

Poppy decided to be proactive. That was her new mantra, proactive. She'd heard it on *Oprah,* or read it in *Cosmo.* Or someplace important like that. Don't wait for things to come to you.

She stepped forward, her eyes locked with Bette's. It was disturbing to admit it, but she was, for once in her life, faced with someone hotter than herself.

"I'm not really in the mood to drink tonight," said Bette.

She turned back to her iPhone.